KURDISTAN + 100

KURDISTAN

+

100

STORIES FROM A FUTURE REPUBLIC

EDITED BY

ORSOLA CASAGRANDE & MUSTAFA GÜNDOĞDU

DEEP VELLUM PUBLISHING

DALLAS, TEXAS

Deep Vellum Publishing
3000 Commerce St., Dallas, Texas 75226
deepvellum.org · @deepvellum

Deep Vellum is a 501c3 nonprofit literary arts organization
founded in 2013 with the mission to bring
the world into conversation through literature.

Support for this publication has been provided in part by grants from the National
Endowment for the Arts, the Texas Commission on the Arts, the City of Dallas Office of
Arts and Culture, the Communities Foundation of Texas, Anaphora Literary Arts, and the
Addy Foundation.

This book has been selected to receive financial assistance from
English PEN's 'PEN Translates' programme.

LIBRARY OF CONGRESS CATALOGING-IN-PUBLICATION DATA

Names: Casagrande, Orsola, 1968- editor. | Gündoğdu, Mustafa, editor.
Title: Kurdistan +100 : stories from a future republic / edited by Orsola
Casagrande & Mustafa Gündoğdu.
Other titles: Kurdistan plus one hundred
Description: Dallas : Deep Vellum, 2024.
Identifiers: LCCN 2024007215 (print) | LCCN 2024007216 (ebook) | ISBN
9781646052806 (trade paperback) | ISBN 9781646053018 (ebook)
Subjects: LCSH: Short stories, Kurdish--Translations into English. |
Kurdish fiction--21st century--Translations into English. |
Kurds--Fiction. | Kurdistan--Social conditions--Fiction. | LCGFT: Short
stories.
Classification: LCC PK6908.82.E5 K87 2024 (print) | LCC PK6908.82.E5
(ebook) | DDC 891/.597308--dc23/eng/20240403
LC record available at https://lccn.loc.gov/2024007215
LC ebook record available at https://lccn.loc.gov/2024007216

ISBNs: 978-1-64605-280-6 | 978-1-64605-301-8 (ebook)

Cover art and design by Justin Childress
Interior layout and typesetting by KGT

PRINTED IN CANADA

Contents

Introduction

TOWARDS THE END OF the Second World War, Iran was occupied by British and Soviet forces; the country would have been too strategically advantageous a base from which to attack the Soviet Union if the Nazis ever captured it, so suppression of Iranian military and police was important to the Allied war effort. In the largely Kurdish city of Mahabad, in the far northwest corner of Iran, the gradual retreat of Iranian (military and police) forces under occupation also left an opportunity for Kurdish separatists, led by the charismatic Qazî Muhammad, to attempt Kurdish independence. In February 1945, confrontations between the remaining Iranian police and the Kurdish people of Mahabad resulted in the deaths of five policemen and one Kurdish civilian, and the complete withdrawal of Iranian presence in the city. Qazî Muhammad, who had previously led the Soviet-backed Komale Jiyaveney Kurd organisation and the Democratic Party of Iranian Kurdistan, seized this moment and, on 22 January 1946, proclaimed an independent Kurdish Republic of Mahabad.

In his manifesto of intent for this new, self-governing republic (a state that included both the city and the surrounding Kurdish towns of Bukan, Piranshahr, Sardasht, and Oshnavieh),

Muhammad issued a number of core commitments that can still be detected – albeit in different forms – in the demands of Kurdish liberation movements to this day. The Republic of Mahabad demanded: autonomy for the Iranian Kurds within the Iranian state; the use of Kurdish as the language of education and administration; the election of a provincial council for Kurdistan to supervise state and social matters; that all state officials be of local origin; and unity and fraternity with the Azerbaijani people.

In April later that year, with the support of the Soviets, Muhammad signed a peace treaty with Ja'far Pishevari, president of the Azerbaijani republic, in which they exchanged assurances that the Azerbaijani and Kurdish minorities' rights in each republic would be preserved. A year later, however, Soviet troops (who had been based in Iran during the war, along with British troops) finally withdrew from Iran,[1] only for the Iranian central government to immediately renege on its withdrawal deal with the Soviets, and months later crush the socialist Kurdish republic, which fell on 15 December 1946. The first 'free Kurdish nation' had lasted for less than a year.

An Iranian military court, loyal to Iran's Pahlavi dynasty, sentenced Qazî Muhammad to death by hanging. He was executed on 31 March 1947, in Chuar-chira Square ('Meydanî Çar Çira' in Kurdish), in the centre of Mahabad.

The legacy of the Republic of Mahabad is still vivid in Kurdish cultural memory, not just for being the Kurd's first modern experiment with self-rule, but also for the values it defended (equality, cultural tolerance, fraternity with the other peoples of the region, and recognition of the Kurdish language). As such, it stands as an obvious point of historical reference for writing about Kurdish futures, a lens through which progressive, positive futures might be seen, even though, as a moment in time, it contains both hope and devastation.

The Kurds are one of the largest nations in the world without a state. They stand alongside other stateless peoples like the Tamils, the Uyghurs, the Rohingyas, the Sahrawis, the Catalans, and many others who have never enjoyed political sovereignty in the modern era. There has never been an independent state called 'Kurdistan'. Instead, the word refers to a geographical area divided between four countries – Turkey to the North, Iraq to the South, Syria to the West, Iran to the East – where the Kurds are the majority of the population. To speak of a single Kurdish literature therefore is ambitious, in the same way that speaking of a single Kurdish resistance movement is, not just because of the internecine conflicts and disagreements that Qazî Muhammad lamented of in his final days, but because of the implicit fragmentation that comes with there simply being so many different versions of Kurdistan: four territories, five dialects (Kurmanji, Sorani, Gorani, Zazaki and Luri), numerous sub-dialects (Hawrami, etc.), and countless combinations of these 'versions' with host nations (Turkey, Syria, Iran, Iraq, and further afield). To fully represent all these disparate sub-cultures in a single anthology is perhaps too ambitious a task, but in the imagined future and in the shared struggle for self-rule, perhaps, some unity can be found. For sure, the one abiding feature across these subcultures has been the tragedies that accompanied this struggle.

In Başûrê Kurdistan (also known as Iraqi or Southern Kurdistan) the struggle for autonomy has a long history of defeats, betrayals, and massacres, including a chemical attack on the town of Halabja in 1988 by the Saddam Hussein regime which killed over 5,000 citizens. The Gulf Crisis of 1991 provided Kurds in Iraq with an opportunity to gain self-rule, complete with a no-fly zone created by coalition forces, paving the way for the creation of the still-existing Kurdistan Regional Government, a federal entity to which a new constitution – written following the fall of Saddam – granted Kurds the right to both self-govern regionally (through a presidential system, PM office with cabinet, and a parliament), as well as representation in the Iraqi national parliament with deputies elected from the Kurdish region. That constitution also granted Kurds the right to stand for the position of president of all of Iraq. Indeed, since the fall of Saddam, all Iraq's presidents have been Kurds.

This being said, even here, with a regional government in place, the Kurds have had a very difficult relationship with the central government. Disagreements still rage, in particular over oil: both Erbil and Baghdad claim rights to the oil-rich territories such as Kirkuk and Mosul, and the Kurds continue to strike direct deals with Exxon Mobil, Total, and Chevron Corp, over land Baghdad claims it controls. These disagreements led to an unofficial independence referendum held in Iraqi Kurdistan in 2005 (which called for independence by a vast majority), followed, in 2014, by the request to hold an official one. That request went unanswered, however, in part because the central government was dealing with attacks from the Islamic State. In 2017, the president of the Kurdistan Region, Masoud Barzani, unilaterally called for a referendum to be held on September 2017, despite widespread opposition by other national and international powers. The referendum went ahead and 93% of the voters chose full independence. The result was not binding and eventually the referendum led to a military conflict between the Iraqi central government and the Kurdish regional government, which lost at least 40% of the region under its control, including the so-called 'disputed territories' (Mosul and Kirkuk), to Baghdad. Masoud Barzani was forced to resign thanks to the consequences of this referendum which, as many observers underlined, was poorly planned, prematurely delivered and, instead of bringing independence, cost the Kurds many of their earlier gains.

Perhaps better examples of the Kurdish dream can be

found elsewhere in Iraq. Two small, self-ruling enclaves in Iraq offer inspiration to the cause: the Martyr Rustem Cudi Refugees Camp (better known as 'Makhmur'), in the province of Mosul; and the region of Sinjar (Shengal) which is populated by the Yazidi Kurds.

Makhmur can be considered the mother of all subsequent attempts at self-governance and the first major success in this struggle since the Republic of Mahabad. The 12,000-plus refugees living there were forced to leave their homes in Northern (Turkish) Kurdistan in the early nineties, after the Turkish government burned their villages, claiming they had been infiltrated by the PKK (Kurdish Workers' Party).[2] In 1997 they accepted an offer by the KDP (Kurdish Democratic Party) to leave the Atroush camp they had initially settled in, to move to Makhmur, a camp built by Saddam Hussein (with help from the UNHCR). The refugees set about converting this area of desert into a camp, deprived of many basic provisions, but liveable thanks to its water supply. Here, the refugees established a horizontal governance body, a council that ran the camp, together with a women's council, and an education system delivered in Kurdish, a language forbidden in Turkey.

Sinjar is tragically best known for the massacre carried out there by the Islamic State in the first weeks of August 2014. Thousands of Yazidi Kurds were killed, more than 6,000 women and children were kidnapped, with most of them being forced to become sex slaves by ISIS mercenaries. Twenty-eight hundred are still missing. Despite all these tragedies, the Yazidi of Sinjar are slowly returning to their land. There, they have established an autonomous administration complete with a defence force.

In Turkey, there have also been successes in the struggle for self-rule. On 15 July 2011, in Diyarbakır ('Amed' in Kurdish), the capital of Bakûrê Kurdistan (Northern or Turkish Kurdistan), the Democratic Society Congress (DTK), a platform for Kurdish associations and movements, together with the main Kurdish party, BDP (Peace and Democracy Party), jointly proclaimed a new, democratic self-government. Democratic autonomy had been exactly the solution Abdullah Öcalan (colloquially known as 'Apo'), the leader of the PKK, had fought for over a decade before – an ambition that had landed him in the maximum security prison island of Imrali, and kept him there since 15 February 1999, like a 'Kurdish Mandela', only one the rest of the world has forgotten about.

Democratic autonomy implies a number of things: 'finding a compromise with nation-states', respecting 'the historical-societal heritage of peoples and cultures' through enshrining irrevocable and fundamental rights in a revisable constitution. 'The foremost conditions of this arrangement are that the sovereign nation-state (e.g. Turkey, Iran, Iraq, or Syria) renounces all denial and annihilation policies, and the oppressed nation (of the Kurds) abandons the idea of forming its own nation-state.' In other words, both parties have to renounce 'statist' tendencies, and we shouldn't expect this to be either an easy or straightforward process. As one commentator puts it: 'EU countries took more than 300 years of nation-state experience before they could accept democratic autonomy as the best solution for solving nation-states' regional, national and minority-related problems.'[3]

The proclamation of 2011 was followed in August 2015, by the announcement by the confederalist DTK (Democratic Society Congress) of self-rule in Sur, a borough of Amed. Around-the-clock curfews were immediately imposed by the central Turkish government on several towns in the region as a result. The curfew in (and siege of) Sur began on 11 December 2015. The siege lasted for more than three months and destroyed much of the neighbourhood. Heavy artillery and machine-gun fire were deployed in clashes between Turkish soldiers and police against the Kurdish militias. The siege ended on 10 March 2016, with defeat for the separatists. At least 200 people, mostly civilians, were killed. The film *Ji Bo Azadiyê* by Ersin Çelik tells the story of the siege and the defence of the borough by Kurdish militias.

In tandem with this, on 14 December 2015, the Turkish central government also declared a 24-hour curfew in the city of Cizre.[4] As with other places, the Turkish military used heavy artillery to bomb residential areas. The violence peaked on 7 February 2016, when at least 178 civilians were killed by Turkish security forces in one day, many of them shot or burned alive when Turkish soldiers poured petrol into basements they were taking refuge in.

Perhaps the greatest achievement of this patchwork of resistance movements took place in Syria, amid the ongoing Civil War (2011-present). With the Republic of Mahabad always as a reference point, and with Öcalan as their leader *in absentia*, the Kurds finally got a chance to implement democratic autonomy in Rojava (now the Federation of Northern and Eastern Syria-Rojava). Against all odds, the Kurds have been shaping and putting into practice a new form of governance in the midst of a bitter war. From the beginning (in 2011), Syrian Kurds opted for a 'Third Way', siding with neither the government of Assad, nor with the so-called 'opposition to Assad', puppets of other states, primarily Turkey.

As the academic Thomas Jeffrey Miley put it: 'It appeared that a revolutionary third way was emerging out of the maelstrom of the Syrian civil war – an effective alternative to the disastrous, negative dialectic of tyranny and chaos in which the region, and even the world, seemed to be increasingly and inescapably submerged. Rojava became a distant, progressive light shining in a dark reactionary night, a rare beacon of hope, from a far away and exotic space. A place onto which European and American leftists could project anti-capitalist dreams and radical democratic illusions. It was somewhat like the Zapatista movement in Chiapas, Mexico, except that Rojava lies at the very epicentre of global geopolitical strife, which certainly rendered the revolutionary developments in the northeast of Syria all the more intriguing, while it also served to multiply their manifold and manifest contradictions.'[5]

Twelve years on, in 2023, the Kurds in Rojava have defeated the Islamic State, in the heroic resistance of the city of Kobane in 2014-15, liberating the Caliphate's so-called capital, Raqqa, in 2017, as well as many other regions up until the liberation of the last IS stronghold of Baghouz in 2019. The Kurds have built schools and universities, and established councils and communes to run cities, provinces, and regions. They were always an anathema to the Turkish government and they continue to be such, which was why Turkey supported (both logistically and economically) the Islamic State (and not only in Rojava as a recent report about the Yazidi genocide in Shengal showed),[6] and why it intervened directly in Syria-occupied Afrin, Serekanîye, and other areas where Kurds and the other peoples (Assyrian, Armenian, Syriacs, Checens, Arabs) live in peace, collectively governing and defending a model they all contributed to build. It is in the liberated Rojava that language (not just Kurdish) and culture (cinema, theatre, literature, music) has most flourished.[7]

This anthology was born from two desires: on the one hand, we found it interesting to challenge Kurdish writers from all four territories (Southern Kurdistan in Iraq, Northern Kurdistan in Turkey, Rojava in Syria, and Rojhilat in Iran) as well as from the diaspora to imagine what Kurdistan might look like a century after the Republic of Mahabad, and that first attempt at independence. On the other hand, this book represents an opportunity for many writers to freely write in their own mother tongue, without (we hope) the danger of being persecuted. Unfortunately, one of the writers, Meral

Şimşek (from the city of Amed), is currently facing trial, charged with 'making propaganda for and being a member of a terrorist organisation.' As 'evidence' of this, the indictment quotes her writings, and in particular the story which appears in this anthology, 'Arzela'. The prosecutor in Turkey included her story as evidence in the indictment against her even before the story had been published in this book. Şimşek explained that 'the utopian country that appears in it was used as evidence. The name of my protagonist, Arzela, is supposed to be my code name. And even though the story is not even set in Turkey, it is presented as a PKK plan for the future.'[8]

The stories of this anthology imagine a future after Mahabad, and are inspired by it. The authors come from all different parts of Kurdistan and write in two of its five dialects: Kurmanji and Sorani. Some don't feel confident enough to write in their own mother tongue, switching to Turkish or English, as if to demonstrate that all forms of liberation (including cultural and linguistic liberation) is yet to be achieved.

The stories by Sema Kaygusuz, Yıldız Çakar, Meral Şimşek and Jîl Şwanî all explore the impact of the ecological destruction of Kurdistan by occupying forces, and yet allow for glimmers of hope for the future. The story by Hüseyin Karabey shows the mountains of Kurdistan offering shelter to eco-activists, just as they have provided shelter for political activists over the years (including many Kurdish political leaders such as Molla Mostafa Barzani, Jalal Talabani, Abdul Rahman Ghassemlou, and Abdullah Öcalan). The story by jailed Kurdish politician Selahattin Demirtaş imagines a child victim of the war growing up to be Kurdistan's head of state and signing a Middle East pact uniting the region in 2046, a century after Mahabad; showing in the process the role the struggle played in liberating Kurdish women.

Although pain, destruction and suffering are common

features in these stories, one other common feature is hope ('hêvî' in Kurdish). Mahabad was a beacon of hope for the Kurds but it was taken away from them brutally. Years after the collapse of Mahabad, the Kurds are still holding on to that *hêvî*. Karzan Kardozi's story resonates with this also: in a post-apocalyptic world, a young girl with green eyes is the only child to survive an unlikely disease; while Qadir Agid's 'The Last Hope' tests this to the extreme: Qazî Muhammad finds himself in a robot-run future city where he learns the curse of Kurds forever being abandoned by their allies has struck again.

One of the characters in Muharrem Erbey's story is named 'Mahabad', reminding us of a tradition that also makes 'Hêvî' one of the most popular names for Kurdish girls. Kurds continue to give their children such names as Zîlan,[9] Dersîm,[10] and Halabja, even though they remind them of such colossal tragedies. For Kurds, the act of hope and the duty of remembrance – that these tragedies don't ever happen again – go hand in hand. Another name of hope you will hear a lot in Kurdish communities is 'Jîyan' (in Kurdish, simply 'Life').

As the stories of Jahangir Mahmoudveysi and Ava Homa remind us, maybe there will come a day when the long sleep will end and the sun will shine over the Kurds, allowing them to light candles for the memories of those lost in the struggle and to celebrate in the squares of Kurdistan those first steps made in Mahabad. The story by Ömer Dilsoz is about a group of Kurds carrying out research into more efficient forms of solar power. In 2146, 200 years after Mahabad, the goal has finally been attained, a statue of Qazî Mohammed is erected and the Kurdish flag raised in Çar Çira Square ('Four Candles Square'), the very place where Qazî Mohammed and his comrades were hanged, and now home to Kurdistan's Science and Technology University in an independent nation. This story also shows how strongly the desire for an independent Kurdistan still burns in many hearts even in a future in which other nation-states have dissipated and merged together.

Nariman Evdike, from Rojava (Syrian Kurdistan), addresses the ways in which several nations, languages and cultures (not just Kurdish, but Armenian as well) have been brutally and bloodily suppressed for centuries and yet have somehow survived and indeed gained greater agency. It is not surprising to read about these issues and concerns in a story from Rojava, because what the Rojava Revolution is doing is precisely promoting and defending the co-existence of cultures, peoples, and languages.[11] Rojava is perhaps today the place where hêvî has its best chance to materialise.

Orsola Casagrande & Mustafa Gündoğdu

Notes

1. Öcalan Abdullah (2011), 'Democratic Nation' in https://www.freeocalan.org/books/downloads/en-brochure-democratic-nation_2017.pdf. For more on Öcalan, see Orsola Casagrande & Ra Page (ed.s), *The American Way* (Comma, 2021), pp345–375.
2. The PKK (Partiya Karkerên Kurdistan/Kurdistan Workers Party) was established during a foundation congress held on 26 and 27 November 1978 in a rural village called Fis (Ziyaret). A central committee consisting of seven people was elected, with Abdullah Öcalan as its head. A leftist popular movement, the PKK is organised around committees (political, cultural, army, women's army, young people, etc.). The PKK's first armed action was in 1984. Initially supporting the reunification of Kurdistan into an independent new state, Öcalan has since the late '90s proposed a new concept: democratic confederalism.
3. Carraher Seamas (2016), 'Birinci Bodrum, First Basement', https://globalrights.info/2016/07/75017.

4. *Global Rights* (2016): 'The Death Basements of Cizre: Five years on, victims are still fighting for justice', https://globalrights.info/2021/02/the-death-basements-of-cizre-five-years-on-victims-are-still-fighting-for-justice.

5. Miley Thomas Jeffrey (2020), 'The Kurdish Freedom Movement, Rojava and the Left', https://merip.org/2020/08/the-kurdish-freedom-movement-rojava-and-the-left-295.

6. Wintour Patrick (2022), Turkey should face international court over Yazidi genocide, report says in https://www.theguardian.com/law/2022/jul/05/turkey-should-face-international-court-over-yazidi-genocide-report-says-helena-kennedy.

7. Festivals in Rojava include: the Rojava International Film Festival, Kobane Film Festival, two literature festivals (Osman Sabri and Martyr Herekol), an annual children's festival, biennial music competitions, the Assyrian Culture Festival, a Women's Festival, a theatre festival (Qamishlo), an annual dance festival, and the Leloun International Film Festival (held in Shehba refugee camps).

8. Kuray Zeynep (2021), 'Meral Şimşek: I will not remain silent', https://anfenglishmobile.com/culture/meral-Simsek-i-will-not-remain-silent-54964.

9. Zilan was a massacre of between 5,000 and 15,000 Kurdish civilians by the Turkish Land Forces on the orders of the army officer (and later president) İsmet İnönü in the Zilan Valley of Van Province on 12/13 July 1930, during the Ararat rebellion in Ağrı Province.

10. Dersîm refers to an Alevi Kurdish uprising against the central government in the Dersim region of eastern Turkey, led by Seyid Riza, a chieftain of the Abasan tribe. As a result of the Turkish Armed Forces campaign in 1937 and 1938 against the rebellion and the subsequent massacre, anywhere between 13,000 and 40,000 Kurds died, with tens of thousands internally displaced.

11. For the 2014 charter, go to:
https://rojavainformationcenter.com/storage/2021/07/
2014-Social-Contract-of-the-Autonomous-Regions-of-Afrin-
Jazira-and-Kobane-1.pdf.
For the renewed 2016 version, go to:
https://rojavainformationcenter.com/storage/2021/07/
2016-Social-Contract-of-the-Democratic-Federation-of-
Northern-Syria.pdf.

Waiting for the Leopard

Sema Kaygusuz

*Translated from the Turkish
by Nicholas Glastonbury*

IN ORDER TO QUELL the excitement of waiting for his new sibling, with whom he would share the lodging house where he'd lived since the start of his mission, the Leopard Warden was rereading his contract with the ministry.

CLAUSE 1 PARTIES:
Whereby the present contract has herein been executed between the Commission for Cataloguing Living Creatures (hereafter referred to as the 'Living Catalogue') as overseen by the Ministry of Environment and Urban Planning of the Republic of Turkey, and the Leopard Warden (hereafter referred to as 'LW143') serving in the Four Mountain Region.

CLAUSE 2 PURVIEW:
Whereby both parties have agreed that, pursuant to LW143's request to the board of Living Catalogue for bio-vivification, LW143 has been informed that the newly vivified human individual is to be thirty years

old, female, healthy, lacking no inner organs, having no physical disability, and that, in accordance with the standard vivification protocol of 2046, she will have fully functional cognitive capacity but will have partial amnesia.

The Leopard Warden had reread the contract so many times over the weeks he'd memorised it, and he patted himself on the chest proudly as he read this clause because he was the reason that a woman who'd died more than a century ago would now be brought back to life. He couldn't keep himself from imagining that someone else in the future might do him the same kindness, that he might be resurrected at the age of thirty, as though he were in the vision of paradise in Islam, many centuries after he died. He slurped down his coffee as if tasting that ancient fantasy. The only fragrant thing in the mountainous region where he lived was coffee. Drinking coffee not only made the Leopard Warden feel human, it also warmed him up to the visual dimension of those harsh lands he had tired of inhabiting. Drinking his hot coffee, he could ignore the wordlessness of the leaden mountains he saw from his window, towering up in cragged bluffs, and he could forget – even for a moment – the misery of the many years he had spent entirely alone in pursuit of a leopard whose very existence was uncertain. Finally, having a companion would make it more bearable as he tried to find a bone or a claw belonging to the leopard he was after. He skipped past the pleasantries of the first part of the contract, moving on to its more distressing clauses on care and relations.

CLAUSE 21 BODY:
Biologically, the 'Vivified Individual' requested by codename LW143 will be a chimeric being because it will bear its own unique DNA as well as LW143's donated tissue and blood. This 'Vivified Individual'

will also carry certain chromosomes in common with the donor, for which reason the 'Vivified Individual' will be considered the donor LW143's sibling as defined by the laws of the Civil Code. As party to this contract, LW143 pledges not to enter into sexual relations, to wed, or to refuse to terminate a pregnancy resulting from any sexual relations with the 'Vivified Individual,' which would violate the bounds of siblinghood. Any form of sexual intimacy between siblings will be subject to criminal conviction without trial as sexual abuse.

The Leopard Warden tossed the contract aside and leapt to his feet. Even though he had read it many times already, he felt nauseous, as he paced back and forth in his room, at the prospect of feeling sexual desire for this woman he would bring back to life, who would genetically become his sister in the process of revivification. He felt humiliated every time he read this section. Because up until the day way back when he had first gone to the Living Catalogue commission with a molar in hand, he hadn't even thought about which gender that tooth belonged to. Aside from expending the right conferred on him by the system to revivify one person, the tooth had no particularly special qualities. All he wanted was a person. All he wanted, the only thing, in fact, as one of the 150 wardens serving in the Four Mountain region, there on that mountaintop where nobody visited and nobody could really live in the first place, was a person. Most of the other wardens in the region had done the same thing. Using samples of blood, bones, and nails from the dead, they had each obtained brothers and sisters beholden to them. Though some of the wardens, at their own peril, must have lived with their revivified individuals as lovers, the mountains would be ashamed of them, even if nobody else noticed. The Leopard Warden covered his face

3

with his hands as he looked at the mountains. In his heart was an arcane shame. Because the thought of such an act, which sullied the pedigree of human existence, awakened the basest desires latent in his flesh.

In order to gather his wits, he returned inevitably to the moment he had found the tooth. As soon as he had learned that this geography had once upon a time been a vast wetland covered in glacial lakes, small waterfalls, and rivers, he decided to dig a well in the field just behind the lodging house. If he had his own drinking water, he would no longer be forced to go to the centre every week, to haul back gallon after gallon of water himself; he would no longer be constrained to the ferrous-tasting, lifeless waters produced in their distilleries. In the beginning, the digging wasn't too difficult. The thirst-chapped earth came up easily with a few light strikes of the shovel. But things became more difficult a few metres down. The deeper the hole grew, the more the sandy layers of the soil changed, and he was confronted by limy, calcareous basalt rocks. The stones he encountered in the depths looked like they had been stacked upon one another, and he had no choice but to pry them out by hand. The Leopard Warden was descending into the past as he dug, into the annals of the earth. As the well deepened, his expectations of water were replaced with something else. A pessimistic feeling, that neither flowed nor nourished like water.

When he reached a depth of seven metres, he was confronted with a sight he hadn't anticipated, a mass grave of bones piled up, delaminated by burning. From this hole sprung not water but a jumble of skeletons belonging, based on the number of skulls in the grave, to approximately seventy people. It took days for the Leopard Warden to compose himself. As he looked at the skeletons of all those people who died embracing one another, they were brought to life in his mind's eye. Some of the skulls had bullet holes; some of the bones had gashes left by sharp blades. There must have been a war, he thought at first. When he realised that among the skeletons in the grave were femurs belonging to children, even to babies, it didn't take long for him to understand that this gruesome scene had been left behind by some ancient massacre.

How many years' worth of a soil shroud had he dug through until he'd reached the grave? A hundred years? A hundred and fifty years? Though he tried to research the events of the region's history by entering its coordinates into the internet, he was unable to find anything earlier than the past fifty years. After Wikipedia had been prohibited in 2017, almost every search engine had been censored by their information filters. He could have tried to access the websites containing the libraries of documents uploaded by underground anarchist groups, but because his computer was directly registered to the Living Catalogue, it would have been impossible for him to break through the firewall without leaving a trace. Not that he had either the knowledge or the bravery to do so anyway. He was an obedient, steadfast, timid man, the Leopard Warden. To him, it verged on insubordination to even wonder about the events behind the mass grave he had chanced upon. In the end, he was left with just a molar. Looking at it through a magnifying glass, he examined the decay in the little cavity inside the crown, trying to estimate the dead person's age. As time passed, the tooth transformed into an indispensable object for him. The tooth's life had come to an end, but it endowed the Leopard Warden's rather ordinary personality with new mettle. Every time he took the tooth in his hands, he was filled with the strength of some divine force, and his sense of self-worth was replenished by its gentle rapture. Thanks to this lifeless, genderless, bodiless tooth, its profundity deepening by the day, the endless cycle of life was in his hands. As the Leopard Warden searched for the leopard in those impassable valleys, those dried riverbeds, those cragged hills surrounding the ruins, that tooth he took from the grave never left his side, because it seemed at once both a miracle and an agonising memory. He felt so bound to the tooth that if anything happened to him, if perchance he were to tumble down a cliff, or freeze in a blizzard, or else be unable to exit one of those passes he entered, being in the tooth's company made him want to inwardly come back to life along with it.

In time, whenever he took the tooth in his hands, a mouth would begin to appear before his eyes, and then a bulbous nose, followed by two dark eyes close together, and lastly, a broad forehead. The face taking shape in his imagination had started to fray his nerves. Six months after he found the tooth, he took it out of his pocket to show his friend the Catfish Warden, whom he'd run into at the centre, and explained the situation. 'Every time I look at this, after a few seconds, I start to see my face.'

The Catfish Warden nodded her head, frowning. 'You feel tied to the tooth,' she said. 'Go back to where you found it right away and leave it there. If you're not going to leave it, though, get it over with and revivify it, or else you'll start hallucinating. If you always see your own face, you'll go mad with loneliness. You know, I haven't looked in the mirror for months now. Why? Because when I see my reflection, I simply can't bear the empty space behind me. I have to go searching for some object in the village ruins to console myself. Recently I found a wooden ladle. The ladle looks at me, I look back at the ladle. Like it's a person. I feel crazy, telling it everything that crosses my mind, my dreams and stuff… Sometimes I raise a glass and sing a song to the ladle. I'm scared to death that one day it'll begin talking back to me.'

Sighing deeply, the Catfish Warden fidgeted with her fingers, calloused from searching for fossils in the riverbeds; her downcast demeanour had sucked the air out of the room. 'They left us to the past, my friend,' she said in a low voice.

'They left us among the dead. We're not supposed to remember anything but they want everything possible to be resurrected. As though we could start all over if we had no memory. But what about that wooden ladle? The life of that ladle? How are we to erase that life beyond language? I feel like I'm going to lose my mind every time I think about it.'

The Leopard Warden was utterly perplexed. The following week, he went to visit the Deer Warden, who lived with one of the resurrected. He wanted to learn from him what kind of experience it would be to live with an artificial sibling. The Deer Warden's home was appalling. He and the brother whom he'd named Plush lived a sordid life together. Plush was a painfully thin man. His eyes were sunken and his gait was strange. He dragged one of his feet with every step he managed to take.

The Deer Warden called him 'it' when he talked about him, 'It came and the whole mood of the house changed,' 'It's an imbecile, never managed to learn how to form a sentence.' The Deer Warden spoke as if he were describing not a brother but some pet he'd been entrusted with. He would rain down commands on Plush, raising his voice when Plush didn't understand him. It was all too clear that Plush had been beaten, and he had developed a pitiable tendency to involuntarily shield his face as a result. By deviating from directives, the Deer Warden had established an outright master-slave relationship with Plush. He was deriving pleasure from this lifestyle. After he forcefully admonished the Leopard Warden not to share anything about what he'd seen there, he explained at length that the resurrected people are truly worthless creatures, that nobody enforces the rules in place, and that it wasn't something to think too much about as a consequence. 'You really ought not to indulge these sorts,' he concluded. 'If you follow the state's rules, they'll get the better of you right away. The rules only exist so we can say there are rules, not so they'll be followed.'

The process of resurrecting the tooth took a very long time for the Leopard Warden. At the forensic centre, they showed him a skull that they modelled with data from the tooth's DNA; a few weeks later, a skeleton measuring 170 centimetres. Though the newly-formed skeleton had as yet no unique qualities, the experts dragged their feet as much as possible in the first stages of the procedure in order to put the Leopard Warden to the test in his decision to resurrect a dead person. In another sense, they were protecting him from 'godliness'. They put him through a series of training exercises to keep him from succumbing to a godly arrogance and enslaving, exploiting, or fomenting insurrection in the new person who was to be his sibling, and in so doing, to make him behave respectfully so that the resurrected person would be a productive and useful individual. Like the Deer Warden had said, they knew all too well how to impose rules. When the expert psychologists gave their approval that the Leopard Warden was ready, a three-dimensional image finally appeared. A dark-skinned, dark-haired woman with sharp cheekbones and a slender face. The Leopard Warden was astonished at the three-dimensional image. 'I was expecting someone more beastly,' he said, 'like the prehistorical wax people you see at the natural history museum.' The doctors enunciated each word as they explained that the resurrected woman had died a total of 108 years ago, in 1938, that she would be no different from the people of the present, that she may have simply had a different relationship with nature and objects. The coming person was simply a modern person who had gone through the same stages of evolution. Neither weaker nor stronger, neither dumber nor smarter.

The experts lectured the Leopard Warden to the point of exhaustion, forcing him to memorise the directives he had to follow. The Leopard Warden found himself in the language of the user guide, dry as a bone, saturated with ethical laws. Each precept was made up of at least four clauses; the words became almost pornographic, unspooled from his feelings, causing his head to spin madly. Even on the subject of the bed his chimeric sibling would sleep in, there wasn't a single paragraph from civil law to criminal law, from property rights to privacy protections, that he hadn't been made to swear upon. The Leopard Warden had to swear on his dignity that he wouldn't use his chimeric sibling as a housekeeper or slave; he had to swear on his honour that he would be responsible for his chimeric sibling's health, care, and nourishment; he promised that he would make his sibling into a productive member of society; he accepted that, if his chimeric sibling were to commit a crime, he would receive the exact same punishment as it would; and, he pledged that his chimeric sibling would adopt the official religion and speak the official language, that it would live according to the fundaments of citizenship in the unitary state, and that it would defend this way of life down to its very last drop of blood. The most compulsory of these clauses, though, was the one for which he had to swear he would never allow his chimeric sibling's memory to awaken. A new person was going to come to life, and so of course its memory was to remain unquestionably dead. The past was not, for any reason whatsoever, to be recollected, to be spoken about, to be brought to the surface with fragments of memory that appear by association. His chimeric sibling was no more than a tooth being brought to life, it had no subconscious or history: that all had to remain underground, along with the rest of the bones. After signing page after page of his contract without objection, like a devoted soldier, he was both a new owner and an official brother. It remained to be seen, though, whose owner, whose brother he would be.

As soon as the Leopard Warden saw his new sibling, he gave her the name Sedef. Meaning mother-of-pearl, it was the only word that suited that phosphorescent gleam, particular to the newly born, in the whites of her eyes. Sedef had a calm, full, nasal voice. Because her vocabulary was still so limited, she'd leave her sentences half-finished, and because she hadn't quite wrapped her head around verb tenses, she had to speak in the simple present.

'I hunger.'

'Then let me make you some porridge, you have to eat easily digestible foods these first few days.'

'Thank.'

Over those first few days, the Leopard Warden was like a tender-hearted father, letting Sedef slowly touch objects as he taught her the meanings of things, allowing her to combine textures and names at the sensory level. All the objects that Sedef focused her curiosity on were born one by one into their names, as if they were coming into being for the very first time. A cup was not just any other cup. It was a crater, materialising out of a topography of memory developing moment by moment between these two siblings. The feeling of alienation that objects awakened in Sedef, thankfully, didn't last long. Whenever she learned a new noun, something superlative would emerge, like the taste of the milk, the colour of the curtain, the transparency of the glass. Adjectives appeared after nouns, followed soon after by figures of speech. A veiled poetry was coming into being in their house. Metaphors that never occurred to him transformed the life he'd built with his sister into crude poems.

'What is this?'

'A mug.'

'What's a mug?'

'We drink coffee and tea from a mug.'

'I like tea. Black tea goes through hot water and turns red.'

'Yes, tea is ruddy.'

'Ruddy?'

'Like red…'
'I like the taste of ruddy.'

The only name Sedef couldn't hold onto was her own. Whenever the Leopard Warden would call for Sedef she wouldn't turn and look but would instead try to figure out which thing the word 'sedef' corresponded to. Apart from her name, she had grown accustomed to almost everything in just a few weeks, except for electronic devices like the telephone or the computer. The natural harmony she forged with things as she picked them up and held them, dug them up and pulled them out, dragged and lifted them, went haywire when it came to something like a digital button. What's more, Sedef had a noteworthy predisposition for taking long, exhausting walks. When she descended the steep, rocky cliffsides, she would enter into a physical dialogue with the stones. With every step she took on the melting snow, she foresaw the slippery loam underneath. Fifty years after the building of the dam, all the springs had dried up and, because of erosion, all the rivers in the valleys had been smothered in mud. Over the years, the creatures endemic to the region had, along with the vegetation, been buried under the earth or else retreated into the unknown. No living thing Sedef would recognise was left. It was for this reason that the swamps where she sometimes mired herself carried, in her barren memory, some primordial meaning. She recognised neither the stones along her path nor the sky above. The mechanic whirring that came from the cable cars descending from the mountains' peaks to the city centre held her perpetually in the listless minutes of the present tense. Nobody else lived in these desiccated valleys or in these village ruins on the escarpments. Except for a couple of other revivified people like her. Community, here, was the pale light emanating from the Brown Bear Warden's house on the opposite escarpment, which she saw from the house on the escarpment where she lived with the

Leopard Warden. Characterising this wasted world in terms of the 'serenity of inorganic life,' the Leopard Warden pretended like death wasn't death.

Instead of using the cable cars that everyone rode to get to the city centre, Sedef would walk for kilometres on end, returning with bags from the market with enviable agility. She asked the Leopard Warden almost no questions. Not because she was without curiosity, but because she didn't know what to be curious about. When the Leopard Warden would stumble on uneven steps out of the house – having turned into a bulky, formless dark green shadow with his thermal camouflage, his gun filled with tranquilising darts and bullet cartridges, and his polar hood swaddling his ears and forehead – Sedef couldn't figure out what she should ask him. Once, though, upon finding a molar in the bathroom cabinet, she appeared before the Leopard Warden and asked him, with the innocent perplexity of a child, 'Whose tooth is this?' The Leopard Warden gulped as he looked at Sedef. The tooth in his sister's hand now afflicted him with terror. 'I found it while digging the well,' was all he could manage to say. Hurriedly putting on his thermal clothes, he murmured a few things under his breath to change the subject. The Leopard Warden had one duty: Waiting for the Leopard. Here's how he put it to Sedef: 'After finding the leopard, my assignment will come to an end, and then we can move to the centre.'

And yet, the word 'leopard' called up no image in Sedef. Whatever it was that was called leopard was nothing more than a vocal ordering of two measly syllables. A brief piece of music, without colour, without form, without scent. Since she didn't know how to read or write, Sedef didn't know by what means she could even pursue her curiosity and research 'leopard.' Over time, leopard evolved from a stubborn word that evoked no associations into a disembodied fantasy. In Sedef's eyes, that thing called leopard began appearing to her swaddled tight like the Leopard Warden, girded with thermal clothes, strange flashlights, and walkie-talkies, masked with digital goggles, with a broad ribcage but narrow legs, seeming altogether like a sibling who spoke softly and always averted its gaze, like a friend who avoided affinity. The Leopard Warden, leaving in the dead of morning and returning exhausted at sunset, was himself, to Sedef, a restless leopard. Sedef, on the other hand, was the other animal at home, an innocent, ignorant, impulsive cub. The secret bond between these two siblings wandered among the farthest reveries, and the feeling of foreignness they felt towards one another simply wouldn't subside.

One day, undaunted by the snowstorm, the Leopard Warden went on a two-hour cable-car ride followed by a four-hour hike, at the end of which he found a dead animal that hadn't yet begun to rot on the edge of the northern mountain's treeline. The horns that emerged straight out of the animal's skull branched out wide before curving back in towards the skull. The black band that extended from its gnashed, bleeding neck to its tail made the animal seem more majestic than it was. The Leopard Warden looked callously into its frozen eyes. Having been born into a lifeless vacuum himself, he couldn't see the melancholy in this lifeless carcass anyway. After all, he lived with the dead alone, the dead who would be brought back to life. The Leopard Warden took a picture of the animal, with its dismembered back leg, and sent it to the Living Catalogue Centre at once. He didn't know what exactly the corpse splayed out on the ground was. It could be a roe deer, or it could be a bezoar ibex. A few minutes later, a call from the centre delivered the news that the animal was a Hook-Antlered Chamois Goat. The chamois was one of approximately one hundred and fifty endemic species that lived in the region once upon a time. Which meant that the rumours as to whether it still lived there were no longer mere legend.

Within the hour, dozens of people stood around the chamois, including the other wardens who'd heard the news. These wardens, responsible for various mammals, drank more heavily, swore more easily, and picked fights more readily than the fish and bird wardens. Often, the first thing they'd do when they came together was to make fun of the women wardens who searched for fossils of salamanders and fish.

The Goat Warden was on the verge of throwing himself upon the animal on the ground and kissing it gleefully. Taking a bottle of cognac from his pocket, he offered it to the Leopard Warden. 'Thank you so much, my friend; thanks to you, I'm saved from this open-air prison.'

As the medical crew transferred the chamois with great care into an air-proof steel crate, the wardens gathered around a fire and began discussing how the goat might have died.

'My bear could have killed it,' the Brown Bear Warden enthused.

The Wolf Warden dismissed him. 'Oh, please. You don't know whether your bear is alive or not, you haven't seen so much as a pawprint. Be grateful that you found a vertebra. If anything did it, my wolf did.'

The Brown Bear Warden was insistent. 'But didn't the Oak Warden say that since oaks grow out of the forgotten depths of the earth, other things might return, too? The Brown Bear is a resilient creature; in any case, it has a fifty-year lifespan. Let's say two specimens survived that bombardment nobody talks about; by now there's at least three, since one of them must have given birth. Didn't you see how the goat's stomach was torn apart? That's the kind of thing a bear can do.'

The Boar Warden listened to the discussion as he glanced through the Living Catalogue Centre's Inventory of National Biological Diversity, finding the entry for the Brown Bear, *Ursus arctos arctos*. 'It couldn't have been a bear, your bear isn't an agile hunter like a wolf or a leopard. It eats birds' eggs and other small prey. If it can't find any food, it'll eat roots, or if it's lucky, honey, though I've never seen the stuff in my life. Clearly the bear's an opportunistic animal. It wouldn't be able to take down a goat.'

The Leopard Warden, doubtful from the start, chimed in. 'How much do you think the bear weighs?'

'Around a hundred and fifty kilos,' replied the Bear Warden.

The Leopard Warden pointed at the place where the goat was found. 'The goat had been dragged here, look, you can see the trail of blood. If a heavy animal like a bear had moved it, there'd have to be indents in the soil. Clearly, it was my cat that hunted down the goat, and then probably tried to bring it back to her den. When she couldn't manage, she left it here, planning to return. Didn't you notice? There's a sharp smell of urine on the goat; she pissed on her prey to mark it. What I mean, friends, is that my leopard is around here somewhere.'

The Wolf Warden was grinding his teeth on a twig he had snapped off the bush next to him. 'Why would she leave her hunt, are you saying that she fled when you approached?'

The Leopard Warden wanted to convince even himself that there was truth to what he was saying. 'The goat was stiff when I found it; it's obvious that a day has passed since it died. I believe that a female leopard killed it, caught it by the throat and snapped its neck. I don't believe she had time to tear it apart. She tried to move it, and when she couldn't, she left it here, among the boulders. Which means she has cubs somewhere far away, defenceless cubs; she must have returned for them, she could be coming here with her cubs. Maybe they're close by. Maybe they're watching us.'

Squirming nervously, the wardens glanced around the escarpment where they stood. The Wolf Warden instinctively took hold of his gun. A leopard with cubs far surpassed any expectations. A living leopard would be so much more significant than every valuable bone, every fossil fragment and shred of fur, every claw, skull and tooth, every discarded, withered, broken, lost remnant that the Living Catalogue Centre intended to add to its Inventory of National Biological Diversity. It would mean that the leopard was, like the wardens, a natural creature. Not a copy, not a corpse, but a living, thoroughbred creature with a lineage. Each of the other creatures, on the other hand, produced out of DNA samples, could be no more than singular resurrections. Though every catfish, every moss, every lizard, every owl produced from fossilised remains was worthy of respect and admiration, they were nonetheless synthetic beings whose privacy had been violated. They belonged not to nature but to an artificial national park constructed out of zoos and botanical gardens. The potential existence of a leopard that had succeeded in surviving on those mountains cast the wardens standing around the fire into a sudden feeling of inadequacy. The cliffside they were looking at now afflicted them with panic. They listened silently for a while to the cracking that came from the earth, a strange thrumming that dissipated into the air. The only thing they heard was the disquiet of being alive. Before long, they hurriedly put out their fire and each made their way back to their lodging houses. On their return home, each of the wardens' senses had long since changed.

For several days after he found the dead goat, the Leopard Warden didn't leave home. He was at his wit's end. He passed his days only drinking coffee and didn't say a single word to Sedef so long as he didn't have to. Sedef, however, seemed to be swimming in language. She would listen to educational programs and seminars that the directives had deemed suitable on the miniature computer the Leopard Warden had gotten for her, her eyes fixed on the screen, and when the seminar programs bored her, she would lie in bed and watch television shows that, again, the directives had deemed suitable. These shows were fictions of assimilation, dramatisations intended to acclimatise people like her to the era in which they'd arrived. They were mostly didactic dramas. Epic stories in which good citizens and hardworking labourers were rewarded and ordinary people each became extraordinary heroes. Sedef would wander through each room of the house repeating every last sentence she heard on her shows with a theatrical flourish, playing one character after another as she resurrected the dialogues she heard with the same intonations in their home. Their home was, in a way, an imaginary film set where every scene was being reshot. In the beginning, the Leopard Warden enjoyed watching Sedef's unrelentingly spirited childhood, because it meant that he didn't have to teach her everything one lesson at a time. But in time, he'd had his fill of hearing the absurd conversations from her shows. The authentic, open-hearted personality Sedef had in the beginning was disappearing by the day, being replaced by an artificial intelligence that spoke in melodramatic sentences. At one point, the Leopard Warden even admonished her to be quiet.

'That's enough, Sedef, I have a headache from listening to you go on like that.'

Sedef approached him, a contrived smile on her face. 'Oh, forgive me, I'm afraid I didn't realise you were there.'

'Of course you know I'm here, Sedef, don't be ridiculous! Besides, it's not even you who's talking, it's the hero of the show you're watching.'

Sedef's wry face turned into a scowl. 'Of course it's me, dear, or my name's not Sedef!'

The Leopard Warden could endure it no longer. 'How do you know your name is Sedef?' he asked, as if to hurt his sister's feelings. He regretted the words as soon as they came out of his mouth.

Sedef frowned, fixing her eyes on the Leopard Warden for a long while. She dwelled for a time on this stinging moment in which her name had become alien to her. Then she went into the kitchen to brew some tea.

A few days later they went out on a walk together. The Leopard Warden was aware that he had put his sister ill at ease but couldn't quite figure out how to put things right again. There was a sharp chill in the air that day that, despite the arrival of spring, pierced through them. The two siblings began to walk, aimless and undirected. Sedef mostly guided the way. After some time, they left the main road, turning onto a snaking path that descended to the riverbed, into parts that the Leopard Warden was more or less familiar with. After an hour's walk, they found themselves in front of a cave, its entrance filled with earth.

Sedef caught a scent in the air, a familiar scent. She looked around excitedly. 'There was a cave here.'

'You're wrong, there's never been a cave here.'

'No, I'm sure, it was here.'

Anxious, the Leopard Warden took hold of Sedef's arm. 'Come on, let's go home, it's getting cold.'

Sedef had fallen silent and began moving quickly in another direction. She was looking for something but couldn't quite put into words what it was. She looked intently at the stones on the ground. She scooped a handful of soil into her mouth. The Leopard Warden began to fret. 'What are you doing?'

'I'm looking for the boulder, there's supposed to be a black boulder here that tastes of iron.'

There was no boulder to be seen; it must have been buried in the swamps. Spitting out the soil in her mouth, Sedef marched towards the swamp. She looked closely at the larvae on the leaves of the cattails as she smelled the air again. She listened at length to the hungry buzzing of the newly hatched swamp flies. The black boulder was right there, in the centre of the swamp, its sharp-crowned apex barely visible on the surface of the muddy waters. No sooner had Sedef recognised the boulder than she leapt, unthinking, into the swamp's waters, while the

Leopard Warden, terrified, tried to grab hold of her. Both siblings were pulled into the soupy mud, into a restless reservoir filled with stones coming alive, a mire that stretched as if opening up, as if swallowing them whole once they plunged in.

Everything was dancing in the swamp. Sedef moved masterfully through the absolute waywardness of the soupy substance as it ceaselessly quivered, leaving behind her humanity and transforming into a heart penetrating into the breast of the swamp. She tried to make her way to the boulder, stretching out her arms as if to tear the rock from its place and take it away. Things would only get worse if she began to flounder. The Leopard Warden tried to maintain his composure. He recognised that the madness that had overcome Sedef, in fact, had nothing to do with the Sedef he knew. Leaving her in the swamp, he managed to climb out, pulling himself up on the cattails.

'Sedef! Don't move, I'm calling for help, hold still!'

Sedef didn't hear him. Engulfed by the swamp, she continued onwards. She was up to her chin in mud. Then, she threw herself forward with all her might, grabbing hold of the bundled mosses that enveloped the black boulder. The bundles came off in her hands as she tried to climb until, ultimately, she dug her nails into the boulder, pulling herself up. She was filled with gratitude. Ascending the boulder, she became a creature not quite human, born of the mud. At the top, Sedef threw her body against the stone, clinging to it as though it would sate her longing. She was seeking a heart there. Her own heart, perhaps.

The Leopard Warden was overcome with horror as he watched Sedef. 'Don't move, Sedef, do you hear me? I'll rescue you from over there. I called my colleagues, they'll be here soon.'

But Sedef couldn't hear the Leopard Warden. Like a believer arriving at her place of worship, she rose to her knees, closing her eyes and placing her hands on her chest. She lowered her head towards the boulder, three times placing her forehead on it and kissing it three times. Out of space itself, she had sliced a strip of time in which tribulation and tranquillity commingled. She had darned for herself an incorporeal chamber into which no one else could set foot. Covered in mud and soaking wet, she and the boulder were becoming sisters. In an inward entreaty she continued repeating the same words, a prayer akin neither to those of Muslims nor those of Christians:

'Purge every passion.

Purge excessive desire.

Purge ambition.

Purge passing whims.

Purge surrender.

Die before death, purge death.

Die before death, purge life.

Purge the world, seek shelter in its essence.

Purge every passion...'

Up until the rescue teams arrived and pulled her out of the swamp with an inflatable boat and chains, Sedef continued her mysterious supplications with the same series of words. As far as it appeared, she was beseeching not a god but the boulder itself. Or perhaps she was repeating what she'd heard from the boulder, imprinting herself on herself. Nobody could make any sense of what she said.

At the end of eight days in which Sedef had been put to sleep with shots of tranquiliser in their lodging house on the mountain, she opened her eyes to see the Leopard Warden holding her hands with tenderness.

Sedef was agitated; she looked confusedly at the nightgown she wore and the objects in her room. 'What happened to me?'

The Leopard Warden spoke calmly, adhering precisely to the directives. 'You had an awful cold, you came down with a fever, you kept talking in your sleep. Thank goodness you're better now.'

'What happened to me?'

'Don't you remember?'

'I don't remember.'

'Good, it's better that way, Sedef. Otherwise they'd have to give you all kinds of medicines, they'd leave you in a daze.'

'Sedef?'

The Leopard Warden lovingly ran his hands through his sister's hair. 'Did you forget your name, too?'

Sedef detested this practical joke. She felt insulted. She jolted up, pushing the Leopard Warden away. There was a vicious glimmer in her eyes as she shouted, 'My name is Xime! Xime of the Abdalan Clan!'

In that instant the Leopard Warden realised that they had entered a path of no return. Deep down he knew now that the Sedef he named was no more than a husk, that the long-awaited, authentic person inside that husk would now, day by day, come to the surface. As the directives would have it, he was to bring her to the Living Catalogue Centre and leave her in the cold hands of the neuroscientists, otherwise he would henceforth be harbouring a stranger named Xime, a violation of the state's iron-fisted martial rule. The Leopard Warden had to come to a decision before Xime was fully recovered and on her feet again. For nights on end he got no sleep at all. Drawing a blanket over his sister, he examined her long eyelashes, which cast shadows on her face in the moonlight. He dried her sweating neck over and over, dressing her in clean nightgowns. He used ice to massage her arms, bruised by the serum injections. He felt bound to her once again. And he felt especially bound to that chimeric component of his sister's body, the same way he felt bound to that inscrutable tooth. For a while he contemplated taking his sister and fleeing these mountains. They could make their way to the Black Sea, resting in city after city until they reached Istanbul. A canal running parallel to the Bosphorus had been dug in the west of Istanbul, and had triggered a fault line in

Northern Anatolia, as a consequence of which there had been a terrible earthquake and the city's population had fallen from 17 million to 6 million. If they could escape to Istanbul, they could disappear from sight in the tumult of the newly rebuilt city. But he didn't dare to even begin planning their escape. He was an ordinary civil servant, the Leopard Warden. He could barely walk down the street without following the directives. If they were caught, they might both end up sentenced to life in prison. He dithered between living with Xime's resurrected memory, thereby violating the state's draconian laws, and living with a vacuous Sedef purged of Xime.

Xime, in the meantime, was so restless. Sometimes she spoke in Kurmanji, a language the Leopard Warden couldn't understand. And she hated everything they had to eat. Soy milk, corn syrup, breakfast crackers, frozen vegetables, ready-to-eat soups – nothing could sate her. She couldn't bear the putrid taste of the foods. She asked the Leopard Warden for various vegetables that nobody'd ever heard of. 'Let's go,' she'd say, 'let's go outside, let's dig up some single-bulb garlic, let's gather acanthus, asphodel, mushrooms, alkanet.'

The Leopard Warden was helpless; none of these plants occurred in nature anymore. All that was left of them were the fossilised remains that other wardens were trying to chase down. The Leopard Warden hopelessly tried to console Xime. Even he didn't believe the words he'd say: 'Just bear it a little longer, Xime. When we find the leopard, we'll leave here.'

'Leopard?'

The Leopard Warden turned on his computer and showed her a photograph of a female leopard, with its black spots; underneath the photograph, it said *Panthera Partus Tuliana*. 'I'm talking about a ferocious cat. It would be enough if I could find even a claw. Then we'd be able to leave here before winter sets in.'

Xime's eyes glittered with melancholy as she studied the photograph. 'Psinge Kou!'

The Leopard Warden grew excited. 'Do you recognise this animal?'

'That's Psinge Kou. The silent cat of the mountains… You know she arrives in the mountains of Dersim when the birds fall silent. She only prowls at night. You mustn't chase after her, otherwise you'll die. Even Jargowit is silent when she walks. It submits to her, waiting for her to pass.'

'Jargowit?'

'The sacred forest.'

'That forest doesn't exist anymore, Xime. There's just a few groves left.'

'Poor Psinge Kou, that means she's prowling at night in search of her forest. During the day she must be in a cave over by the Cliffs of Sinan.'

The Leopard Warden leapt to his feet in excitement. He paced from room to room for a long time without speaking. For some reason, he didn't dare say what was passing through his mind. That night, the two siblings sat on the divan by the window, watching the sky until morning. There in the velveteen skin of the sky, millions of stars glittered.

Hours later, with sincere innocence, Xime raised the first question any human had ever asked: 'Why are the nights dark? With so many stars there shouldn't be any night.'

'The universe is expanding, Xime. The path travelled by light is stretching further over time. In every instant, we're moving farther away from the stars you see.'

Xime fell silent in the gloom of that thought. Comprehending at last that the past is still in passing, she lowered her face to the ground. 'Those in the sky and those on the earth are the same. Time passes but bones remember all.'

Xime was right, memory was itself a light travelling its path. The Leopard Warden mustered up the courage to ask, 'Do you remember where the Cliffs of Sinan you mentioned are, Xime?'

'I can find them. My uncle died there.'

As dawn broke, Xime stared off into the distance and began forming sentences, half in Kurmanji, half in Turkish, under her breath. Her mind was bare. Every word that spilled from her mouth drew up another word from somewhere inside her. It was as if her language was being born all on its own.

'My uncle and my father hid in Jargowit as they fled from soldiers. The soldiers chasing after them set the sacred forest on fire, so nobody could hide there. The two brothers had no choice but to ascend the Cliffs of Sinan. As they searched for a cave to hide in, they saw a female psinge kou, alongside her cubs. When the cat rose to her feet, my father drew his knife, out of fear... instinctively... not to kill her... My uncle grabbed hold of my father's hand, it took all his might to pull my father out of the cave. To the edge of the cliff. But in one leap, the cat came after them. A yellow creature with black spots, her eyes the colour of honey. The length of two men from nose to tail, her ears erect. That's what he told me. She focused on my father since he'd drawn the knife. Showed her teeth before letting out a roar. When my uncle realised what was going to happen, he beat his chest as if to say, leave him alone, come after me. Psinge kou pounced on my uncle. My uncle had given himself to the cat to save my father. Once the cat leapt onto him, he wrapped his arms around her neck and pulled her toward the cliff. They tumbled through the air, crashing into the rocks on the way down. That's how my father was saved. He saw his brother and psinge kou below, corpses wrapped in embrace. The two most beautiful corpses the mountains had ever seen. My father, of course, didn't leave right away, he slept for days in the cave, snuggling with the two cubs left behind. Sometimes he'd hunt boar to bring them, sometimes deer. He played the father to those two psinge kou cubs, left without their mother. Months later he returned to us as a predatory cat, prowling silently. He didn't just leave his brother at the Cliffs of Sinan, but his children. The leopard you're after must be one of those cubs. My sister. And whether you like it or not, your sister too.'

The Leopard Warden felt flustered, but as a man of duty he simply couldn't internalise this abstract sisterhood. 'Would you take me to those cliffs, Xime?'

'I'll take you, but you have to promise you won't shoot her.'

'I'll just put her to sleep, I promise. But anything could happen on the way. There are minefields, meadows covered in fungus, swamps, riverbeds filled with soil, forests turned to ash... you might get sick again when you see them.'

Xime shrugged. 'I haven't healed anyway,' she said, 'these bone-dry mountains make my lungs burn.'

Before embarking on their journey, Xime and the Leopard Warden waited for the mudslides in the region, brought on by the pouring rain, to abate. Because Xime refused to ride the cable car, they were going to travel on foot. It took them a while to ready all their camping supplies. In the meantime, Xime had been cutting her sheets into strips, dipping them into the margarine she melted on the stove and forming them into long, narrow cones. The Leopard Warden couldn't make any sense of it. Leaving Xime to her own devices, with the absolute silence of the observer, was a way for the Leopard Warden to ignore everything she did. He did nothing to hinder any of his sister's mysterious actions, and yet, by remaining completely silent, he was preventing her from putting them into words. Every memory that might awaken meant a narrative, and every narrative meant a historical event. And the Leopard Warden didn't have Xime's courage to bring history back to life. After all, he had found Xime's molar in a mass grave in his backyard.

They left together one morning when the weather had warmed and the earth had begun to dry out. Xime walked ahead, the Leopard Warden directly behind her. Xime descended towards a dried creekbed. There was no water. But it was clear that waterfalls had once run through here; a tall stone there had been marked by the water's striations. Xime lit one of the oiled cones she'd prepared and, sidling up to the stone, placed it in one of its small hollows. Pressing her head to the stone, she prayed inwardly. Perhaps she made a wish. She asked something of the stone. Maybe she even gave something to the stone, too. The Leopard Warden glanced around anxiously. 'That's enough, Xime, please, if someone sees us we'll have no way to explain what's going on.'

They spent the night in a narrow tunnel deep in a valley that cut through the riverbed, in a hollow where the stones spoke silently to one another. The air was so cold. Xime fell into a peaceful sleep nonetheless. The Leopard Warden, on the other hand, kept guard, two guns in hand, one filled with lead bullets, the other with tranquiliser capsules. The following day, they climbed towards a different mountain. It seemed to him like they were going back the way they came. Still, the Leopard Warden asked no questions. This time they arrived to a place that had once been an oak forest, where new saplings were sprouting from the withered oak roots. Xime took a deep breath, smelling the air. She was spirited, full of life.

'This is Jargowit,' she said. The forest was not in its place. They stood in an imaginary forest. Passing through that absent forest, they arrived at a glacial lake. There was no more than a small puddle in the very bottom. The lake was like an eye gouged out. Dark green aquatic plants with thick leaves still lined its perimeter. Xime collected a porous rock from the lake's edge, held it against her chest. That night, they pruned the thorny briar from the nearest flat area and set up their tent together.

As the sun was setting, Xime pointed at a mountain to the north, its three peaks lined up one after another. 'That's where the Cliffs of Sinan are, the den of psinge kou. That's what we're going to climb.' Xime had developed a startling sense of self-confidence since they'd left their lodging house; she wasn't searching for the place they were going, but finding her bearings by the altitude. The Leopard Warden, on the other hand, had collapsed out of exhaustion. He was quick to fall asleep as the sun sank.

When he awoke, Xime had lit a small fire to brew tea and prepared breakfast, roasting the tubers she had pulled from the roots of the thorny briars. Her hands were covered up to her wrists in scratches from sifting through the thorns. Despite that, there was an incomprehensible joy about the woman. It was as though the bond of siblinghood they shared was growing stronger. This time, though, the roles had been reversed, and Xime was the true host.

Before they would climb the Cliffs of Sinan, they had to travel through one last dark pass where the caves followed one after another in gyres, which served as a shortcut that saved them from an otherwise very long route. The Leopard Warden was astonished. They'd crossed through this pass that appeared on no satellite images, this place that nobody had yet discovered, where water trickled from the stones. This was where the dried cataracts had hidden their water. They listened to the sound of the water flowing below, as though at any moment it might split through the ground and spray into the air. After a hard hour's walk they encountered the headwaters, where the water flowed drop by drop. The area around the headwaters was darkened by soot. Traces of fire. Melted candles left by people of the past coated the stones in a layer of waxy, shiny residue. Xime produced another cone and lit it. She kissed the headwaters three times and placed her forehead on it three times as well. This place was clearly a private temple. They were making a sacred pilgrimage on their way to the leopard, asking nature's permission with every step.

Upon ascending the Cliffs of Sinan, the peak was silent. Xime had brought them to the edge of a cliff. The Leopard

Warden glanced around, out of breath. He regretted having come here, felt like he'd been tricked. He looked despairingly at the cable cars, no more than tiny boxes off in the distance. They had defied not only the directives but the borders as well. The Leopard Warden could no longer hide his anger. 'Where have you taken me, Xime? Are you sure the leopard is here?'

Xime gestured at the sun's slanting descent, asking him to be patient. She told him that the psinge kou would appear after the sky darkened. She would have to leave her den and pass here in order to hunt. Once night fell, they put on their pitch-black coveralls and, without lighting a fire, in complete silence, waited for the leopard to appear. Clinging tightly to his gun, the Leopard Warden's fingers had gone numb. Pain shot through his back from sitting in the same position. Xime was sitting straight up, holding her breath as she waited. The following morning, the Leopard Warden awoke in a rage. He no longer believed Xime and felt like an idiot for falling for her delusional story, letting her bring him to these perilous cliffs. Xime must have had a plan. Maybe she was planning to kill him and flee. He regretted that he'd never suspected this rebellious, hard-headed woman or her eccentric behaviour. He listened until dawn to his sister gently snoring, curled up asleep in her coveralls. He searched her face for any sign of betrayal, but all he saw were her eyelashes, trembling as she dreamt. In that moment, he heard a furious growl. A deep growl that gave birth to the day, that made the sun rise. The Leopard Warden slowly got to his feet, feeling something between terror and reverence. He looked now at the creature, almost unbearably beautiful. At the leopard he had dreamed of for years. The imperium in her shining eyes brought the mountains to life, and it made his knees buckle. He had entered the creature's dominion. He couldn't believe he was standing so close, that she was so alive, that she was so real. Xime opened her eyes, and said to the Leopard Warden, 'Shhh, don't move a muscle.' And yet, the

Leopard Warden's face now wore an expression she had never seen before. He was transforming from a persistent warden into a sovereign hunter. Raising his gun to the creature, he couldn't repress his greed, which had set its eyes on the leopard. The leopard snarled even more ferociously. She must have recognised this way that humans look. She stretched her neck and tensed, readying to pounce. Shocked, Xime looked at the leopard, and then at the Leopard Warden. Even though she'd intuited the murderous expression on his face, she had no way of knowing what command his finger on the trigger would follow. Right as the Warden fixed his target between the leopard's two eyes, she leapt at him with a roar. In an instant Xime threw herself between them. She wrapped her arms around her chimeric sibling's neck, pulling him down the cliff. Tumbling down the cliffside, crashing against the rocks on the way down, she left her true sibling in her den at the top of the Cliffs of Sinan.

The Wishing Star

Jîl Şwanî

THE MESOPOTAMIAN MARSHES, WHICH I think should be renamed the Mesopotamian River, grew as the ocean levels rose. On the day we were to row through them, the weather was calm and the sun shone. Our guide, who laughed when we told him we were to write a piece about the Kurds, told us we could get close to Baghdad in his boat. Daniel, my companion, spoke Kurdish, Arabic, Turkish, and even some Kurdish sign language. He was my translator and general bridge with the societies we were to meet and was himself half Kurdish. His father had escaped in the mid-twenties, after the Turkish expansion project, and he grew up speaking his Kurdish tongue at home. Although, before we arrived, I was unsure how far that language would carry us in the mountains of Byara.

Our guide through the marshes was a middle-aged Arab man, whose hair was a yellowish white from his chain-smoking, and his skin was dry and coarse from his many hours in the sun. He turned to us and laughed when we passed by the green shrubberies on the banks of the marshes, 'God loves irony, doesn't he?' Daniel translated for me. I asked the boatman what he meant by that.

'Look at all this green. Beautiful, but useless. We can't survive on these thin leaves,' he said, then added, 'I'd recommend you spend all your money on food in Baghdad before you go to the north.'

He didn't speak much after that, and we didn't want to ask more questions. He was a man who went up the marshes and then down to the port once more, and that was all he knew. When we docked in Baghdad, he suggested a marketplace, and to be safe, we bought some canned food to take with us, but only enough that didn't inconvenience us or our luggage.

It cost us hours, four maybe, and a lot of money and persuasion until we found someone willing to drive us to Byara. Most of the drivers laughed at us when we told them our destination, and those who didn't walked away very quickly. I realised before our trip that our project wasn't an easy one. My editor told me several times that I could go to anywhere else, and when that failed, he pulled up several articles about journalists who went to Kurdistan with the hope of a story and never returned, 'The last journalist to go there did so in 2042, and now, four years later, no one has heard a word from him.'

'I don't care,' I told him. 'I'm going.' I smiled and my editor knew there was no point in arguing with me.

We waited until the next morning to drive out of Baghdad because the driver told us it wouldn't be safe to go to the north at night, 'The Turks patrol for smugglers along the highway when it gets dark.' About ten minutes into the drive, the driver turned to us and asked us how long we would stay there. 'A month or so, possibly,' Daniel told him. The driver then asked whether we had bought food, and once again Daniel answered.

'A month's worth?' asked the driver.

'No, maybe enough for a few days.'

'You won't survive on that.'

Daniel translated, and I asked the driver whether he'd ever been there.

'No, no one goes there. But those who escape; first thing they do is go to restaurants, get on their knees, and cry and beg for food in some gibberish language. Every time.'

Daniel told me perhaps it would be wise to stock up on more canned goods, and at first I didn't agree. 'He's probably got a deal with some shopkeeper to bring travellers to him,' I said. But Daniel insisted. We stopped at a market and bought lots of canned goods and packed them into our bags of notebooks and pens.

The one thing that marked our proximity to Kurdistan, more than anything else, was the landscape. Daniel was first to notice, and he pointed it out to me. He told me his father's stories about his homeland: the tall mountains, the green plains and valleys, the cold rivers, and the clear blue skies. And yet, as we went closer and closer, the land became all shades of beige. The occasional bits of green that we saw on our trip up became nonexistent the further north we went, and the mountains were tall, but they in no way resembled what I thought them to be. They were dry and lifeless, with the occasional black spots.

The driver took us as far as he dared go, and told us we needed to cross the rest of the way on foot. It was thirty-two kilometres that we needed to walk, and beyond that, we had to watch out for patrols from the Turkish army. With our luggage, and the relentless way the sun beat us down, we knew it was to be a two-day, perhaps three-day, trip, and most of that would be at night.

We set ourselves between two hills, and lay on top of our black bags to hide them underneath our beige clothes. We ate a meal of canned food, and waited until it was dark enough that we felt comfortably covered by the night. We walked thirteen kilometres before we collapsed in a valley near a dried-out river bed. The semi-cold stones were a welcome break from the parched, sun-baked soil that lined the inside of our shoes, and we slept on them for a solid five hours, before the sound of men and their military boots woke us up. Daniel was first to rise, and he shook me until my eyes were open. We got to our feet and ran to hide underneath the valley wall on the opposite side, underneath where the sounds came from. As they walked above us, a few pebbles rolled down to the valley, and their conversation echoed against the limestone. They didn't stop, nor did we give them reason to, and were beyond the reach of our ears in about ten minutes. We remained in our spots for longer than that, however, and afterward, for as long as there was light, we looked for crevices to hide in.

We were back to hiking as the sun went down again, and we were three kilometres closer before, once again, the sound of patrolmen put us into hiding. This time, we found no place to take cover, and Daniel suggested we get behind our black bags and lie down, and hope that the darkness would do us a favour. The patrolmen came within spitting distance of us, but thankfully their conversation was so engaging that they didn't pay any attention to their surroundings. We continued for a few more kilometres until we saw the towering mountains of Hewraman. At first glance, I was intimidated by their height, but looking over to Daniel, and seeing his enormous glee, made me feel more at ease. But I swear, when I first saw those peaks, I thought these mountains could challenge the skies and the sun for dominance over the firmament.

'We found our friends,' Daniel told me.

On the mountainside, there were many little holes to hide in. When the first of the morning light came, I looked back at the ground, into the hole we had slept in, and saw not soil but soot.

During our second meal in Kurdistan, Daniel looked to me and said, 'It's odd. I haven't seen a single insect or animal so far.' I hadn't thought of that until then, but he was right; the land was dead.

The remainder of our way, we were unbothered by patrolmen, and when we first saw the mud houses of Byara, Daniel stopped and kneeled down. He kissed the ground, and a few of his tears wet the dusty ground of what was once a verdant Eden. We took refuge at a nearby mountainside and, in the morning, went to the houses.

The first house we knocked on, nobody answered. I heard the scuffle of feet from inside, and I'm sure I caught a pair of eyes through the small square window, but we understood we weren't welcome there. The door on the second house opened immediately, and in the doorway I saw the shape of a person that resembled Gollum more than any human I'd ever seen. From the balding spot that took with it all the hair from forehead to crown, to the greyish skin, the protruding bones on his face and arms, and the dirt-ridden clothes, I was immediately gripped with a fear that I hadn't known the whole way there. I also noticed on his left arm a burn mark the size of a tennis ball. I took a step back and looked around, only to see that now all the windows were lined with prying curious eyes. I almost told Daniel we should leave when he spoke. He said something in Kurdish, which he later told me was a simple greeting, and after that the grimace on the man's face disappeared, and in its place was a broad smile and a tearful pair of eyes. The man didn't reply, instead he spoke with his hands, 'Welcome,' he signed.

He invited us in and gave us each a glass of water and a piece of bread which was as hard as the mud bricks of the house we were in. 'Forgive me, we don't have anything else to offer,' the man said in sign language. Daniel translated everything for me, and I told the man that he need not worry. He enquired about us, and Daniel replied, and I looked around the house. There were three mattresses on the floor, two bags in the corner, next to which were a frail woman, with strands of hair dangling below her cheekbones, and two skinny children huddling next to her and leering at us. The house was small; there was only the room in which we sat, and beyond two piles of clothes, and another, third bag, there wasn't much else. Daniel bumped me on the hand and I paid attention to the man again. He signed frantically, and his smile became larger than before.

'I told him we are journalists, and he said he will help us with whatever we need.'

'Ask him if it's safe for us to be here.'

'The soldiers come once a week, and usually don't make surprise visits. We can hide you and host you for as long as you need.'

'Can you take us around the village and help us gather information?'

'We can go after you've eaten,' he replied, then pointed to the piece of bread and glass of water.

Daniel said it would be rude of us to not eat, so we finished our breakfast, and then set off with our host, Shad.

We left all our things, save for our passports, wallets and a single notebook and pen, at Shad's house. Shad accompanied us to a few houses, and everywhere, they spoke the same way he did, with their hands. I asked why it was nobody used their voices, and he paused before he replied, then told us,

'We don't have tongues. Is this not known to you?'

'What does he mean they don't have tongues?' I asked Daniel.

The man opened his mouth, and inside there were only a few rotten teeth and the stub of what once was a tongue.

'What happened to his tongue?'

'None of us have tongues. Those of us who were born before the expansion had it cut out when the Turkish army came, and those born after the expansion have their tongues ripped out after birth.'

I asked Daniel if he was sure that's what he said, and he asked the man again, and we got the same answer. I wrote it down in my notebook, just below my descriptions of the village and the houses, looked at the man, and asked one last time, imitating a scissor cutting out my tongue, and the man nodded in response.

'The younger ones here won't be able to understand you,' Shad told Daniel. 'They only know sign language.'

In the evening, most of the village gathered around us at Shad's house. Our congregation was illuminated by a small fire, behind which Daniel and I sat, and after they answered most of my questions about their lives, they asked whether Daniel knew any stories or songs in Kurdish. Daniel answered that he knew a song, but didn't have a good voice, but they didn't care, 'We just want to hear it,' Shad told him.

Daniel, after humming and hawing for a minute, began his song. It was an old song named 'Estêrey Awat', 'The Wishing Star', by Adnan Karim. Our small audience, those who understood the language, began to cry, and the younger ones who didn't, had their parents translate for them into sign language. Pretty soon, they all began, in a whispered hush, to hum along, and Daniel had to stop to dry his own eyes.

The villagers gave up their own mattresses that night to accommodate us, and before we slept, Daniel turned to me and said, 'We should give them our food.'

'It will last them a day. And then we will starve with them.'

'They're starving now.'

I didn't want to reply then. Daniel was thinking with his heart and not his head, and that was to get us nowhere. If we starved like them, we couldn't get our job done, and I told him that.

'If they starve to death, our article won't help them.'

'There are millions of others like them.'

'I'm giving them my food.'

In the morning he did give them his food, and although they were starving, they refused at first, and only after Daniel's insistence did they give in. Afterwards, Shad took us on a fifteen-minute walk to the edge of the village, and told us to stay still and not to worry. From afar, a small red fox approached us, and Shad picked it up and brought us back to the village. In the village, a herd of children ran up to us with big smiles and started petting the fox. The fox didn't seem to mind, in fact, it played along. The children had small portions of bread in their hands, and after petting the little creature for a while, they fed the fox the bread.

I asked why they didn't hunt the fox for its meat, and Shad replied, 'They've taken everything else from us: our mountains are black with their bombs, our walnut trees were plucked from the land, our land is barren and dead, and we can't even speak in our language anymore. The sun, fire, and the foxes of our old stories are all we can give our children.'

'Do you tell the children the old Kurdish stories about foxes?' Daniel asked.

'That's why they love the fox so much. They think it's as cunning as the foxes in the stories,' Shad smiled.

After a while, to the annoyance of the children, Shad picked up the animal and took it back to the edge of the village, and from there the fox went back to its hole and we returned.

Over our dinner of canned beans, supplemented by a small slice of bread, I asked Shad about his burn mark, and he said, 'I had a tattoo of the word "daye", mother, in Kurdish. When they saw it, they burned it with a torch.' We gathered around the fire again that evening and Daniel sang for them, and the villagers, especially the children, rejoiced and tried to sing along in their own way with him.

Early the next morning, Shad woke us up and said he needed to hide us for a few hours because the soldiers were to come and do a headcount. We hid in the mountains, and watched as the soldiers brought out bags of bread and distributed them among the families: from what I counted, for every mouth there was one bag, and when they were done, they noted the number of people, and then left in their trucks.

For two weeks after, we continued to gather information and build our article. It was difficult to say what was important and what wasn't, because everything they told us seemed to have a place in the story and, after those two weeks, I told Daniel that we might end up with a book instead of an article. He implored, again, that I give away my food, and I again said no, although, there wasn't much left of it anyway by then, and I doubted it would make a difference.

One morning, when we went to find the fox with Shad and bring it back for the children, before the fox showed up, we heard the sound of patrolmen in the distance, and Shad told us to run and find a hiding spot. We ran not too far, found some boulders and sat behind them. We peeked around from time to time and saw the patrolmen walk up to Shad and talk to him. The patrolmen spoke in sign language and Daniel told me they were asking what he was doing out there. They didn't harm him and they didn't threaten him, but as the fox ambled toward them in its usual manner, and rubbed itself against Shad's legs, the patrolmen asked him about it. Shad said it was just a hungry animal looking for a meal, but the patrolmen knew better. Without warning, one of them pulled out a pistol and shot the animal in the head, then they made Shad pick it up and took him and the animal with them.

We waited for some time, but Shad didn't return. When the sound of the patrolmen disappeared, we made our way back to the village, hurriedly and constantly looking over our shoulder. We explained what we'd seen to the villagers, and two of the elders escorted us back to their house.

That night, we didn't convene by the fire to tell stories and sing songs. The parents took their children inside, and we didn't see anyone until morning. Before we slept, Daniel suggested perhaps it was time for us to leave: 'We're endangering them by staying,' he said. I disagreed. Our job was to help them, although I felt, seeing their reactions to the news, that they were angry with us. Every night since our arrival, they wanted to sit with us and answer our questions, but it was different now. Nobody came to visit us, and our old hosts, despite feeding us, didn't speak much to us.

Before sunrise, the two old men woke us up and, from the other side of the village, I heard the loud ruckus of engines and a crowd of people moving about. The men took us into the mountains and handed us a bag of bread.

They gave us some of their clothes for us to wear, and told us they would return for us later, but that we were to stay there until they came. They returned some hours later, and before they approached us, they looked around the area, then gestured that we come forward.

They took our old clothes and burned them in a fire, and when they returned, they explained that there was a raid early in the morning. The villagers were interrogated, some beaten, and some threatened, but they gave nothing away. The face of the old men then changed, and they told us that the military men had taken away our bags with all the notebooks in them.

'All of it?' I asked, and the old man nodded, 'What did you tell them about the bags?'

'Mahabad Xan, Shad's wife, told them they were Shad's belongings. They took her as well, but spared her children. Don't look sad,' the older of the two said.

He looked down to the ground for a second, and explained, 'When they take someone away, we don't see them again. Mahabad knew that. She made her choice. She's a strong woman; she's named after the Kurdish Republic and has fire in her blood. She and Shad made their choices. They both want this article to be put before sympathetic eyes.'

'Would you all be safer if we left?' Daniel asked.

'We aren't safe either way, Kak Daniel. If your work is made, maybe we will be better. That's what's important.'

Our weeks of work, my food, and the relative safety we had up until then was gone. Daniel told me again that night that we better leave, for the safety of the villagers, and this time I gave it more thought, but I knew leaving meant going home empty-handed.

'Shad and Mahabad's death would be for nothing,' I told Daniel.

'More will die, I know more will die.'

'If we get our work done, we might save more than just these people here.'

'You care more about your article than the lives of these people. The whole reason you came here was to write a piece that no other journalist could. Don't fake altruism now.'

I didn't reply. When I picked him for this trip, I did so because I thought that having someone know the culture, beyond just the language, would be to my benefit, but Daniel always thought with his heart.

'We can recreate what we lost from memory. I can write it all down for you here,' he said.

'We're not leaving empty-handed.'

'Fuck you. I'm not staying here if it means we'll be the cause of further deaths.'

'You're scared, that's all. Sleep on it and let's see what happens tomorrow.'

The next morning, we didn't have time to discuss anything. The two old men came to us, like the previous day, and guided us back into the mountains. We stayed quiet during our five hours of hiding, and when they returned, they told us the soldiers had come back and looked through the houses for undesirable objects. It was like that for the rest of our stay there.

The villagers became too scared, or too careful, to sit around the fire with us at night, and Daniel refused to translate for me when I wanted to bring them together to answer my questions. We went another week and a half with nothing to show for our stay, other than massive weight loss and scruffy beards.

One day, while laying in a mountain cave, looking down on the dilapidated remnants of the old town of Byara, Daniel asked me again why we were still there. He argued that we weren't getting information; that we were risking being caught and further hurting the people. I wanted to tell him to stop asking me that question, but with the constant growling of my stomach and the pain in my back and ass, I didn't bother. He went on about how we could still write a book, and we could still bring attention to what we saw, but every time I tried to agree with him, every time I wanted to tell him that I, too, wanted to go home, the empty pages of my notebook screamed at me. My editor warned me of this, but I smiled. I thought of the many journalists who came down to Kurdistan for a story and all those who disappeared in these mountains, and I wasn't going to be one of them.

'If you want to leave, then leave,' I said to Daniel.

'And you'll stay and do what? Learn sign language and spend your day gazing down at the people from the mountains?'

'I'll figure it out.'

In the evening, the two old men sat with us in their house and ate with us. We had tea that night, something I hadn't tasted in nearly a month. They told us the soldiers gave them the tea to soften them up. 'They think we'll talk if they bring us gifts. They think we're children,' they both laughed. Their laughter was more like a silent hiss with bouts of coughing than real laughter, but the small joy on their faces was as genuine as any.

Three weeks into our cat-and-mouse routine with the soldiers, I looked at my notebook and saw I only had eight more pages of work, and what both Daniel and I traded off for those eight pages was chunks of hair loss from malnutrition, protruding ribs, and figures so skinny that our rags of clothes hung off our shoulders like curtains around a window. I read through the eight pages: there was, in total, seven paragraphs of useable facts, and the rest were descriptions of the land; I didn't know why I needed so many words to describe dusty brown hillocks, and yet I seemed to have had filled nearly five pages with it.

Eventually the land, despite my creative use of language, wasn't describable anymore, and when that happened, Daniel and I lay on the soil and talked about food. He told me about his favourite desserts: chocolate eclairs. He described to me his favourite cafe: walls of cream-white, brown tables, a barely audible bit of swing music playing in the background, and a glass case full of sweet pastries, all the while the space was filled with the aroma of freshly ground coffee. The eclairs, he said, were soft and flaky, and the chocolate was like pudding. I told him about my favourite meal: cheese pizza with a sauce that exploded in the mouth with the tang of the tomatoes, and the subtle fresh bites of the basil leaves. I cried that night. I cried for pizzas and I cried for eclairs with chocolate. Daniel, I think, cried, too. I didn't ask him about it, and neither did he, but when we were back on the mountain we talked again of food.

After five weeks, the two old men sat us down one evening. They laughed when they told us we looked like two hungry street cats, and when they asked about how much work we had done in those five weeks, their faces changed. They didn't seem sad. They looked like they heard what they expected to hear.

'Ferhad and I have made a decision. We ran it by the people of the village, and they agreed with us,' the older man spoke, and I thought he was about to tell us we should leave. 'The soldiers aren't leaving, they are sure there's something going on here. If not that, then they've been ordered to find something and won't leave until they do. Ferhad and I think it's time you took our places. The soldiers don't know any of us, they do head counts, and walk around, but that's all they know.

They search the houses and spit inside them, but they don't know whose house is whose. Ferhad and I will leave tonight. We'll walk south, and if we're lucky we might find ourselves in the care of a kind stranger. That's not important. What's important is, with us gone, you two can stay without changing the headcount. You look like everyone else here now, you don't have to hide in the mountains anymore. You can walk around and work in the mornings until you've gotten what you need. And then you can go back and publish your article.'

'Are you sure you didn't misunderstand them?' I asked Daniel. He nodded, albeit after a brief pause.

'We can't let them do that,' Daniel said finally.

'Tell them.'

'It's not your decision to make, my boy,' Ferhad, the younger of the two said.

'You'll die if you leave, or worse, get caught.'

'I'm 71 years old, and Azad is 76. In a few years, we will be as good as dead. We were born free, and in our freedom neither of us travelled further than Slemani and Sina. It's not your decision. We want to go.'

They went house by house that night, and said goodbye to everyone. Each family gave them one loaf of bread to take with them for their journey, and when they came back around to us to say goodbye to us, Daniel kissed their shaking hands and called each of them, 'Bapira,' Kurdish for grandfather. The two old men held Daniel and kissed him on the cheek, and had a brief exchange that Daniel didn't want to translate for me. I hugged them, too, and thanked them for all their help. They smiled at me, and signed something. 'They're thanking you for your work,' Daniel told me. I nodded and shook their hands one final time, and then they left. Daniel and I waited outside the house and watched them disappear into the mountains.

We didn't sleep that night; Daniel insisted that he teach me some basic sign language, just in case I was approached by the patrolmen. I never got to use those phrases, but the next morning, when we lined up for the headcount, I felt somewhat better knowing them.

For the headcount, each household stood in front of their doors. I stood before the old men's house, next to another old man who came to stand with me, and Daniel walked to the other side of the village. A young soldier, perhaps in his early twenties, walked around and counted us. He pointed with his finger at each person as he whispered numbers to himself, and once in a while paused and stared someone down. Looking at his face as he approached me, I doubted this boy could throw a punch, let alone pull a trigger. His face was beardless, with red cheeks. He still bore the expression of a child, something that was mostly visible in his eyes. He avoided our eyes, fearful, I assumed, and when he paused to stare at someone, I noticed he did so in a pattern. For every six houses that he passed by, he stopped at the seventh and did his shtick to appear intimidating, but if someone caught his glance, he went away faster. He paused on me, and I looked back at him, and I saw his cowardice: his lips might as well have been quivering.

A few hours later, Daniel came to the house and said we could visit some of the families and ask them questions. On our walk there, I saw the military cars on the edges of the village, and I asked in a whisper if he saw the fear in the patrolman's eyes. 'Yeah, but it isn't all fear. The villagers told me he's Kurdish. He's ashamed at doing the job,' he answered.

We entered one of the houses, and before we got to ask our questions, the family set before us glasses of water and bits of bread. Like Shad did the first time he welcomed us into his home, this family also apologised for the humble meal they presented us, and Daniel quickly told them that they needn't say anything like that. The father, along with their teenage daughter and the mother, answered our questions. When we asked them about their family history, they both started crying, and the daughter looked down at the floor. They told us they had two miscarriages and lost a baby due to malnutrition and that they're struggling with diseases too.

That week, every family we visited gave us similar stories: everyone had lost loved ones due to the lack of food and medicine, especially babies who were more fragile than others. At some point, I stopped writing the stories, and began writing down the numbers of people who'd died due to these reasons, and after a second week of interviews, Daniel and I tallied the dead, and learned that in the past five years more had died in the village than there were people currently populating it.

One evening, when I was talking about the structure that I had in mind for the book, something occurred to me, and I asked Daniel, 'Why do you think they don't escape?'

'I asked a few people that. They don't have anyone to rely on outside, not to mention escaping with children, especially diseased children, through these mountains, it's next to impossible.'

The continuous work helped us in more than one way: we forgot about our hunger for long periods of the day, and the more we worked, the nearer we felt to home, and now that the notebook was nearly filled up, I began to think about the journey out of Kurdistan.

When we met up after the headcount on one of the final days in Kurdistan, I told Daniel that I estimated our departure to be in a week's time. Like all our days in the past two and a half weeks, we made the rounds and went to each house with a list of questions, and pen and paper ready to go. After two houses, when we were back out in the village, I noticed some of the patrolmen following us with their eyes. We exited the third house, and as we made our way to the fourth, two of them, a tall dark-haired, mean-faced one, and the boyish looking one that did our headcount, approached us. We stopped in front of them, and then they began to ask us questions. I didn't understand, and so avoided their eyes. Daniel answered everything for us, and then, before I realised what was happening, the dark-haired one punched Daniel square in the face, knocking out one of his teeth and putting him flat on his back in the dusty path. The patrolman then turned to me as he pulled his arm back for a second round, but I recoiled away and put my hand in front of my face. Daniel got back up and put his arm around me and escorted me back to the house. I asked him what had happened, and he replied, 'I told that little jash¹ he should be ashamed of himself.'

'Why did he not hit me?'

'I told him you have learning difficulties and that's why you're not talking.'

For a second I almost laughed, and I would have too if it wasn't for Daniel's bloody lips and frustrated, heavy breathing. 'I wish I could have him, just me and him. He's so scared, he wouldn't even scream for help,' he said.

He continued muttering angry remarks to himself as he cleaned up his face, and then we heard a large thud on our door and it swung open. The two patrolmen entered and looked around the room, and I noticed the Kurd had the imprint of a red hand on his cheek. They came quickly to us and patted us down and then searched the house, not that we could hide anything inside. The dark-haired patrolman then turned to Daniel and signed something. It was, despite the situation, a little hard not to laugh: his face was angry and his veins were popping, his shoulders were moving back and forth furiously, and his general demeanour was that of a thug, yet his hand moved with the agility and steadiness of a ballerina as he made each word. They made a few empty threats and then left after slapping Daniel around for a little.

Daniel didn't sleep that night. He whispered angry comments on his floor mattress, and I woke up a few times because of him. The next day, we went about business as usual.

We planned on having four interviews, but it didn't pan out that way for us. The first house we went to, we only spent fifteen minutes there, before the two patrolmen from the previous day kicked down the door. In a rush, I shoved the pen and notebook into my pants, and hoped it wouldn't be too visible when we stood up. It was, in a twisted way, lucky that we had lost so much weight; because the way our clothes looked on us, like oversized dresses, the notebook and pen were invisible to the soldiers, and when they patted us down, they didn't want to put their hands near our groins. We went home, and stayed put for the rest of the day, hoping to try again tomorrow. But as tomorrow came, and we visited a new house, the same thing happened again. The third day was more of the same, and by the fourth day, both Daniel and I knew our time in Kurdistan was up.

We made arrangements that night to leave, and like they did with the old men, many of the families gave us bread to take with us, but unlike them, we couldn't afford to go house to house to say goodbye now that we'd become persons of interest for the military.

As soon as the sun set, Daniel and I walked out of the house and continued nonstop until we saw the early orange glint of the rising sun. We traversed away from Byara, by my estimation, a good twelve kilometres that night. Despite not having the weight we came with, our weakened bodies and malnourished muscles could go no further. When we sat down that morning, we both heard creaks and snaps in our bones, and we felt that if went any further we would crack our legs and backs.

We slept a few hours in a cave not far enough from Byara as we'd have liked, and woke drenched in our own sweat. We both wanted to leave the cave, just for a minute, but neither of us dared to. We knew that the headcount was going to show two missing persons, and they would already have their eyes on us. We knew there already must have been a search party prowling the area to find us, and as uncomfortable as the heat inside the cave was, and as thirsty as it made us, neither of us wanted to risk a breath of cool fresh air.

We went back to sleep in a puddle of sweat, and in the evening, we shuddered as a light breeze entered the cave and cooled us down. It was the coldest I had felt in all my life, and although still sweating, we clung on to each other for warmth for a few minutes. When it became dark, we helped each other up to our feet and began to hike again. We descended the mountains, and arrived at a plateau populated by dried-out trees. The ground was uneven, and I rolled through its crests and falls without much awareness of our surroundings. My mind was elsewhere, I didn't know where, but it wasn't where my body was, and then Daniel brought me back. He pressed down on my back and pushed me to the ground. I heard the sound of cars and boots all around us. I tried to focus on the noise, to hear where it came from specifically, but it seemed to be coming from everywhere. We crawled away and found a hiding spot underneath a broken log, and remained there as the sound came closer. Daniel looked up and tried to plot out a path out of there, but as he looked ahead, behind, left, and right, he found nothing. His breathing became heavier and his hand on my back grew in weight. He looked at me, a few tears in his eyes, a few rolling down his cheeks, and his dark hair, thick with sweat.

In a whisper he said, 'You will publish the book. Yes?' I didn't understand. He asked me again, as he clawed at my back, 'You'll publish it. You'll make sure we do something good. Alright?' I nodded. He nodded. He got to his feet and ran as fast as he could. When I no longer could hear his footsteps, I heard a loud cry. His cry took with it all the cars and patrolmen, and as the noise subsided for a moment, I looked around and saw the clearing that now surrounded me. I sprinted away, and went as far as I could. I heard gunshots. I paused and looked back. They sounded far away. I continued.

I didn't see or hear anyone until sunrise. I had run the whole way, and now I didn't want to stop. I was out of the mountains by this point, near the valley where Daniel and I slept months ago, and on the dried-out river bed, I saw two bodies. I approached carefully, hugging the walls of the valley as I ambled toward them, and I recognised the corpses of the two old men. They lay face up, looking at the sun that now dominated the sky. I held my hand over my mouth and I cried for a minute. I said the word that Daniel used, 'Bapira,' grandfather, and got on my knees and talked to the sky. I dried my eyes and continued.

I couldn't feel my legs, and my skin and lips were parched. My vision was blurry, but I recognised the tarmac road when I arrived. A car passed by, and I raised a hand. They stopped, opened their window and talked to me, but I couldn't understand. I passed out.

I woke up in a hospital in Baghdad. They told me I'd slept for three days. I couldn't move for two days after that, but when I could I called the embassy. I made it back home with my notebook.

I wanted to rest when I got back home, but my mind wouldn't let me. I started writing the book straight away. I passed out more times than I could count in those six months of sitting in front of a keyboard, but I managed to finish the book. After my editor read it and said it was good, I crawled towards my bed and slept.

I spent the next three weeks mostly sleeping. I ate little, because my stomach couldn't handle much food, and I spent my waking hours looking out my window at the sky. Sometimes, when the sun was setting, I watched it slide down the horizon until it hid behind the tall buildings, and I waited for the stars to appear.

The book came out with both my name and Daniel's as well as a dedication to the people of Kurdistan, under the title 'The Wishing Star'. It became a success and a bestseller. I did more than thirty interviews, and when the politicians couldn't ignore it anymore, I was invited to the parliament and the president's office to talk about it. Other countries approached me, and I talked to them too. The people in the media constantly talked about me, most of them heralded me a hero though some called me a sneak. The Turkish government put out a warrant for my arrest, but they couldn't reach me. They put out statements and propaganda videos; some news websites broadcast them, and some invited me on to comment on them. On one such occasion, I shared the screen with a prominent politician. During the interview she agreed with all I had to say, and afterwards, backstage, I asked her if she had plans to take action to help the people of Kurdistan. She smiled and said, 'You've made good money with your book, you've become a household name, you can work anywhere you want now. Accept that you won, and keep doing your interviews.' Then she walked away.

After all those months of work, the sacrifices, the multiple talks and interviews I did, and everything else that was done, a few governments finally spoke out. They condemned the government of Turkey for their treatment of Kurds, but then continued working with them. I went on more talk shows to say that condemnation wasn't enough, but after the hype around me and the book died down, all that was left were the condemnations. And in the end, the condemnations did nothing. In the end, nothing changed.

Note

1. Kurdish word literally meaning foal of a donkey. Used colloquially as a term for Kurds who betray their people and work with the enemy.

Friends Beyond the Mountains

Ava Homa

Inspired by the activist Minoo Homeily.

MY MOTHER'S TURQUOISE DRESS swayed with a graceful rhythm as I clapped along to the beats of dohl and zurna. Confidently, she climbed onto the stage and took her seat with the panel of other invited speakers. We had all come, attired in our finest ankle-length dresses, to watch my mother, Shno, or 'Daya gian' as I liked to call her. An aroma of freshly baked pastries wafted through the bustling throng. Sweet treats had been distributed through the crowd and we all savoured the buttery layers as they melted on our tongues. Together with thousands of others in the city of Sena, we had united in the town square for a series of events, celebrating Kurdish creativity and honouring the momentous centenary of the Republic of Mahabad. The crowd had been entertaining itself for hours. A group of young people were dancing shoulder-to-shoulder, forming a spiral of joy around a massive holographic bonfire. It had been three years since the long-awaited overthrow of the Islamic Republic of Iran and the success of the Democratic Party of Parsi that had promised a federal government and self-determination for all ethnicities.

Across the wide expanse of Kurdistan, and undeterred by the arbitrary borders that sought to confine us, people in all corners of our beloved homeland were right now gazing at holographic projections of prominent Kurdish women, figures who had fought for both gender and ethnic equality, refusing to compromise one pursuit for the other. Everyone from Adela Khanem[1] to Sakine Cansiz[2] levitated above town squares across Kurdistan, shining as bright as the sun on our national flag.

Although it was January, the new AI-controlled artificial weather systems maintained a semblance of eternal spring across the country: a symphony of life where flowers bloomed, and green shoots sprung up, straightened and opened. The seasons, ravaged by environmental disasters, had completely lost their natural rhythm. In their place, this new simulation had been implemented sixteen years ago, shortly before I was born and, though it brought me joy, it saddened my mother who had known what real seasons felt like, and cherished her memories of snow, fresh buds, and the fragrant white wisteria flowers with their long clusters.

After the great women of history had spoken, my mother was called up to the podium. I felt like I was flying as I watched her walking gracefully towards the microphone, masking her nervousness with a broad smile.

Daya gian showed how the algorithm she'd written could forecast the economic and political effects that different investments can, and do, have on different communities. She quoted the statistics that the former Iranian government was known to have spent on suppressing minorities. Using her app, she demonstrated, with a very fine degree of accuracy, how the whole of Iran would have benefited from investing in Kurdistan, how the national economy would have bloomed, and a significant portion of political, social, mental, and even health issues would have been averted.

As she spoke, the memory of a recent interview on national Iranian TV came flooding back: 'Yeah, right!,' the smirking news presenter had scoffed at my mother's arguments. 'A Kurdish utopia, a win-win situation! That's quite the fantasy!' I could still hear his chuckling.

I clenched my teeth as my mother continued. Her work had already earned her some recognition, at least within scientific circles. The praise her algorithm received, its ability to accurately predict socio-economic outcomes based on hypothetical inputs, meant thousands of people across the globe were turning their attention to the Kurdish situation and even watching celebrations like this one.

'You'd rather harm yourselves than let us thrive, is that it?' Daya gian had responded to the Iranian TV presenter that day.

Daya gian's presentation was continuing when the sky suddenly went dark, casting the entire city into shadow. The deafening sound of jets and the screams of frightened people running in all directions filled the air. 'Daya gian!' I yelled and ran, in the smoke, towards where I assumed the stage was. Fighting against the tide of panic, I found myself checking my device to see what was really happening, but we'd all been disconnected from the world, it seemed: the internet had been shut down. Terror engulfed the square, and my heart raced. 'Daya gian!' I screamed again and again at the top of my voice.

The lights flickered back on but amid the chaos, my mother was nowhere to be found. 'What happened?' I asked no one in particular, imagining a nationwide crisis.

'Over there!' someone shouted and we all looked up to witness a fleet of hoverjets descending on the foothills of Mount Awyar,[3] to the west of the city. Heavily armed Mehr Guards, formerly known as Revolutionary Guards, poured down the hillsides like ravaging locusts descending on their prey. The sight sent a chill down my spine. They were here to take away our short-lived autonomy right on the hundredth anniversary of Mahabad Republic, yet again characterising us as the 'unpeople' whose land and natural resources were to be looted, creatures to be driven out into the open and exterminated.

Life, as I knew it, was taken from me in 2046; the blue skies became smoke-stained, the smell of blooming mulberries and poppies mixed with gunpowder. I searched every corner of our town for my mother. At a time when wealthy Persians were taking vacations on the moon – where, unlike here, clean air and water were available on tap – we had no choice but to fight for the very right to exist.

The Kurds, like many others, had participated in the demonstrations that eventually brought the Parsi Administration to power. How could we not? The Islamic Republic that had ruled Iran for almost 67 years had also tried to stamp out any glimmer of Kurdish self-assertion; when they found that they could not, they had ensured that the region fell behind, underdeveloped, and afflicted with obsolete technology, red tape, slow or non-existent internet, and the cheapest narcotics.

When the Islamic Republic was finally overthrown, chaos ensued in many parts of Iran but in the Kurdish region, the *benka*, or local councils, collectively managed our cities. We cherished this hard-earned freedom. Many of the political parties that had united to overthrow the Islamic government now found themselves suppressed and took refuge in our cities, where freedom of expression still prevailed.

But on that evening, as the hoverjets and drones swarmed over the town, the prosperity and optimism that had so recently sprung up in our city was suddenly snuffed out. I headed home, hoping to find mother there. Bullets buzzed like flies. Daya gian was nowhere to be found.

The morning after Daya gian vanished, the echoes of gunshots still reverberated through the town. From the moment I woke, my heart pounded, as if echoing the heavy shelling outside, but my thoughts remained fixed on a single question: *Where could she be?* Desperate for answers, I donned my khaki pants, cautiously manoeuvred through the chaos, and sprinted, street by street, zigzagging through the crossfire, towards the hospital. With each step, my reality blurred with the memories of video games I had once immersed myself in. It dawned on me that the distinction between horror and entertainment lay in your proximity to the events unfolding.

I witnessed the apocalypse as I ran past or hopped over the wounded and the dead, covering my ears to prevent being deafened by the shells, chasing an imagined reunion with my mother. A trip to the hospital that, in peacetime, would take only ten minutes, took more than an hour – I had to wait for the armoured cars to pass by, crouch down or crawl along low walls, then stop, look around carefully and run again.

As I sprinted and sought refuge, my eyes caught sight of a perfectly wrapped piece of chocolate lying on the ground. Intrigued, I paused, scanning my surroundings for any signs of danger. When the absence of gunshots reassured me, I retraced my steps and eagerly retrieved the sweet treat. It offered a fleeting moment of bliss amidst the desolation.

As I sat, enjoying the rich flavours of the truffle, the moment was interrupted by the sight of a tall figure on the opposite side of the street. In an instant, he crumpled to the ground, blood trickling from his forehead and pooling in his open eyes. Horror engulfed me, and I instinctively threw myself to the ground, my body trembling uncontrollably.

The fragile line between life and death, between being a mere observer and a victim, hung precariously in the air. If today was to be my last day on earth, I vowed to dedicate it not to self-preservation, or even to finding my mother, but to reaching out and offering a hand to anyone in need.

I ventured into the streets where bullet-ridden walls stood as silent witnesses to the relentless onslaught. Long stretches of them had toppled over already. Shots rained in from both the ground-level and above. That's how the Mehr Guards, armed with tanks, drones, and hoverjets against an opposition relying on mere rifles, went about slaughtering us.

When I finally arrived at the hospital, I met Leyla and Dilan, two girls about my own age, who were there to volunteer at the hospital and had been told to wait for the head nurse, Narin. Meeting the two courageous girls brought me some comfort. I told them that I too was there to serve. Together, we stood at the threshold of the hospital. Shifting from foot to foot, I looked up at the building as if it were a temple in which I could be elevated.

Narin showed up, petite with a skinny face, she looked charismatic, formidable, and slightly intimidating. She sized each of us up and started assigning tasks: 'Leyla – it's Leyla, right? – go help register the new patients; Dilan, check to make sure the patients take their medicine on time – you'll find the schedules on the charts by their beds.' When the two were gone, she came forward and put a hand on my shoulder. 'I know it's maybe too much to ask a person your age, but ....'

'Anything!' I said and then blurted, 'They kidnapped my mother. I'll do anything.'

'Oh, my goodness... You're Shno's daughter!'

I nodded, 'My name is Hataw.'

'I can trust Shno's daughter!' She paused, her eyes piercing and searching. 'I have a hunch one of the doctors, the one that just arrived from Tehran, Dr. Sadeqi... I could be wrong, but I think he's a plant.'

I took a step back and her hand fell from my shoulder. It suddenly occurred to me that if we succumbed to this invasion, she and I and all the other volunteers could be identified and persecuted, or worse. But that was not Narin's primary concern.

'He might hurt the patients,' she said. 'You'll assist at the operating room and keep an eye on him. Good?'

'But… how can I tell if he's doing something wrong?'

'You will.' She pulled me towards her and gently squeezed my skinny arms poking out of my khaki T-shirt. 'Just be there and watch him, watch other nurses' reactions to him. Do your best. You have to be observant. Astute.'

I didn't know why Narin picked me out of all the volunteers for this job, or maybe she had assigned a few of us for the same task. Either way, her trust warmed me and gave me resolve.

Over the following days, I spent a lot of time with the surgeons, learning the names of the equipment they used, and washing and sanitising them. Before long, I was scissoring the patient's clothes, often bloody, undressing them, covering them with sheets and standing by to assist the doctors, especially when Dr. Sadeqi was operating. He was kind to me, ruffled my hair and even recited classical poetry out loud. I was afraid one day he'd find out we had distrusted him and it would break his heart.

The hospital was in a building that had once housed a large, wealthy family; there was a high wall running around what had been a dusty courtyard, then three floors of bedrooms, kitchens, closets, and sitting rooms. Underneath had been a spacious cellar. Today, the mansion was more crammed with people than it had ever been; it was overflowing with patients, doctors, nurses, volunteers, every yard of available floor space taken up by stained blankets shaped into beds for the groaning wounded.

I hurried down the hallway to the morgue. My arms ached as I carried the buckets from the operating room, heavy with amputations. Inside were ash-pale fingers, feet, ears, hands, sometimes a whole forearm or lower leg, whatever the doctors decided was unsalvageable. Dr. Sadeqi was on duty today, so there were more than usual.

The first time I had to take body parts to the morgue I was haunted by it. The legs and three fingers of a thirteen-year-old girl named Sharmin had been amputated after a mortar shell struck her. Despite these tragedies, Sharmin's bed, the only pleasant spot in the hospital, was where everybody would gather to laugh and relax for a few minutes. At a young age, Sharmin had become the most inspiring figure in the hospital. A hand-written placard behind her bed read: 'Kurdistan, my love, my legs are my gifts to your freedom.'

After having carried away so many body parts, I was no longer as horrified. In the yard, some were wailing, some screaming, some shaking in quiet sobs.

Amid all the chaos, I was reminded of something my aunt used to say. 'There were two types of barbarians in this world: those who were already in charge and those who were trying to be.' My aunt, as a young woman, had fought examples of the second type: Daesh, the Islamic State, a violent group that hadn't yet ascended to what they presumed was their rightful throne. My aunt's all-female YPJ was naturally looked up to, saluted for being the freedom fighters they were.[4] But to their horror, as news of them spread, the women found themselves turning into global objects of male fantasy: the girl with the gun, the brunette bombshells, the ones who would send a hundred savages each straight to hell. But what mattered was that the brainwashed Daeshis, who didn't fear death, were terrified of Kurdish women. They genuinely believed that, if they were killed by them, their God would slam the door of paradise right in their face, denying them their precious seventy-two virgins.

The first types of barbarians, by contrast, those already in charge, had allies, nuclear powers, diplomatic ties, and representatives in the United Nations. Their state brutalities were the ones the world was already used to seeing, or didn't see anymore, or yawned when they saw. So we were shunned when we combatted the second group. That's how the man-made world worked and that's how people in war-free countries were too busy being in denial or already overwhelmed by bills and pills to stand up to injustice.

The hospital gates opened, and a van entered full of howling young men, their clothes and faces stained red. The crowd of relatives stopped crying and helped carry the men inside. Since no beds were available, and the 3D printer allocated for printing new beds was out of order, they had to lie down on the floor and wait for a doctor to snatch a minute to examine them. The van they arrived in had been sprayed with bullets and five men were injured. One of them was a man about my age with glistening dark eyes whose leg was bleeding. The bullet had struck bone, and he was in more pain than the others; already he had a high fever and was hallucinating. I put his feet in cold water to bring down his temperature, but he kicked and yelled, still in his dream, cursing his fate and spilling the water. I held his hands firmly, but he pushed me with his greater strength, and I fell back, landing hard on my rear end. His friends, who had minor injuries from shrapnel, started laughing. I gave up and left to help a more cooperative patient, leaving the young man to the care of a stronger nurse.

Because of the bombardment, most of the staff had not come to work at the hospital. I, though, was a brash teen full of lofty ideas about service to the cause. I was not alone; many adolescent boys and girls were there to offer their help, and other adults volunteered as best they could. The roads were blocked, and food and other necessities were not allowed into the city. All the warehouses and online shops had shut down. No one had wireless connection throughout the assault. People, who still remembered how, baked bread in their houses and sent it to the hospital. They invented recipes to make use of whatever they had in the house.

After tending to a second casualty from the van, I remembered that I had left the bucket in the yard and ran back to retrieve it. When I arrived at the morgue, two women and an old man in traditional attire were standing at the door, holding large, heavy containers. Only two hours before they had been here with an earlier delivery of ice to help prevent the bodies from decomposing. I assumed they lived nearby – how else could they have risked crossing the streets twice a day? – but I never asked. They had a rustic bearing to them and lacked the city-dwellers' self-centeredness. 'Thank you! Thank you!' I muttered to them, still gasping.

'Narin told us to take some of them.' The man rubbed his salt-and-pepper beard.

'Take some of what?' I asked as I turned the key in the lock of the morgue.

'Some of the bodies that we identified.' He wiped his forehead with his sleeve. 'To be buried in their parents' yards and gardens. She said the hospital had no more room.'

The thought of families having to turn their gardens into their loved ones' graveyard made me shudder. The putrid smell struck us all when I opened the door. Not having eaten or slept much in the last week, I felt sick to my stomach. The other two women stoically scattered the ice over the bodies. I remembered one of the twins who seemed at peace. The image of their tall, pregnant mother took shape before my eyes. She had been shot crossing the street to buy formula; the doctors tried to save her babies. The next time I passed by her bed, her eyes were closed, and a twin was wrapped in a white sheet beside her.

'Families need to find help to dig the graves,' the old man said. 'Graves,' he repeated.

'Thank you,' I said; illogical, perhaps, but I had nothing else. With bullets and missiles flying through the city, people couldn't get to the graveyards without risking another loss.

Iranian satellites monitoring every movement could easily

distinguish civilians from fighters, but they deliberately targeted unarmed people to break the resistance.

I set the bucket of limbs down in the morgue and locked the large padlock on the metal door behind me.

'I will come back when I find a truck or something,' he said.

I nodded. It was hard to find old cars that worked with gas and could still be used. All the electric ones had been shut down by the central government.

The three of them left and I watched them go, carrying the empty containers, their backs perhaps a little less bent than they had been a few minutes ago.

I went inside to give the young men antibiotics and check their temperatures. 'Soran is calm now,' one of them said, winking and pointing at the man who had been kicking and yelling a couple of hours ago. So, he was called Soran. I started washing his feet in the cold water; though he didn't resist, he still seemed to be unaware of his surroundings. His friends were stifling laughter and I knew something was going on. Anyway, it was getting dark and Soran needed an operation urgently.

Dizzy, unfocused and tired, I headed straight to Narin's office. Even though I washed my scrubs so obsessively that others made fun of me for it, I felt unclean; the hospital had no showers, and I didn't want to leave while there was still a wound I could clean, a hand I could hold. But I had already been at the hospital for a week, day and night, and I needed a few hours off. I could have asked the people with ice containers to let me shower at theirs if they lived nearby. Or I could knock on any door in this street. Ever since the government's assault, even apolitical people who didn't dare leave the imagined safety of their homes, welcomed those taking a more active part.

Narin didn't notice me right away, being too busy turning a dial on a strange old box to hear me come in. She was a collector of all things antique and manual, things that my generation considered a waste of space. She came from four generations of women fighters and looked to history to predict the future. She had replaced the batteries in what she told me was a 'radio' and suddenly we were hearing the Mehr Guard officers barking orders through their wireless bluetooths.

'Kill'em all!' a commander shouted, and I envisioned him with a long red tie, looking different from the long-bearded, stinky Islamic Republic soldiers, but fuelled by a similar bigotry.

'The hospital, sir?' a meek voice asked the commander, only to be immediately berated for doubting the order.

'Where in the world do people attack hospitals?' I asked, incensed. When Nurse Narin had first ordered us to turn all the lights off after dark (leaving only the life support machines connected to the hospital's mini-fusion generator), we all protested. 'They won't bomb a hospital. That would be a war crime,' I had said.

Narin shook her head in reproach. 'Why else do you think the government pulled the internet?'

That night, Kurdish fighters shot down drones targeting the hospital. Horror filled the city like a mysterious, infiltrating ether.

The rest of the world, had they learned about Iran's brutal and unjustified attack on the Kurds, wouldn't protest. China, the world power, had no pretence of defending democracy and human rights. The Europeans, sick of the Islamic Republic and excited about new trading opportunities with the secular government, could happily turn a blind eye, like they had done for so long with Saudi Arabia and Israel. Iran's only fear was that Russia, no longer having Iran wrapped around its finger, would immediately take advantage of the turmoil, and settle a score. As Kurds, our only hope was that our sisters across frontiers would notice, leak it to the international media, and send reinforcements.

I wasn't sure how to ask for a break without making Narin feel that I was bailing on her in the middle of a crisis. She turned off the radio and faced me. 'Are you keeping an eye on Dr. Sadeqi?'

'Yes, I am,' I said. Watching the bespectacled old doctor with his hunched back was my most challenging duty. The rest of the doctors and nurses who arrived at the hospital from Tehran all seemed nice, and I liked them, but Narin couldn't bring herself to trust this one and I had faith in her judgment. 'I should go now.' Thinking of Dr. Sadeqi made me realise I had to keep working. On the way back to the operating suite, I went to the bathroom to wash my hands, and for the first time, in front of the mirror, wept.

Soran and his friends were still lying on the floor. In the pre-op room, just outside the operating theatre, a few patients were waiting, and I had to prep them. The next in line was a man who had been shot in the stomach; I tried to help him undress. He was engaged to one of the nurses, a lovely woman who kept saying she had no interest in politics but who barely slept and was always busy taking care of the injured.

Dr. Sadeqi, who had just finished examining the young men, came into the pre-op room, and asked me to help the nurse's fiancé and then go to clean and dress Soran's friends' injuries. When I took hold of the man's hand to pull it around my shoulders and help him up, I felt that it was cold and lifeless. I touched his wrist in terror; he had no pulse. I held my fingers before his nose and didn't feel his breath. Dr. Sadeqi came forward and examined the man. 'Internal bleeding,' he announced, looking more indifferent than the walls.

The deceased patient's fiancée arrived at that moment and started shaking the man. When she saw no reaction, she burst into loud sobs that made me feel short of breath, my throat tightening. The man had bled to death. The nurse stopped sobbing and began shrieking; a woman who had saved so many lives failed her own fiancé, lost her man while helping someone else who had seemed to be in greater danger, the woman who thought politics wouldn't affect her if she just kept out of it all. Cold sweat formed on the insides of my thighs and my back.

Suddenly the loud roar of an airplane shut everyone up and we all crouched down, covering our heads and ears. An explosion shook the walls and shattered several windows. Soon after, Dr. Sadeqi left for a break, the lights were turned off and Soran was rushed in for his operation so no other patient would bleed to death.

I was almost done cleaning and dressing the young men's wounds when I noticed that, despite the recent attack, Narin was heading out on her rounds to check on the patients being kept in underground hospitals around the city. As soon as it was safe enough to move one of the injured Peshmarga, Narin would send them to one of these safe-houses to be cared for. The Peshmarga weren't just our defence force; their name literally means 'those who face death,' and Narin knew they would face it once again, after the invasion ended, even if they fully recovered. The church and schools of the city had become safe havens for the Peshmarga.

Some residential houses would also take in patients, let them rest. Sometimes the injured were taken to one of these places for temporary care until the opportunity came to transport them to the hospital. Sometimes patients who had not been fighters were sent out to the same safe-houses just because no beds were available in the hospital for non-urgent cases. The number of injured brought to the hospital was beyond count. Young men and women who had dreamed of a free and democratic Kurdistan were brought in, teetering between life and death, blazing in excruciating pain. There were more patients than our equipment and staff could handle, and our efforts were sometimes pointless.

'Hataw, Hataw,' Narin suddenly called to me. She pointed

to a spot behind me. 'Go and hold her hand and don't let go of her.' When I turned, I saw Leyla lying on a bed, a white sheet covering her body. I recognised her delicate face and light brown hair, lips that looked paler than her skin. Leyla, the volunteer I met on my first day at the hospital, had been shot in the head while helping collect the dead and injured from the streets. The emergency room had no space, and she was left alone while the staff tried to help those who still had a chance. How Narin could remember Leyla amid all the mess and send someone to attend to her was beyond me.

I held Leyla's icy hands and nervously touched her face, her feet, her hair, her hand, the lines of her nose and broad forehead, all lifeless and cold. Despite the crowd, my tears sneaked out and rolled down my face. Leyla had turned up here to help others and now no one was able to help her, no matter how much we wanted to. I stayed with her for over an hour, unable to leave her alone.

Finally, a tearful man appeared by her side, eyes looking like buckets of blood, narrow lips quivering. '*Kanishkakam. Kanishka nazarakam.*' My daughter. My darling daughter. His shoulders shook. A faint smile appeared on Leyla's near-death face. I walked away when their hands locked. I wasn't far when I heard the first of the father's loud sobs shudder through the hall. She had held on until she saw his face.

In that moment, a longing for my own mother suddenly overwhelmed me. If she had not sought refuge in one of the hospitals, my heart whispered that she must be confined in a prison, hidden away from the world. Since arriving here, I'd rarely had a chance to pause and process my emotions. Instead I was like a stone, hard and cold, focused and pragmatic. I did sometimes catch myself staring blankly, vaguely, helplessly at nothing in particular. What had happened to us? We had put our lives on hold and focused on ending the reign of the fanatical theocrats and on bringing peace and justice to our beloved ancestral land, but history had reared its ugly face once more, in its endless cycle of repetition.

Two more weeks went by and I took to strolling aimlessly from room to room, watching the sleeping patients. It was night when the terror that cloaked our world turned faint and invisible. An ominous menace was delivered in the rhythmic tick-tock of the clock and the chirp-chirp of the crickets, the moaning of patients, the shock and disbelief of those who reached into the empty space where an arm or a leg used to be, the quiet sobs of a mother who had just buried her daughter in their front yard and was now watching her other child as if she could protect them from the enemy's arsenal if only she stared long enough at them without blinking.

Soran was sleeping, but his fever was high, and he was still incoherent. I continued washing his feet to bring down the fever; he resisted, and I held his hands. This time, he calmed down and I gently massaged his legs and changed the damp cloth I had placed on his forehead.

With his hands in mine and nobody around, I looked at his face; his red lips opened and closed and a few incomprehensible words leaked out. His fever was still high. I continued to wash his feet from time to time, trying to bring down his temperature. When he stirred drowsily, I would reach out and hold his hands until he quietened again. A few times, I thought I saw him begin to open his eyes; but when I looked into his face, it was blank and calm. Once again, I dampened the cloth I had placed on his forehead. He moved, and I took his hands again, watching his face carefully. His chest heaved up and down gently, rhythmically; sometimes a syllable seemed to take shape on his lips, only to fade again. It was terrible to think that he might never walk again. If only he had been born somewhere else, somewhere peaceful. If only I had been born there too. If only we had met there, maybe in a class, maybe on the street, him chatting with his friends, our eyes meeting from across the crowd...

Startled, I realised that his eyes were open, looking into mine. Clear and deep. His hands stirred. Looking into his eyes again, I saw a twinkle and suddenly understood. 'You weren't really asleep!' I accused.

'I was,' he protested, but the corner of his mouth twitched up. 'Kind of,' he amended.

'When did you wake up?'

'Well,' he said, 'the first thing I can remember is feeling your hands.' He paused. 'They're very nice hands. Healing hands, I suppose. They brought me back from the fever.'

I felt a sudden wave of warmth wash over me, and went to pull back, but he didn't let go of my hand. I was suddenly conscious of my messy hair, my wrinkled shirt. Soran wasn't looking at those, though: his eyes were locked on our hands. Very gently, he squeezed them. 'Thank you.'

'It... It... It was nothing,' I stuttered. What was going on? My face felt like it was in a furnace, like I was the one with the fever, while he looked calm and cool, staring up into my eyes again. This was strange. I was used to swiping pictures when considering potential boyfriends, video chatting, certainly not feeling someone's hands, the electricity they could induce in my body. My generation was more used to sex robots, convinced that humans no longer really needed a lifelong partner, that it was old school, a form of entrapment. Here was this wounded human, melting me with his charm, making me want to be near him.

'You're very pretty,' he said, then immediately let go of my hands, pulling back. Embarrassed. 'I'm sorry, I shouldn't have said that. I'm still a little woozy.' He yawned elaborately. 'Maybe I should just rest.'

I couldn't help but smile, even as I glanced about. Everyone around us was quiet, either unconscious or caught up in their own thoughts. 'How will I know you're not faking this time?'

He didn't answer me, not directly. Instead, keeping his eyes closed, he said, 'I remember them saying, when I still hadn't opened my eyes, "You idiot! Why'd you go and shove a pretty girl?" Was that you?'

'I guess,' I said.

'I won't do it again,' he promised. On impulse, I reached out and took his hands again. Squeezed them. He squeezed back.

I wanted to throw myself into his arms, tell him how connecting to strangers had sustained me in this apocalypse. But I found myself rushing down the hallway instead. My heart was singing, though, and I could not wipe the smile off my face.

Later that night, a pickup truck arrived, carrying the gruesome remains of bodies torn apart by cluster bombs, yet another war crime. I was tasked with taking these shattered fragments to the morgue, but the thought of facing the darkness alone sent a shiver down my spine.

In the midst of the hospital, I overheard whispers and soft laughter emanating from Sharmin's room. Dilan was there, in mourning no doubt for her friend, Leyla.

'Dilan, will you come with me to the morgue?' I asked.

'But I have to stay here,' she said. 'Go yourself, go. You're Mistress Brave around here. Go.' Dilan stifled a chuckle.

Reluctantly, I gathered my resolve, picked up the bucket containing the dismembered body parts, and ventured into the corridor. What seemed like a routine task during the day, turned into a haunting experience under the cover of darkness: to approach a pile of corpses, add more body parts to the pile, some partly eaten by stray dogs. The high windows of the morgue had been shattered in the recent shelling, so I no longer needed to fumble with the key; I approached the broken doorway and simply tossed the body parts through the jagged remains of the window pane. The macabre act was a grim testament to the savagery surrounding us.

Turning back, I bumped into something soft, causing me to scream in fright – my first scream since the invasion started.

'Hahahah.'

I recognised the laughter. 'Very funny!' I yelled at Dilan, hating her prank.

'Oh, it is. You have no idea, Mistress Brave.' She was doubled over with laughter, holding her belly.

Her laugh reminded me of Daya gian's. My anger turned into embarrassment, and I started laughing too. 'Buffoon!'

With her awkward, gangly frame, there was something clownish about Dilan. The laughter was a relief. These past few weeks, my life had felt like a jungle where I was surrounded by wild hungry animals that could tear me apart at any moment, yet here I was, sharing a spoonful of honey with another precarious life. A small moment of joy, our defiance against the injustices.

Returning to my station, I lay, staring at the plaster ceiling. Despite the fatigue that engulfed me, I realised that in these past few days, an invisible wellspring of energy had fuelled my work. Only three weeks ago, I had been obsessed with who had said what about me online. How strange that I had matured in the span of three weeks; my mother would be proud of me, I thought. I sent her a prayer as I fell asleep, bracing myself for whatever tomorrow might bring.

When I woke up, Soran was nowhere to be found. Narin had safely transported him and others to hidden locations, away from the danger posed by the Mehr Guard.

When Narin finally asked, 'Who's going to deliver blood and medicine to the underground hospitals?', I eagerly volunteered.

Sitting in the back of the ambulance, surrounded by boxes of medicine, I felt a mix of determination and anticipation to reunite with Soran. Across from me, Dilan rested with her chin on her chest, seemingly exhausted. Playfully, I teased Dilan about her uncanny knack for finding opportunities to take a nap, a light-hearted attempt to even the score after her teasing from the previous night.

The city's largest hill, *Ban Bashgah*, was occupied by the armed guards, equipped with modern weapons and scopes, ready to shoot anyone who dared to venture into the streets below. That neighbourhood had become a haunting place, littered with lifeless bodies that no one could retrieve. Only the stray dogs found solace in the abundance of carcasses.

My jesting came to an abrupt halt when I gently nudged Dilan and noticed drops of blood running down her forehead. I let out a scream. How could this be? A bullet had silently passed through the already shattered window of the ambulance, striking Dilan in the back of her head. The gunshots I had heard seemed distant and inconsequential until this moment. I felt like I was losing my mind. Did she pass away peacefully in her sleep, unaware of the pain that awaited her?

On arriving at a school-turned-hospital, we carried Dilan's limp body onto the driveway. I went into autopilot, hastily handing the medicine to the man seated at the makeshift reception area, a plastic chair serving as his temporary station. Then I started scanning the rooms, searching for Soran through the strong antiseptic smell. The beds – simple metal frames – were adorned with multi-coloured sheets and blankets donated by local families. A woman tended to her injured partner and a young boy, feeding them soup on one of the beds. The rest of the underground hospital seemed to fade into the background as my focus remained fixed on finding Soran.

Finally, I located him. Soran was still confined to his bed, unable to walk or move freely. The neighbouring bed displayed a disarray of blankets, newspapers, and a half-consumed juice box, indicating the imminent return of a fellow patient. Impulsively, I threw myself into Soran's arms, aware that this was inappropriate. His gentle hands caressed my bare arms while he kissed my hair.

He was shocked when he saw my wet eyes. Because my face was buried against his chest, he hadn't seen or heard my tears. He paused. I sensed that he wanted to kiss my lips. I wish he had. But he was too alarmed and confused to move.

Our moment was interrupted as the absent patient returned and the blaring sound of an ambulance horn pierced my ears. I didn't get to tell him that I'd just lost another friend, or that I could be next. I had to rush back to the hospital where every corridor was lined with anguish. Every second mattered, for there were always lives to save.

Upon my return, a wounded Peshmarga with bloodied arms was brought into the room. Despite his obvious agony, he maintained a stoic composure, biting his lips to suppress the pain. However, as soon as Dr. Sadeqi touched his injured left arm, a blood-curdling scream filled the air.

'This hand has to be amputated or you'll die,' the doctor's words cut through the atmosphere like ice. I stood there, struck not only by the severity of the situation but also by the callousness with which Dr. Sadeqi addressed the suffering patient. My mouth opened instinctively, but no words left my lips. I attempted to meet the doctor's gaze, searching for some semblance of empathy, but he averted his eyes. In that moment, I sensed an undercurrent of hatred in his countenance as he prepared to sever the Peshmarga's arm. The young man's torn lips, the crimson-stained sleeve, and the fear that filled his eyes were too much to comprehend. With trembling hands, I carefully cut off the man's shirt, seeing the dangling arm that was to be amputated near his shoulder. If Daya gian were here, I'd ask her what to do. Suddenly, I felt her near me, confirming my intuition.

I took off my mask and scrubs, fleeing from the room and the hospital. Despite the bullets whizzing through the streets, I sprinted until I reached Narin's home. My heart pounded as I banged on her door, a flurry of emotions engulfing me, uncertain of my own actions and motives. It took her a while to respond to the relentless knocking.

'What is it?' she said as she opened the door in her sleeping robe. Her eyes were bloodshot.

I couldn't speak, couldn't even breathe.

'What?' she repeated, now awake and anxious.

How could I explain? I lacked evidence, only a hunch that gnawed at me.

Dr. Sadeqi had the power to incapacitate the young Peshmarga, and I stood there trembling, unable to find my voice. Narin briskly pivoted on her heel and disappeared back inside, leaving the door slightly ajar. I was left wondering what her intention was, before finally remembering to breathe. Soon after, Narin re-emerged, clad in an earth-tone dress. I took off running, and she followed suit.

As we reached the operating room, I became insignificant in Narin's eyes as she focused on examining the patient, whose arm had not yet been amputated. 'I will stitch this arm,' she declared.

I glanced at Dr. Sadeqi, expecting him to object, to insist on removing it. But he remained silent and simply left the room. Throughout the night, Narin tirelessly and meticulously sewed up the dangling arm.

The world beyond may have been technologically and scientifically progressing, but here, in my world, any breath could be my last. My mother's whereabouts remained uncertain, but my path now lay clear before me. Above, in the upper branches of a cedar tree, the moon emerged from behind the lingering fog.

Notes

1. Adela Khanem (1847-1924), also 'Lady Adela Jaff' (sometimes referred to as 'the Princess of the Brave') was a Kurdish ruler of

the Jaff tribe and one of the Kurds' most famous female leaders. Being herself from the Sahibqeran family, she married the leader of the Jaff tribe, Osman Pasha Jaff, became its effective leader before her husband's death and continued as such after it.

2. Sakine Cansız (1958-2013) was one of the co-founders of the Kurdistan Workers' Party (PKK), and leader of its women's movement. Following the Turkish military coup of September 1980, she was imprisoned and regularly tortured for many years in Diyarbakir prison, where 34 fellow inmates died of torture between 1981 and 1989. A close associate of Abdullah Öcalan (also known as 'Apo'), she was shot dead in Paris, France, on 9 January 2013, along with two fellow female Kurdish activists, Fidan Doğan and Leyla Şaylemez.

3. Mount Awyer (known in Persian as 'Abidar') stands to the west of the city of Sanandaj, in Eastern Kurdistan (northwest Iran).

4. The YPJ or Women's Protection Units ('Yekîneyên Parastina Jin') are all-female militia (part of the Rojava's Syrian Democratic Forces) that were instrumental in claiming control back from ISIS in the Syrian civil war.

My Handsome One

Selahattin Demirtaş

*Translated from the Turkish
by Amy Spangler*

WHEN WE TRY TO recall our earliest childhood memory, we
can never be exactly sure. Our memory misleads us. Which of
the hazy black-and-white images floating through the fog is the
earliest, we wonder?

Our home was in Lice, a small, verdant town in Diyarbakır.
During the summers, everyone slept on the earthen roofs of
their single-storey houses. For beds we had what we called
'thrones', which were like enormous, four-legged tables made
of wood, sometimes with an iron frame, surrounded by a
railing to keep us from falling off. The throne I shared with my
mother had a thin iron frame. It was light grey, its paint chipped
off here and there, and rusted in the spots where there wasn't
any paint. On the roof opposite, my uncle slept together with
my Aunt Pakize, and their baby, Welat, on their own wooden
throne.

I'd learn much later that Welat's name had been officially registered as 'Vedat'. Kurdish was forbidden. I must have been around six years old at the time, and hadn't yet heard a single word in any language other than Kurdish. Life had a lot to teach me, but most of all, it would teach me what it meant to be Kurdish.

That morning, it must have been especially cold, because I'd snuggled up real close to my mother. I woke up to the low, deep howl of a bird. It was an owl, perhaps an eagle owl. The mulberry tree in our courtyard was so huge, it towered a good four-to-five metres above the roof. But the bird wasn't in our tree. Perhaps it had perched on the walnut tree in our neighbour Xaltîya Susê's courtyard. The sky was clear as could be, with stars raining down. It felt like my mother and I were sleeping right there amidst the stars. As if I could reach out and touch them, that's how I remember it:

The leaves of the mulberry tree begin stirring ever so gently, and there's a rustling sound. The cool wind blowing down from the giant mountain behind us carries the scent of fruit and oak trees. I used to love that scent. I recall inhaling it deeply into my tiny lungs. Then, all of a sudden, I realise that I really have to go. I quietly slip down from the throne and head to the toilet. I need to climb down the wooden ladder that's propped against the eaves. I take each step carefully to keep from tumbling down.

I'm not even halfway down the ladder when the sound of a distant explosion demolishes the dawn's magic tranquility. And immediately in its wake come volleys of gunfire. My mother's woken up and is yelling and screaming as she searches for me. My uncle, holding Welat, and my aunt make a dash for the ladder. I'm scared stiff, frozen halfway down it. When my uncle reaches the ladder and sees me, he calls out to my mother. And so, all together, we climb down to the courtyard before making our way into the small, windowless storage cellar. For nearly an hour we wait there, crammed together in that tiny space where there's barely enough room to store food, let alone us. Though I'm scared at first, after a while, I too calm down, pacified by my uncle's reassurances and soothing voice. Though I still really have to pee, for a while I'm so scared, I forget. When my fear subsides, I start squirming again. Realising my predicament, my mother whisks me off to the toilet. Out in the courtyard the sound of gunfire is much closer and more frightening. I must have been six years old, yes, that's right, because they'd taken me along with them once, that year, to visit my father in prison. I guess I must have heard similar sounds before, because I knew what they were. But I can't recall anything earlier than this. Or perhaps I'm confusing the order of events.

I was born into war. And so I thought war was just a natural part of life. The truth is, I had no idea what 'war' even was or who was fighting. War was something natural, like rain, or the wind. You know how when a baby gazelle is born, it knows instinctively that it needs to flee from lions, well, for me, war was the lion always lurking in the woods. It was bad, and we had to flee it, that's all I knew. Whenever we heard gunfire, we were to run straight to the cellar.

It was with my father's death that my fear of war turned into rage. I may not have known exactly who or what war was, but I understood that it had something to do with his murder. After my father died, I was no longer afraid of anything. Because when I went to see him in prison he had told me, 'Don't be afraid, my girl, don't you be afraid of anything.' Though I couldn't understand at the time what he was saying. Because he'd spoken in a different language.

He was in prison for a year. I remembered him at his most handsome. At first, I hadn't recognised him from behind the thick, dirty glass. I had clung to my mother's skirt and cowered behind her. The man before me had his hair shorn short, no moustache, and a thin, sallow face. For a moment, I felt he was a stranger, but his eyes belonged to my father, they were my father's eyes. We were only there for a few minutes before the soldiers swept in and forced us to leave.

Outside, my uncle scolded my mother. 'Didn't I tell you not to speak Kurdish? See, you got us kicked out straight away.' My mother was crying so hard she couldn't speak. She bit her lip to keep from screaming, holding her mouth shut with one hand. Her other hand was in mine. Without realising it, she squeezed my hand so hard that I too was crying along with her, from the pain.

My mother picked me up and tried to calm me. That's when she told me what my father had said to me inside: 'Ne-tirse qîza min, ji tiştekê re ne-tirse.' I immediately stopped crying.

I'm sixty-eight now. The only photo left of my father is a black-and-white headshot. In the image, he has a moustache, and his hair is combed to the side. His eyes hold a deep sorrow, and he's very handsome. I've carried this photo with me my entire life. It's the photo I hold in my hand now as I look upon the sparkling Aleppo night extending before me, from the balcony of the hotel where I'm staying. It's the only photo that encapsulates my childhood, and that has given meaning to my life since. It's the image of the man who still says to me with sorrowful eyes, 'Don't be afraid, my girl, don't you be afraid of anything,' a photo of my hero, who was tortured to death in Diyarbakır Prison at the age of twenty-six.

'I'm not afraid, Dad!' I say, talking to myself. 'I'm just nervous. Tomorrow is a big day. For my people, for all the peoples of the Middle East, and for our country, Kurdistan, Dad.'

The phone in my room rings and I go inside to answer it. It's the Minister of Foreign Affairs. 'We're ready to start the meeting,' he says, adding that they're waiting for me. For me? Gulazer Sozdar, Kurdistan's second female president.

*

At the hour-long meeting, we review the final preparations. The agreement we're to sign the following morning will be a turning point for the entire region. We add the finishing touches to my speech for the signing ceremony. Everything is more or less ready, and we return to our rooms, having agreed to meet for breakfast at nine.

My plan is to take a shower and go straight to sleep, so I can wake up refreshed in the morning. But when I lie down after my shower, I toss and turn. I can't manage to fall asleep. I get up and go back onto the balcony. It's after midnight now, but Aleppo is still buzzing with life, still sparkling. It's impossible to believe that just twenty-five years ago this city was in ruins. This city, which had been devastated during the Syrian civil war, with not a single building, not one road or piece of infrastructure left intact, was now a veritable carnival. Even at this hour, the streets reverberated with the jubilant sound of people's voices. Thousands of people from all over the world had flocked to the city to witness the historical event that was to take place the following day. And the people of Aleppo, as if to avenge those dreadful, agonising days of the past so full of misery, were singing and dancing in the streets.

I take a deep breath, inhaling Aleppo's jubilant air, and a feeling of serenity fills me. All living creatures on Earth deserve to live in serenity. None more so than the heavy-hearted peoples of these blood-soaked lands, who had been left yearning for peace for so many long years. And now here we are, all together, fervidly welcoming the serenity that is, finally, ours. *Now we too have a great democracy,* I think to myself, *and we have every right to boast.* But my joy is accompanied by a faint sadness, coming from within, somewhere deep inside. Because this serenity has come at a heavy cost. The more I think about all those we lost, the heavier my sadness becomes.

It seems to me that only the new generations – our children and grandchildren, that is – those who never knew war, will truly be able to savour this new era. All the pain that we endured, was it not so that our children's world might be different from that of our own childhood? The mighty struggle we put forth, all of our labour, our resistance, was not all of it for them? So that they might break out in beaming smiles and dance freely. This world now belongs to them, I sigh.

I recall my childhood again. I pick up the headshot I'd placed on the table and go back out onto the balcony. I take turns looking at my handsome one, my father, and at Aleppo. The sound of my mother's screams, her wailing, when they brought his body to Lice, rings in my ears, intermingling with the boisterous laughter rising from the streets of Aleppo.

It was three or four months after we'd seen him in prison. They brought my hero to our house in a coffin. Soldiers stood guard at the head of every street, they weren't letting anyone go to the mosque or the cemetery. A crowd of relatives and neighbours filled our house. Our courtyard was crammed full of people. Everyone was sobbing quietly, except for my mother; she was howling like a wounded gazelle. The soldiers didn't allow the coffin to be opened. There was a scuffle in the courtyard. I was nearly crushed in the uproar. One of our neighbours picked me up and took me inside. The soldiers wrenched my father's coffin from us, beating off anyone who tried to stop them, tossed it into a GMC, and sped off.

I watched all of this from inside, through the window, silent with fear. I recall bits and pieces of what came after, perhaps most of what I remember actually consists of things I heard once I'd grown up:

The soldiers want to take my father to the cemetery and bury him as quickly as possible. But my father's friends and the people of Lice refuse to accept this. They say they can't allow for him to be buried without first performing the funeral prayer and carrying out the proper rituals in accordance with our traditions. A huge crowd gathers, and the soldiers begin opening fire. The people then begin throwing stones. All of this continues until nightfall. A number of people are injured, either shot or beaten with the butts of rifles. But in the end, the soldiers are forced to concede, because the people aren't backing down, no matter what. The next morning, after performing the funeral prayer, they bury my handsome one, shouting out slogans all the while.

I was at home the whole time this was happening. I had neighbours with me. My mother and my uncle and all our other relatives were out. Only my aunt, Welat's mother, and Welat were with us. The day after the burial my mother took me to the cemetery. I was so small but that day, standing at that gravesite, I buried my father deep inside my heart.

*

I barely got a wink of sleep before it was time to wake up. When the alarm on my telephone went off, recalling where I was, excitement and nervousness overcame me once again. I needed to act quickly, there were only two hours left until the ceremony. I opened the balcony door to air out the room before heading for the shower. Apparently no worse for the previous night's jubilation, the streets of Aleppo were already coming alive. The coolness of morning was about to surrender to the heat of the sun. It took me less than half an hour to get ready. When I reached the hotel lobby, the Kurdistan committee was there waiting for me. We had breakfast together and then set out for the ceremonial venue. All along the way we passed through streets adorned with flowers, balloons, and the flags of myriad countries. As our convoy made its way down the main boulevard, which had been transformed into the hanging gardens of Babylon, masses of people waved and applauded boisterously. The Kurdistan flag at the front of our convoy blew gently in the breeze, returning their ebullient greetings. I watched the crowd with joy in one eye and sorrow in the other, but tears in both. I recalled the days of my youth. All the marches and rallies I'd attended, and the excitement, fear, and courage that accompanied them.

*

We didn't stay in Lice long after my father was killed. A few months later, my uncle rented a place in Diyarbakır City and moved us all there. My mother and I stayed in one of many rooms surrounding a courtyard, and my uncle and his family lived in another. There were several other renters besides us in the other rooms. It didn't take me long to become accustomed to our new home. All of the other people had, like us, been forced to migrate, their villages either evacuated or burned down. I started primary school. For the first few years, language was a challenge for me, like it was for everyone else. Because everything at school was in Turkish. Still, we managed to pick up some here and there. Middle school is when my lessons started taking a backseat to my interest in our people's struggle. Everyone was talking about the liberation movement, about going to the mountains, about guerrillas. Such talk filled me with elation. Though I didn't fully grasp what was what at the time, I gathered that this struggle had something to do with my father's murder. And that politicised me, and I became more and more engaged. I still didn't know what I was going to do though, after all, I was just a child. I spent my high school years continuing on the same quest. Now and then, I took part in rallies, illegal Newroz celebrations, and funeral marches, but it was never enough, never enough to put out the fire burning within me.

It was at university that I learned about the organised

struggle. I'd gotten into the Faculty of Medicine at Dicle University in Diyarbakır. The students there were already well-organised and wielded a certain amount of power, and it wasn't long before I joined them in the movement. I took part in a number of student actions, and when I reached my fourth year, I decided to drop out and become a guerrilla fighter. I'd promised myself that as a guerrilla, I'd never fire a shot at anyone. I intended to provide medical support to the soldiers and to people in rural areas. But my plan was thwarted. The house in the village, where we spent the night with two guerrillas and couriers who were going to take us to the camp, was suddenly surrounded, and we were taken into custody.

I spent eight years in prison. I met hundreds of women in the five different prisons I was incarcerated in, and it was there that I achieved true political consciousness. For years without fail, my mother came to visit me. She worked at cleaning jobs and the like and stayed politically involved, coming and going to local party headquarters. My mother was my greatest support and source of morale. Her, and the headshot of my father. I had the photo on me when I was arrested, and they confiscated it, but then they gave it back to me before they sent me to prison. I kept it with me the whole time I was in there; whenever my heart grew heavy, I'd take it out and look into my hero's eyes and all my fear would disappear.

After prison, I began to engage in the legitimate political process. Those too were tough years. The war was still raging, and oppression continued in full force. But the world was changing rapidly. The Kurdish people's struggle was gathering more and more support, and gaining more and more sympathy worldwide. In Rojava and Syria, and in Iraqi Kurdistan in particular, major political developments were happening. Though oppression in Turkey had reached its peak, hope for a solution continued to grow in tandem with the resistance. Once the ban that barred me from officially participating in politics expired, thanks to a student amnesty, I was able to return to the Faculty of Medicine, where I picked up my studies again from where I'd left off, and eventually graduated. I went on to become a doctor at a private clinic in Diyarbakır. And then later, I was elected co-mayor of Lice for a term.

In 2025, when multiple wars in the Middle East came to an end, I was the president of the Kurdistan Chamber of Medicine. By that point, a whirlwind of political activities was underway. Across Turkey, Kurdistan, Iraq, Iran, Syria, Jordan, and Egypt, major steps towards democracy, and revolutions in civil liberties, were taking place, that would radically transform the region's social structures. While the Middle East gradually became a place of increasing prosperity, welfare, peace, and democracy, the European Union was slowly emerging from its own recent crisis. And it was in precisely those years that the discussion about forming a Middle East Democratic Union began. The idea was to build a democratic structure modelled on the European Union experience, only more durable, based on welfare rather than trade.

After long years of debate and preparations, a consensus was finally reached on a series of topics like forming a joint Middle East Constitution, setting up an MEU Court of Human Rights in Halabja, a Middle East currency, a central MEU Parliament with one foot in Cairo and one in Baghdad, drawing up a Middle East Convention on Human Rights, establishing a tariff union, and abolishing borders.

Following the conclusion of these discussions in 2045, I was nominated and ran for president in the Kurdistan elections, to become Kurdistan's second female head of state. Now, on the 100th anniversary of the Republic of Mahabad, as I approach the ceremonial hall where I, together with my council, will sign, in the name of Kurdistan, the agreement marking the official declaration of the Middle East Democratic Union, my heart beats so hard I fear it might burst from my chest. In the car, I sweat from excitement. But I'm not afraid. In my hand I hold the photo of my hero, my handsome one.

At the entrance to the hall, before getting out of the car, I kiss the photograph one last time and hold it to my chest, over my heart. A massive crowd greets us with slogans, applause, and flowers. All are animated with festive spirit, and the faces of one and all radiate with happiness. Everyone from age seven to seventy is joyfully crying out, 'Long live freedom and democracy!' We struggle to make our way through the crowd.

As I'm about to enter through the door to the hall, I think I see my father there in the crowd. For a moment our eyes meet. I'm certain it's him. He's young, and good-looking, exactly like he is in the photo. He smiles at me, and blows me a kiss. I smile back. Then just like that, he disappears. 'I'm not afraid of anything, Father, and I love you dearly,' I say, my voice imperceptible there in the crowd. Two tears roll out of my eyes. This time, they are both tears of joy.

The Letter

Nariman Evdike

Translated from the Kurmanji by
Rojin Shekh-Hamo

IN A DEEP SILENCE, on the fourth floor, in a cold, dull room, Zayno was dying. Her breath seemed to be stuck in her throat, neither coming in nor going out.

Jeen stood at her mother's side, awaiting her final breath, vigilant for the moment of departure. Zayno and her daughter lived in a strange land, and here they were in a hospital of a strange and distant city. The word 'strange' used to make Jeen laugh whenever she heard it. She was intrigued by the fact that, after so many years, Zayno still used it to mean foreign. She stood near the window, her eyes staring out into the night though her ears followed only Zayno's breath. It had been 40 years since the five-year-old Jeen left her homeland with her mother and father and came to this strange place, and ten years now since Jeen's father had left them to take his place by God, leaving Zayno – because Jeen lived in another city – all alone.

The sound of Zayno's breathing ceased. The final breath had been taken and then released. Jeen turned towards her and muttered, 'Mum… Mum!' But Mum did not answer; neither with her breath, nor with one gesture. Mother Zayno was gone.

In order to get back to her life and work, Jeen wanted to go through her mother's things and clean up the house as quickly as possible, so that once she closed the door she would never have to open it again. Thus, she delved into Zayno's belongings and a flood of childhood memories came rushing back. Yet none of them stirred anything in her. She wanted to draw a line under the situation as quickly as she could. Jeen lived like a dry tree; with no feelings or spirit, so memories alone had no effect on her. Only one thing caught her attention among all the clutter, namely a tattered old box. She'd never seen it before, and her eyes fell on it instantly. Whenever she tried to put it to one side and get busy with something else, she'd be drawn back to it. Eventually, Jeen just dropped everything and walked over to it like a child heading over to the breast of its mother. She placed the box on her lap and slowly opened it.

Inside she found a letter and an old photograph of a handsome young man. Jeen didn't recoginse him, but was struck by how good looking he was. Smiling, she put the photo aside and turned to the letter. To her surprise, the envelope appeared unopened and its contents remained presumably unread. Impatiently she tore it open and attempted to read it, but the contents were indecipherable. Surprised, she said to herself: 'What language is this? Some of the words are familiar, but so many are not!'

Jeen was forty-five years old and unmarried; she never dared mix with her immediate community and had no friends to speak of. She enjoyed her own company and found social interaction difficult. That's why she was so impatient to pack up the house and get back to her solitude. But the letter she held had stopped her in her tracks. Questions were clashing against each other in Jeen's head, one after another.

What was this letter? Why did Mum never open it and read it? And most importantly, what was this language? What did it say?

Jeen took a breath and after thinking a while and getting on with other packing, she took the letter to her computer, transcribed it into Google, and translated it. The language was confirmed to be Kurdish, more specifically, the Kurmanji dialect. This was the old tongue Zayno had always spoken around the home, and that Jeen had used herself, informally. But it had never occurred to her that it would have been classed as an official language and she was now suddenly curious about it.

That night she couldn't sleep. She sat at her computer till dawn, learning about the language and its speakers. The letter only consisted of a handful of lines and they were as follows:

'Mrs. Zayno,

According to our enquiries, the young man you asked about was last seen in the city of Halabja three days before the fateful incident. Therefore, we do not believe him to still be alive. The names of all those who survived that dark fate are known to us. As everyone knows, the chemicals the regime sprayed over that city, stripped us of everything: pebbles, wood, earth and sky; everything was killed.'

On reading these words, new and different questions jostled in her head. Her brain became a field of questions: *Who was the young man? Why was Mum looking for him? Where is Halabja?* And *what was the incident that brought everything to a head?*

In order to answer any of these questions, Jeen returned to her research. This felt like the first time that she had ever broken with her daily routine of work and rest. She kept reading and researching for days. Her life seemed to disappear into the lines of text. And it all led to a new thing. Jeen did not know what it meant to be a Kurd. She did not know the suffering inherent in this identity. She knew, of course, that

Kurdistan had been divided into four quarters and that she was from the western one, Rojava, where the seven layers of the Earth had once run with crimson, though now it was coloured with spring flowers. The thing that she didn't and couldn't understand was why Zayno had distanced herself from this life and history for so long?

Bewildered by all these questions, Jeen resolved to find out who she really was. She realised now why she had been alone all her life. She would return to her homeland, in particular to its westernmost part. She booked a flight, and reconnected with a number of old family acquaintances, and within a week she was back in the land of her ancestors; western Kurdistan.

Jeen began a new life there; everything was different for her. The language that letter had been written in – which she'd always treated as a private, intimate ritual – was suddenly the official language of an entire people. Schools, universities, media stations – everyone used it.

Jeen set about looking for her mother's family. She was desperate to meet them so that she could see Zayno anew, through their eyes. After a long search, she found an address for her aunt. Without hesitation, she went to visit her. Aunt Zerê received Jeen with a warm and sorrowful heart. When she embraced Jeen, she broke down into tears: 'Oh Zayno! Why did you do this to us, and yourself? Why did you kill us with yearning for you and for this young lady...'

Zerê's tears became like a flood and her eyes like flowing springs. The woman was younger than her sister, Zayno, and had lived through a lot, having never left Rojava. Jeen launched into her questions – the very questions that had brought her here into her aunty's arms. Aunt Zerê responded graciously, adding, 'Listen, my daughter, there's no secret to any of this. We started a mighty revolution many decades ago and suffered greatly to get where we are today. You can see with your own eyes: we have become an independent state. We no longer fear anyone. We do not tolerate any form of oppression, from anyone. Your mother's story is not different from the story of the revolution, my child. She resisted, the way we all did, but when she failed, she fled.

'Your mother, my dear, was strong and graceful. And she was knowledgeable about the age she lived in, unlike the other girls of her generation. She studied, against our father's wishes, and followed her own path. She fell in love with a friend called Jiwan, who was known for his good looks. It was true, my girl, he was handsome, but our father disapproved.'

At this, Jeen interrupted quizzically, 'But why?'

Zerê caressed Jeen's face and continued her story, 'Jiwan was a young man of partly unknown background. His father had appeared in the village one day without explanation and one family, the Ehmê family, had agreed to take him in, later marrying him to their daughter. None of us knew where he had come from because neither he, nor the family who took him in, ever talked about it. Jiwan's father and mother went on to live a happy, comfortable life together, but the one who didn't live comfortably, because of his forbidden love, was their son, Jiwan. Back then, that's all we knew, but later we found out about the real story of Jiwan's father: that he was Armenian who had fled from the Ottomans' annihilation of his people; that he sought refuge in the Ehmê household and they, in turn, raised him without telling his story to anyone. This way, the godless Ottomans pulled up every Armenian root.'

With these words, Zerê fell silent and could hold herself together no more. Her tears stopped anything else from being said. The photograph from Zayno's box sprung to Jeen's mind. Quickly she rummaged for it from among her things and held the old, worn picture up for Zerê to see, saying, 'This is Jiwan, isn't it?' Zerê raised her head and, on gazing at it, an anguish from the very depths was unleashed; her eyes said *yes*.

In her research before she came here, Jeen had read a little about the Armenians and their annihilation. Her heart was heavy, but she needed Zerê to finish the story: 'So what happened, Aunt Zerê, what did Mum and Jiwan do?'

Zerê took a deep breath and continued, 'My sweet niece, your grandfather was a stubborn man. When he said no, that was final. Poor Jiwan didn't give up and sent many people to try to talk him round, but it was all in vain. My father wouldn't capitulate until Jiwan was left with no choice. Not knowing what else to do, Jiwan left the country. I didn't know where he went, but one thing I did know was that your mother didn't stop looking for him until one day she received a letter. Your mother lost all hope when that letter arrived, saying, "This is the last letter I will ever receive. I will neither read it nor open it." And it was. Any letter she read after that was just a heartbreak for Zayno. She was beaten.

'Several years passed with Zayno receiving proposals from suitors almost every week; she rejected them all. And each "no" felt like a new defeat for her father. Then one day your father appeared and for some reason your mother said yes. Maybe it was because he had a plan to emigrate to Europe, and all she wanted to do was leave.'

As Zerê finished her story, Jeen threw her arms around her and closed her eyes. She didn't let go, as if she wanted to hug back into her all the years she had been away from her sister.

Jeen knew now why her mother had kept her so far away from this part of her life, and why Zayno's own life with her father had been so spiritless. But her parents' coldness had affected Jeen's life too. Here though, things would be different. She could begin to get to know herself differently. The lonely days were over, and she would never set foot on that dark, dusty path again.

The Story Must Continue

Muharrem Erbey

*Translated from the Turkish
by Andrew Penny*

I AWOKE TO A strange morning. 15 May 2045 was my twenty-first birthday and it began with my mother shouting at the top of her voice: 'Damn you! Look at the message he sent me, and after all these years!' She hurled her mobile phone at the couch, where it bounced onto the carpet. I picked it up and read the message. *'Dear Gülay, I am embarking on a long journey to find myself, to fill a void. I am leaving the City of Unhappiness where people devour each other, like creatures of consumption, acting as if they are smart, but are unable to be themselves. Instead I'm going somewhere less smart to find myself. Don't look for me, because you won't be able to find me. I love you all. When I find myself and attain peace and serenity, I will return to you. I'm not asking for forgiveness. Just understand. That's enough.'*

With thousands leaving the planet to settle off-world colonies, igniting new interplanetary wars, with developments in artificial DNA threatening the biosphere, the Governor of the Metropolis of Amed Province has abandoned his post, his home, and his family, saying, 'I'm going to find myself.' For weeks I had been asking myself: *How can he just meditate and wallow in weird self-help books all the time?*

Just then, there was frantic knocking at the door. Armed personnel from the Governor's office poured into the house. The Commissioner of the Protection Force asked for my father.

My mother sobbed: 'Your boss has gone. He has abandoned the lot of us.'

When the Commissioner asked, '*Where* has the Governor gone?' My mother replied, sobbing as she retired to her room, 'He has gone to the middle of nowhere to fill the vacuum inside him.'

When the Commissioner persisted – 'I don't understand, where has he gone, *where*?' – I realised it would be me fielding the questions from now on. People were constantly coming and going, officials arriving at the house all morning. Announcements were being made by wireless and security measures were increasing outside. The deputy governor arrived.

'Where is Mr. Governor?' he asked.

I piped up: 'We don't know where my father has gone. We gather he left early this morning. He sent my mother this message.' I forwarded the message from my mother's phone to the deputy governor. The men looked at each other, grumbling, then left. A few vehicles remained in the street outside. Neighbours arrived, but my mother refused to leave her room. No one had a clue what was going on and everyone was dying to know. One of the neighbours called to say a flying outside-broadcast vehicle was hovering before the front door. When I opened it, a flying robot greeted me. I slammed it shut and immediately lowered the curtains with the remote control.

We didn't hear anything from my father for days. He had apparently succeeded in evading all the cameras at the security points. From the house cameras, we saw that he had left wearing old clothes and a hat. At a blind spot in another street he had changed his clothes. After that, we didn't know what he had worn or what he looked like. He had left his mobile phone in his study and prised out the compulsory chip in his arm with a sharp kitchen knife and thrown it in the bin. There were drops of blood everywhere. He had left his chipped cards in the house. We were suffocating from the crowds of relatives and high-level officials in the house. The strange thing was that no one believed that someone with the authority of the Governor of Amed Province would willingly just abandon everything and vanish. 'There's something fishy about this,' everyone was saying. My mother and I were well aware that the visitors had not come to console us, but to get to the bottom of it all. Even the relatives whispered to me when we were alone, 'What's really going on? Tell us, we won't let on.'

The Minister of State, who'd been abroad, arrived with his wife. He embraced my mother, saying, 'Rest assured, we will find our governor.' But they didn't. My father had worked out in advance how to hide, how to be invisible; he planned the whole thing. I was worried something might happen to him. All the news channels showed the footage of him leaving the house. Some conspiracy theorists said he had been abducted by Iranian agents, others by agents of the Turkish state. Others claimed that he had been taken by kidnappers who had been active recently, and that they would soon make contact, specifying a ransom. If I had known where my father was and that he was happy where he had gone, I would have been content. Eventually we would find a way to communicate. I used to ask him if he ever got fed up with all the bureaucracy, the officialdom, the insincerity of it all, and he'd reply, lowering his voice and smiling, 'Don't even go there, Mahabad, my daughter. But one day I'll run away.'

One evening, about a month after my father disappeared, there was a knock at the door. It was a friend saying she had seen my father changing his clothes that morning at the blind spot not seen by the cameras. She said she had seen him going through the bushes to the other street in women's clothing. I asked her why she hadn't told us before. She replied, saying that my father had seen her and sworn her to silence, and that for a month she had been in two minds about whether to keep her word, eventually deciding to break her promise.

I forgave her and embraced her. 'You're a very good friend. Don't tell anyone,' I said. I asked her which way he had gone, to which she replied that he had gone behind the gardens of the houses. She described his clothes. A friend who had a house in that vicinity came to mind. I went to see her and checked their camera footage. A person trying to walk like an old woman could be seen in the footage from that morning, passing behind the houses and heading towards the hill. I stared for a long time in the direction that person had been headed. Then I returned home, put everything I needed into a backpack and, without telling a soul, decided to walk the route taken by my father.

I walked for hours, attempting to work out where he was trying to go. From time to time, clouds of yellow dust scorched my nostrils. Sudden gales and showers signalled that the weather was about to change. After a long two-day walk, I came to a mountainside. I lifted my head and looked into the distance. I could feel my father's presence. I saw a shack in the distance and walked towards it. I walked up the slope, climbing higher and higher, gripping rocks and tree branches. When I reached the shack, a large dog barked at me. I decided to sit down, cross-legged on the ground, and simply wait. An hour later, the door of the shack opened and a woman came out. She was an ordinary, poor woman, but with an air of self-confidence. She came towards me. She was carrying a bucket full of water. She placed it in front of me and waited. I looked at the bucket for a while, then picked up a leaf from the ground on my right and placed it carefully on the surface of the water in the bucket. The woman picked up the bucket and went inside.

She returned and asked me in Kurdish, 'Who are you?'

'I am the Amed Provincial Governor's daughter. My name is Mahabad,' I said.

'And who is the Governor?' she asked.

'At the moment, he is someone who is missing, and I am looking for him. Is there anyone inside?' I asked.

'Yes, there is,' the woman said.

'What's his name?' I asked.

'The Man with Fiery Eyes,' she replied.

'Can I see him?' I asked.

The woman said, 'No. Only he decides who he sees.'

'In that case, I will wait for him,' I said.

The woman went inside and shut the door. I closed my eyes. After a while, a storm broke out. The gale tried to drag me from my seat, but did not succeed. The dogs began to bark ferociously around me, baring their teeth. They slavered over me, their saliva even landing on my face. Eagles flew low overhead. Their shrieks tore at my ears. I didn't move a muscle. Snakes hissed as they slithered over my knees and still I didn't react or utter a sound. I waited. It was evening and the temperature was dropping. As darkness fell, it began to freeze. I couldn't feel my hands or my feet. I was shivering. A short time later, sleep came over me. I knew that I was going to freeze to death out here but I couldn't move. Nor could I prevent myself from falling asleep. My eyes slowly closed. I felt a quilt being put over me. I was walking in a deep vacuum. I saw lights. A yellow light that coiled around me and took me inside it. I was melting. Consciousness abandoned me and I was lost. I knew I was heading towards death. A warm feeling embraced me. Then everything went black. When I opened my eyes, my father was beside me. When I saw the look on his face, I remembered the first time I asked him about my name.

'Dad, what does my name mean?'

'My dear Mahabad. Your name means "Moon City." It is

the story of all of us. The history of the Kurds. To be without stories is to be completely alone in the world. Our forefathers used to say: "Steer clear of those with no past." Hang on every word I say. The best response you can give to those who want to leave us without stories is to not forget our story and to pass it on to our children and grandchildren. We have lived in these lands for as long as human history has existed, all of these lands – as far as the eye can see, all the way to the snow-capped mountains, and beyond, and in all the villages, towns and cities, around them. Mahabad is in a magnificent valley to the south of Lake Urmiye in Iran, which we call East Kurdistan. Its old name was Piranshahr. The Kurds organised and, with the support of the powerful Soviet Union, declared an independent Kurdish Republic in Mahabad on 22 January 1946, under the leadership of the learned Qazî Muhammad. The Kurdish Republic of Mahabad wanted autonomy for Kurds in Iran, the use of the Kurdish language in education and government, a local assembly, the election of state officials and the introduction of a legal system that treated everyone equally.

'Muhammad was an enlightened man, sending his own daughters to school, which was very progressive for the time. Classics of world literature were translated and published in Kurdish and schools provided an education in Kurdish. A Kurdish theatre and opera house were also established. The flag of Mahabad incorporated the nib of a pen, the sun and an ear of wheat. With the founding of the Mahabad Kurdish State, the backward Kurdish tribes lost their authority. Soon these tribes began to talk badly of Muhammad and made a pact with the Shah of Iran. Throughout history this kind of treachery has cost us dearly. We were always broken into pieces because we could not act together. When the Americans and the British supported the Shah, the Soviets were unable to resist and they withdrew from Iran. When Qazî Muhammad realised the Iranian army and the tribes were on their way to ransack the city, he agreed to surrender in return for the troops being withdrawn. Iran accepted this proposal. On 17 January 1947, the Iranian army took over Mahabad. But Qazî Muhammad and fifteen administrators were hanged in Çar Çira Square on 30 March that year. Qazî Muhammad wrote a letter to the Kurds containing recommendations before he was hanged.'

My father took down a book. *"The symbol of success for every nation is unity, cooperation and solidarity,"* he read. *"When you don't ensure unity you will suffer the oppression of the enemy and be crushed.[...] If the tribal leaders hadn't sold themselves to the Iranian government, this calamity wouldn't have befallen us. My bequest to you is this: educate your children. Apart from education we lack nothing compared with other peoples. In order not to fall behind those other peoples, study. Studying is the most effective weapon against the enemy. Be sure and know that if your harmony, unity and education are good, you will gain victory over the enemy.."*

Seeing my father standing at my bedside, I reminded him of that old conversation. 'Do you remember when you told me about Qazî Muhammad and how he had been hanged on account of the betrayal of those around him? For years, I never really understood what betrayal was. But I think I understand it now.'

'And what was it, daughter?'

'To leave people you love in the lurch and go away.'

'But I didn't betray you. Years ago I found myself on the bottom rung of a ladder I neither liked nor wanted. I couldn't turn back and I couldn't let go. The further I progressed the more impossible it became to turn back. You were not the problem. *I* was the problem. I didn't escape from you, I escaped from the Governor of Amed. You have to understand me. We even talked about it occasionally. I felt suffocated. I couldn't be myself. Remember: politics, like religion, is a drug. When you use it you become addicted. It becomes impossible to turn back. Two months ago, I made a speech in London. Do you remember? Whatever happened to me, took place there.'

'Yes, I remember. I watched a video of it online.'

'Dear guests, as the Governor of Amed Province I greet you.

'Modern man has, in the last two centuries, destroyed and devoured the world we live in. Today our homes boast hundreds of items of technology that are supposed to make our lives easier, but render the wider planet uninhabitable. I yearn for the days when there was only one electronic device in our homes: the radio. Every Wednesday afternoon in our house in Saray Kapı, in the Sur district of Diyarbakır, the words "Temaşevanen heja, hun radyoya Erivane gohdar dikin, [Dear Listeners, you are listening to Yerevan Radio]" would transport us to a different world. The Kurdish language was banned in Amed.

'In a land called Yerevan, however, songs were sung in our language. The technology that brought this to our house left me awestruck before the vastness of the universe. The radio was enchanting. We would pump water from the well into an earthenware pot and cover the pot with muslin to ensure no dust or insects fell into it. Water was sacred to us. It was the most important thing in our lives. With most of our water sources exhausted, as Governor of Amed Province, I am now trying – with the same earnestness as when I carried that pot all those years ago – to make sure that not a drop of water from the river Tigris is wasted. We have depleted the world in pursuit of profit – we have destroyed it. Pollution is at its highest ever level. For three days now in London, I cannot go out on the street without taking a clean air capsule and putting on a mask. The few occasions when I took it, I was suffocating. More than half the world's species are on the brink of extinction. Does anyone here remember crocodiles, lions and tigers, elephants, leopards, lynx, vultures or eagles? We can still save the planet. But life is not possible without clean air and water. Today we are aware that the eyes of Europe are on the water resources of Kurdistan. Fresh water is being bought and sold across the world. But once upon a time there was an abundance of water, flowing from springs, brooks and rivers. We are ready to share our water resources.'

'On the plane back at Heathrow,' my father said, reflectively, sitting in the chair beside my bed, 'an announcement was made in Kurdish explaining what button to press to activate the seat belt. When I pressed it, the belt flew round from my left side and clicked into place on my right. Just at that moment, the watch phone on my wrist quivered and I put on my headphones. As I spoke by video, the plane suddenly took off vertically. Your mother was calling to me from the garden while shouting at the grandchildren whizzing backwards and forwards on hoverboards over the pool. "Esteemed Governor," she teased. "How did the speech go?" "Well, I think," I replied. "When will you be back?" she asked. "I've just boarded, I'll land in Amed in an hour and ten," I said. "What did you get the grandchildren?" she asked. "There's a new hologram, you create a jungle from 10 wild animals, then you fight them," I replied. "Sounds cool," she said. The line went dead.

'Announcements were made. We were passing over the Balkans. The ten-year war was showing no sign of ending. The captain announced in Kurdish that, thanks to the plane's special protective shields, any object would be deflected easily. Robot cabin crew were serving meals. I asked for a chicken tablet and water. I placed the tablet on my tongue and washed it down with water. The screen on the back of the seat in front opened and I touched it with my fingers. I pressed the "book" button and opened up the section of *A Thousand and One Nights* that had been translated into Kurdish. I was just about to lose myself in the story recounted in Scheherazade's own language when the person sitting next to me fainted. A robot cabin attendant came and took the passenger to the back of the plane. The monitor on the ceiling of the plane was updating the news. *BREAKING: Ganymede X91 Colony requests assistance from Earth after rival Titan Y98 Colony officially declares war. "Earth will be next," X91 Governor says. amid fears around Titan's secretly developed weapons.* My eyes closed and I dropped off.

'Suddenly, I heard a woman from the market in the neighbourhood near our house calling up to me. "You don't belong up there. Why don't you listen to your heart?" she was saying. A short while later I awoke as the plane shuddered violently. An announcement was made saying we were going through turbulence caused by unexpected weather. Shortly after the plane landed at Amed airport, and I took a hover-taxi home and forgot about the dream.

'The next night, however, I had the same dream. Once more, the woman was telling me to follow her, free my heart and replenish my soul. When I awoke I was shaken. But once more, I forgot about it. Two nights later this woman again appeared in my dream in the same place, saying: "If you don't come to me, I will come to you." When I woke up, I grappled for a time with the absurdity of the dream. Then I got up, left through the back door, to sidestep my security detail, and went to the market in disguise. I saw her. She was selling pottery. I watched her body language, the way she sat down, the way she touched the pots. I was entranced. I went over and greeted her. She smiled at me and continued working. She bore the innocence of an early human. I squatted down beside her. She offered me a piece of bread, which I took and ate. I just watched her. She didn't speak to me. I can't explain the energy she gave out. I couldn't drag myself away from the aura she emitted. After a time I got up, bought a few things from the market and returned home.

'The next day, I again left home early wearing a hat, glasses and cloak and went to the market to see her. She was one of the most extraordinary women I had ever met. Her way of sitting, her attitude to life, was amazing. She was from a different dimension, but no one saw or realised this. Is this possible, I said to myself. I can't explain it – the way she touched the earthenware, the way she picked it up and handed it to the customer, the way she explained it, put it back on the ground, the way she looked at each piece. How a person can love the work they do that much – I wanted to be in her place. I went over and sat next to her. She touched my shoulder with her hand. I was shaken for a moment by the energy that entered my body. It was as if she had stuck a needle into me rather than touched me. I couldn't get up. I asked her name. She replied without looking at me, "Efruze." Then she said, "I'm glad you came. Look, your breathing is better already. Come every day.'"

'Compared to all the people who bow and scrape to me, this woman's naturalness, sincerity and lack of expectation really affected me. *What shall I do now?* I thought. I didn't want to leave, but I had to. I was afraid someone would recognise me. When I got up and my feet started to drag me unwillingly towards home, I looked back and Efruze was smiling at me. I didn't know whether this was love, desire, or something divine. All I knew was that a human being who was ignorant, sincere and full of energy, had exerted her influence over me. I didn't go to the market for a few days. Three days later I was about to leave the house when I saw Efruze standing on the other side of the road with a staff in her hand. I couldn't believe it. She was standing there looking at me. As I took a step towards her, my guards took her by the arms and brought her over to me. She whispered to me, "Your heart will give in if you carry on this unhappy life. Don't be stubborn." I told the guards to leave her alone. She returned the way she had come.

'That evening, while attending some function, I had a heart attack. They took me to hospital, where I received treatment and quickly recovered. I came home in the middle of the night. I forgot to tell you: After I went to the market the next morning, your mother asked, "Where did this morning's shopping come from?" I replied, saying, 'I'm bored, I come to life when I go to the market.' When I got to the market the following day, the woman wasn't there. I felt a void inside me. I felt inadequate and didn't know what to do. I went to her usual place and sat down as if she was there beside me. I could still feel her energy. Eventually I got up and walked home. That night, Efruze appeared to me in a dream. She was leaving the market, making her way through the back streets, quitting the city, heading for the mountains. Then she disappeared into a shack on the top of a ridge, at which point I woke up. The next day when I went to the market, again she wasn't there. It was then that I decided to go the way Efruze had taken. I made my preparations and, the following day, left the house. I followed the route I had seen in my dream and came to her.

'When I got here I found myself. I was frightened at first. Then I started to fall for Efruze. Now I'm in love with her. I understood that each new rank, each new promotion was slowly killing me. She brought me back to myself. With each day, now, my health improves.'

I paused before replying. 'What is this woman filling your head with up here?'

'Nothing. Efruze just does her work. She makes earthenware pots from the clay she brings from the other side of the mountain. Then she puts the pots in the oven she made, throws wood on the fire underneath and bakes them. Everything is natural. She nourishes her dog and three cats with love. She leaves out bread for the birds as if they're her children. She quietly waters her garden and the flowers. She prunes the trees and the weeds, and cleans the house like a poet writing a poem. She adorns the garden like an artist painting a picture. She doesn't talk very much. In fact, she mainly talks to me through the energy she gives off, through her body language. She carries out her tasks as if she is performing a prayer. That is what I've observed. To me, she gives short clipped answers, but to the living world around her, she is constantly in dialogue. She exists and breathes through the natural world. I soon realised, rather than being alone, she actually has lots of friends. One day she turned to me and said, "You people who live in the cities – there are two unattainable things you never remove from your minds, from your lives."

"'And what are those?" I asked.

"'The past and the future," she said, "You are forever in a flap, either about the past or the future. You never see the present. Those who don't seize the magic of the present are not really alive. You don't feel the spirit of the universe, its entirety. You aren't trying to be part of the universe, you're merely trying to possess it."

"'So what are we supposed to do?" I asked.

"'You need to open your heart in order to see and understand the universe. To do that, you have to kill the old you. Are you prepared to kill the old you for a new you?"

"'I don't know," I replied.

"'You must know. You must want to change," she said.

"'Only your heart will pick up on the signs the universe is giving you," she said. "You make such a noise that it is impossible for you to hear this voice in your heart. You don't listen to nature or your soul, those things that will most nourish you spiritually and physically. You have gone to outer space, to other planets, but you are still distant from yourself. You follow your ambitions, not your heart."

"'What should I do?" I asked Efruze. "How should I listen to my heart?"

"'Get up before dawn like me. Sit and close your eyes. Listen to the silence. Hear yourself breathe. Don't think, and open your heart to tranquillity and all the sounds of nature.

Remain sitting until it gets light. You sleep through the best and most nourishing time of the day. Civilisation and technology have dulled your senses," she told me.

'Dearest Mahabad,' my father said, turning to me as if from a daze, 'you see, I get up early each morning and meditate. I feel an energy rising from my heart to my head. We just take short breaths. But breathing is energy. We don't live in the right way. We don't breathe properly. We don't walk properly. Everything is different here, including my diet. We eat plants, vegetables and fruit. I don't eat meat. My stomach is comfortable. I feel lighter. I observe life, nature, everything here. It's an amazing thing. I listen. Efruze is re-teaching me life. She has taught me to share what I have with other living things. One night, when I woke up I felt she was embracing me. But it wasn't an ordinary embrace. I embraced her, too. An unfathomable energy accumulated between us. I felt relaxed. The laws of the universe have whispered to us to share what we have. But we don't hear. We inflict cruelty on other creatures. How have we done this? This world, this universe belongs to all of us.'

'Father, you confuse me,' I replied eventually. 'I came here to bring you back. Yet you say you're happy here. But that doesn't mean you've haven't still abandoned us...'

'Mahabad, a person should be wherever they're happiest. A person should promise their partner happiness, not marriage. When there is no more happiness, commitment to one's partner ends. My marriage to your mother ended long ago. She didn't love me; first she loved her husband and then the Governor of Amed province. We disseminate the lie of happiness. Your mother loved the opportunities I provided. She loved my position, my rank and milieu. She never loved me. I am aware of this. I want to be understood and loved. I want to be myself. We think very logically, but if you think less logically, communication between minds becomes easier. Happiness increases. We have destroyed the world. We can't breathe. Life needs to start afresh. Either that or we shouldn't complain about the path to extinction. Mahabad, in seven months' time it will be the hundredth anniversary of the Mahabad Kurdish Republic. I have a request to make of you. On 22 January 2046, go to Mahabad. Kneel down in the Çar Çira Square and pray for Qazî Muhammad and his fifteen comrades who were hanged and pass on my thanks. They opened the way for us. Don't forget, this story must continue with you. This is my last request of you.'

I Have Seen Many Houses in My Time

Karzan Kardozi

I HAVE SEEN MANY houses in my time, traveled to many places, seen many cities, towns and villages since my childhood, and each time I've revisited them I've noticed many changes, from tragic to joyful, but one house, that has always stayed vivid in the memory – despite all the changes – has suffered so much, merely thinking of it makes me gasp for breath.

The house, or rather, the mud-house, as it was, is located in the upper northern part of the Shadala village, these days just a 45-minute car ride from the city of Slemani, though time was it took half a day to reach it. The house with its mud roof, grey walls and large rooms, overlooks the whole village from its elevated position. The first time I visited was many years ago: I was a little kid of seven; it was 2026, shortly after the Cataclysm. No one knew where the virus had come from and how many people exactly had died. After a milder pandemic a few years before, people were complacent when this new strain arrived. Everything collapsed within a few months. Those of us who survived fled to the Qandil Mountains, built small communes, and gave up the use of money, trading our services instead.

I remember vividly my stay in Shadala, playing football on the roof of that mud house with other kids. Every few minutes the ball would roll down onto the ground, down into the village, and through the streets; one of us would always be blamed and forced to embark on the long journey of fetching it back.

For the next few years, every summer, my father and I would make this trip to Shadala; my grandmother was from there, and most of my father's distant relatives still lived in the village. Our family originally came from the city of Mahabad in West Kurdistan, but left because of the war in 1946, settling in Shadala soon after. When my father was young, he left to study medicine in Slemani. Then came the Cataclysm, and the relocation to the Qandil Mountains which is where I was born. My father was among the few doctors who survived the Cataclysm; each week he would travel to a different village in the Kurdish mountains helping in whatever way he could. When I turned seven, he took me to work with him for the first time, the village we visited was Shadala. He wanted me to become a doctor like him, and since there were no more schools, the best way to learn was to travel with him.

The mud house belonged to kak[1] Rasoul, a distant cousin of my father's. I'll never forget that first visit.

When we arrived, my father left me alone in a small room, as he went with kak Rasoul on his rounds through the village. I sat in a corner, shy, not knowing what to do, until a short woman of forty, kak Rasoul's wife walked in and, seeing me alone, shouted to her son, who was outside: 'Come and play with Doctor Sharif's son'. From then on, I became known in the village as 'Doctor Sharif's Son', and even to this day, as if my father were some kind of legend.

The boy, Rejan, was the same age as me, skinny with green eyes, pale and slightly fragile looking. We hit it off straight away. He told me about a beehive they kept, and being of a mischievous nature, I wanted to see it. He agreed to show me, but the whole way there kept telling me not to touch it. Being the sort of kid I was, when I got there I picked up a stick and immediately jabbed it into the hive. Suddenly, bees were everywhere, attacking from all sides, biting and buzzing. I started screaming at the top of my voice, with Rejan all the time trying his best to comfort me: 'It is nothing. Look, I've been bitten many times.' He took a handful of mud and put it on the places where I'd been bitten, comforting me: 'It's nothing; it's nothing.'

Five minutes later I was sitting on a big soft carpet, eating lunch with the family back in the mud house, surrounded by the smells of freshly baked bread, goat's milk and cheese, honey and hot tea. On the mud walls hung three portraits; two young boys and a little girl. In the corner, the mother was sewing little socks for Rejan, occasionally looking up at us with a smile.

After dinner, I couldn't but help ask my father, in a whisper, who the people in the pictures were. 'They were the children of kak Rasoul,' he said, but looking around the room, there were only Rejan, his older brother, Ibrahim, and his younger sister, Suzan, and none of them looked like the children in the pictures. 'Where are they now?' I whispered to my father. 'They're dead,' he whispered back.

On the way back home, my father explained to me the tragic story of kak Rasoul and how typical it was for so many villagers. As a young man, he had married his cousin as there were so few survivors from the Cataclysm. Living in the countryside, the place lacked medical facilities, and even in the cities, back then, there was no access to things like genetic testing for newly-wed couples. Their children were born with a sickness called 'Thalassemia', an inherited disease occurring primarily among people of Mediterranean descent, caused by a defective formation of part of the haemoglobin molecule, and increasing the numbers of red blood cells. The only treatment is to have blood transfusions every month.

Kak Rasoul and his wife had three children in quick succession, but each of them died in their late teens, a tortuously slow death, for the multiple transfusions needed to sustain their lives had led to an iron overload throughout their organ tissues and eventually the destruction of their heart and other vital organs. They kept having children, hoping at least one of them would be born healthy, but none were. Each month they all had to have blood transfusions, but it was hopeless, the parents knew by the time they reached around eighteen, they would be facing a slow, painful end. There was no treatment available that would sustain them beyond that age.

'Will Rejan die when he is 18?' I asked my father.

He was silent for a while, then simply whispered, 'Time will tell.' I felt desperate and sad, knowing that the young boy whom I had just become friends with, so full of life, would probably die by the time he turned eighteen, and no one could do anything about it.

I left for America to study a few years later, forgetting all about Rejan. I became a doctor after my father died.

Twenty years after my first visit to the village, I found myself returning to the house again, the same mud house, with the roof overlooking the village. As I entered, I heard the same 'Doctor Sharif's Son' echo through it that I used to hear. They recognised me at once: the mother kept looking at me, 'Look how you've grown! You're so tall!' There was sadness in her voice; her hair was starting to grey and her green eyes were full of sorrow. There was the same smell of freshly baked bread, goat's milk and cheese, honey and hot tea, but also there was something different. Beside the portrait of the three children, hung a portrait of little Rejan. He had died ten years earlier.

We began to reminisce, in front of the paintings; I recalled Rejan's winning smile, and his melodic voice, how he'd comforted me when I was stung by the bees: 'It's nothing. It's nothing.' Suddenly I had to leave the room, as I knew if I had stayed any longer, I would burst into tears. I guess I reminded the mother of Rejan, or perhaps she knew a little about my grief too, but as I left the room, she burst into tears as well. I could hear her outside.

At dinner, I sat beside Ibrahim who, despite being older than Rejan, had outlived him. And yet now, at 23, he already looked like an old man: his face wrinkled, yellowish, with no other colour in it. Yet, he was as cheerful as Rejan, laughing all the time in a sing-song voice that reminded me of his brother. His younger sister, Suzan, also looked much older than she should have; but her green eyes, just like Rejan's and her mother's, captivated me. Both of them were still living from one transfusion to the next. I looked at the mother in the corner, who was now breastfeeding a new baby, a new girl. Kak Rasoul kept saying that the doctor had told them that his new girl didn't seem to need any transfusions, and was healthy enough to live a long life. But there was always the element of doubt.

A few years later, I once again visited the little house. It was for the wedding of kak Rasoul's nephew. I had promised the groom I would be the photographer, and was busy taking pictures of the happy couple when, a beautiful, green-eyed little girl, maybe seven years old, ran up to me, asking loudly in her sing-song voice, 'Are you Doctor Sharif's son?'

'Yes, I am, and who you might be?' I replied.

'I'm Suzan',

'Well, Suzan Khan, who is your father?'

'My father is Rasoul!' So there it was, little Suzan, with the same green eyes and living smile as her late brother. 'Can you take some pictures of me, please?' she asked. I took more than a dozen, all the time a dreadful thought creeping closer in the background: Is she sick too?

That evening, I went back to the house – no longer a mud house, but a contemporary, two-storey, brick construction –

fitted with all modern conveniences. Walking back into the main room – the dining room, I guess – I saw once more Rejan's mother: she was sitting on a sofa sewing, the television was on, little Suzan was watching a cartoon of *Tom and Jerry*, on seeing me, the mother stood up: 'Doctor Sharif's Son!' Her hair was completely grey now, she was suddenly an old woman.

I sat beside kak Rasoul at dinner: the room thronged with wedding guests, coming and going, their laughter filling the house. I had a burning desire to ask kak Rasoul about little Suzan: was she sick or not? But I didn't dare to. Looking at the portraits on the wall, there were now seven pictures, besides Rejan's: images of Ibrahim and Suzan, plus another little girl that I didn't recognise. Seeing me looking at them, kak Rasoul asked, 'You were friends with Rejan and Ibrahim, if I recall?' 'Yes,' I replied, but feeling uncomfortable, I tried to change the subject: 'I didn't realise Suzan was your daughter, I took some great pictures of her.'

Kak Rasoul was a cheerful man; he seemed to be forever smiling; you would have never guessed he carried with him the agony of losing seven children. 'You know, my little Rejan had the same eyes as hers, he was beautiful like her, and he was so smart, he had the mind of a grown-up. One time, I took him to the city to get a blood transfusion, it was during the time of the Cataclysm. We went to all the main civilian hospitals in the city, but they were out of blood. My little Rejan was already weak, and couldn't walk, so I carried him on my back. I feared for his life, and grew desperate, searching from one hospital to the next, but he was the one comforting me. "We will find it, Daddy," he kept saying. I managed to get a piece of paper from a doctor, authorising us to get a transfusion from the military hospital. Back then, the Azadi Park acted as the military hospital. We had to walk an hour to get there, the whole way with Rejan on my back. He kept kissing me on the neck, saying, 'We will find it, Daddy.'

'When we got to the hospital, the place was like hell on earth: choppers were flying in and out continually, bringing in the sick and removing the dead. The road leading up to the hospital was even worse, littered with dead bodies in between sick people waiting. When I saw that, my knees began to give in, I told Rejan that they would never give us blood with all these people waiting, but he kept smiling and saying: "We will find it, Daddy." We went to the office of the hospital's chief physician and, at first, he refused to do anything for us. But when he caught Rejan's eyes, his heart softened. He led us to a refrigerated room, and handed us two bags of blood. When he gave me the bags, I broke down, overcome with gratitude that little Rejan would live another month. The boy was so full of life, always happy and smiling. One of his favourite things was chocolate candies; there was a shop in the village that sold them. One day he asked me to buy him some chocolate candies, so I took him. There was a group of Peshmerga stationed near the village back then. One of them was outside the shop, and when he saw Rejan, he started to hug him instantly: "I have a little boy just like him in North Kurdistan." He took the boy who so reminded him of his son into the shop and told him to choose anything he wanted. "I'll pay for it," he said. But Rejan refused to pick anything. He didn't want the soldier to spend his money on anyone but his son. He waited for the man to leave before he picked the chocolate candies, and I paid for them. That is how he was; he always thought of others before himself.

'A week after he died, when the same Peshmerga heard about his death, he came to our house. Before he reached the front door, he crumpled to his knees, cursing and crying, hitting the mud with his fists. I had to go out and comfort him. "Come now," I said, half-jokingly. "You should be comforting me, not the other way round." He kept crying for the rest of the visit, telling me that he had seen many of his friends die in battle, but never cried like he did for Rejan. "Why did God take him away, he was so innocent, so full of life?" Every Friday until the day he left to return to North Kurdistan, the soldier visited his grave. I wish I knew where he is now. He was a gentleman. Maybe I could meet the son that Rejan so reminded him of.'

As I looked at Suzan, watching the television, I couldn't hold back any longer: 'Does Suzan also need the monthly transfusions?' I asked, immediately feeling ashamed for trespassing on their privacy.

'No, thank God. God gave her to us healthy.' At that moment, the little girl, knowing we were talking about her, ran to her father, and threw her little arms around his neck. Kak Rasoul was beaming with joy. 'Do you know who this young man is who's taking all the photos today?' he asked her,

'Of course,' she whispered, 'he is Doctor Sharif's son.' They both smiled.

Suddenly I couldn't bear it anymore. In that moment, the tragedy and the joy of life seemed to cascade into one another, and, combined, they were too much to bear. I picked up my camera and ran out of the house – the mud house, as it once was – and gasped for breath in the cold, wind-swept night.

Note

1. kak: a Kurdish prefix meaning brother.

Arzela

Meral Şimşek

*Translated from the Turkish
by Andrew Penny*

2046

Right in the middle of the city, crouching among piles of concrete as if playing a game of hide-and-seek, is the wooden house where I have taken refuge, like a swallow in the trunk of a tree. After years of living in the belly of a mountain, I feel, for the first time in a long while, comfortable. I have a rocking chair like the one I yearned for in my childhood. After I left the stomach of the mountain and returned to civilisation, a group of young people came to visit me. One of them was called Berfin.[1] She had a dignified bearing, befitting her name, with long brown hair and hazel eyes. The way this woman in her early twenties looked at me in admiration warmed my heart. Just before they left, Berfin gripped my hand and said, 'Arzela, before you went into the bowels of the mountain was there anything you wanted but were unable to possess?'

After pondering this question for a moment, I said that my dream had been to own a blue rocking chair. This lovely woman of Kurdistan did not forget my wish and recently sent me a blue rocking chair for my sixtieth birthday. Who knows how difficult it must have been to find it. These days everything is metallic and cold, as if the colours of the universe have waned. Everything makes me shiver these days. Being deprived of the smiling face of the sun for so many years has made me all the more sensitive to the cold. Consequently, I want everything around me to be made from wood. Even though it has been turned into pieces of furniture, I still get the feeling the wood is putting down roots. It makes me feel safe and I don't shiver so much.

Early one morning there was a knock at the door and I found an enormous parcel, with the following message, written in letters of three different colours:

'To Arzela, believing in my heart in a free country, Berfin.'

The courier, realising I wouldn't be able to carry the packet indoors, lugged the chair, that would bring a deep blue sky into my life, over to the window. This blue was a fantasy designed to wipe away the sadness of yearning for a sky amid the tired, broken skyscrapers that surrounded me on all sides.

It was the depths of winter – climates had changed considerably – and the sun seemed to have lost its power. It had been nearly a year since my return but I had yet to really fully experience its radiance. Everything and everyone there was so alien it left your sense of belonging broken. Only the wooden house offered a refuge where I didn't feel suffocated. Such houses were constructed for those who had emerged from within the mountain. Most of us refused to live in the enormous skyscrapers. Here I can breathe at least, and, moreover, I have a sky-blue rocking chair.

One overcast night, I sat myself down in my blue dream and began to observe the world outside, as much as I could see it. In daylight, or in places where high-powered lights are used, I still have to narrow my eyes. But at night I can truly see. There is a sharp chill to the air. The dancing snowflakes fail to light up the night or indeed my heart. All the city's thwarted hopes crowd my palms. I sit, withering in the meaninglessness of being human. All the fables of creation resonate in my ears. All the tears ever shed, from the most ancient times to the present moment, gather suddenly in the courtyard of my face. The lamentation and divine laughter multiply. Oh, what a carnage-laden enigma is it to feel!

All the women whose souls have been whipped, all the children, all the men, the universe itself, they all call out to me in a giant chorus: 'Hey you! Do you hear the sound of the flames crackling in our souls?' I cannot say that I hear. How many of the infinite instances of pain crammed into the universe am I supposed to sense? Which one do I have the capacity to sufficiently comprehend? What I have personally lived through is rendered meaningless in the face of such pain, I become the nothingness of pain. In Johannesburg, I am hit by a gram of gilded dust: a dark rage envelops my skin.

In Nanking, the naked bodies of women thrash about in blood: the pangs of womanhood grip me. However many grains of wheat exist in the world, they all commit suicide before my eyes. From the hands of tens of thousands of Indian children, a yellow death enfolds its ache in my craw. Ah, Halabja hits the jugular of my heart with the stench of pitch-black apples![2] The Zilan stream turns to blood and pours down my temples.[3] A fire in Amuda descends from my hair into my lungs.[4] I fall to the ground from the legs of women in Dersim. I am squashed in and frozen. Unknown corpses are being dragged along the border, my heart is being plundered. I am learning all the languages on the face of the earth accompanied by the lamentations of Kurdistan. The shame of the slaughtered, fertile world envelops my fingertips. Is there an end to the shame? No. The shadow of the shame lengthens on the faces of the clocks. Every pain I learn about marginalises another pain, and the world is rapidly disowned. However much pain there exists, whether human or divine, flows from my head and I'm drowning. My anger splinters all boundaries. *If only I could flow to ancient times,* I say. I don't know how much pain there is there, I'm scared, and I take refuge in the bowels of the mountain.

I must sleep! Tomorrow is the big day! Tomorrow is the big day, I must sleep!

I have never been a good sleeper, but on this occasion I woke out of excitement every hour then tried to get back to sleep. Thus, eventually, it became seven in the morning, according to the digital clock on the wall. In the bottom-right corner of the clock was the date: 22.01.2046. What a magnificent day. I opened the curtains. It must be a miracle: the sun was showing its beaming face. I went to the wardrobe and took out a flowery dress I'd had made when I was young and had only had the chance to wear once. It was made from material in three colours, I was a slim woman back then, now I was even thinner. I thought it would fit. Many of my belongings had been preserved, in memorial to us, when they thought we had died in that mountain. Seeing this, when I returned, had both saddened me and made me feel happy. I put the dress on. Although for a moment I thought it was too ostentatious for a sixty-year-old woman, I didn't take it off. Today was just the day for me to wear it. The sun had brought a glimmer of spring at last! I looked in the mirror. The dress looked loose on my aging body, but on fastening a velvet belt it fit better. It was as if my long, grey hair that reached below my waist was dancing with my dress. I combed my hair, tied it up and went over to the coffee machine. I have still not mastered the use of this electronic equipment. Although most of the things in my house are designed to appear old, there are some that used new technology, which I find difficult. As soon as I managed to get the machine to work, an exquisite aroma of coffee engulfed me.

I poured myself a cup and with small steps moved over to my blue chair. Many flavours, such as sugar and salt, have exited my life. It wasn't by choice but by habit, having spent years in the bowel of the mountain where nourishment could only be drawn from a very limited variety of food. I am so used to privation that sweet things are now repugnant to me. Outside was all hustle and bustle. I sat in my chair and began to sip my coffee. Vehicles hovering in the air flew past at speed. I just couldn't get used to them. In front of every building, or rather, skyscraper, there are lift entrances through which the vehicles can be accessed. For me, the sight of them is peculiar, even sad. As if it is not enough that the enormous skyscrapers shut out the sky, these vehicles suspended in the air have to conceal what's left of the sky's blue. When I first returned to the city, it hurt me to see it in this state. People had less space in which to live, which is why as many tall buildings as possible had to be built, and vehicles had been lifted into the air, so as not to occupy the limited space at surface level. Many cities no longer existed, having been entirely destroyed. There were vast areas – thousands of square kilometres – where not a single thing could live. I haven't seen these places yet. As I put the coffee cup on the couch, I caught sight of the clock. My friends were about to arrive. Despite all I have been through, I am lucky. I have dozens of friends from my time under the mountain. These wooden houses were specially built for us to be near to each other, as most of us were nervous about living at altitude. Being so high up is not something we could easily adjust to.

From the window, I saw my friends had arrived. What a picture! The women had turned the three colours into a rainbow emblazoned on their bodies – the colours of the motherland: green, red and yellow. As for the men, they looked so dignified. Most of the young ones we had raised together. They had had dozens of parents. I smiled as they got into the car lift. I only thought of lifts being for the high buildings. We sped out towards the city centre in a long convoy of vehicles. Amed[5] has become so modern and alien there hardly seems to be any trace of its past. If it weren't for the city walls, I wouldn't believe it was the same holy city. We arrived at the square, which was packed, and passed through a path that opened up for us. As soon as we reached the platform, erected in the middle of the square, the crowds began shouting in one voice:

'Hey you,
Who brought the light from the belly of the mountain,
The three-coloured, mother-of-pearl dawns will one day
     find strength in your voices,
And that day is today.
It will come into being with the birth of the mountain,
The free homeland of our dreams!'

These lines echoed with such power and conviction, the blue of the sky seemed refreshed and the sun showed the face it had concealed for years, shining as if reborn. The pale expressions I had seen until a few days before had been replaced by glittering smiles. It wasn't just the people in this square who were applauding, it was all the people of Kurdistan who had for thousands of years of tyranny been forced to bid farewell to the sky. In face of this rebirth, all the fables of creation bent their knees. The fact that today was the hundredth anniversary of the Kurdish Republic of Mahabad first established on 22 January 1946, but demolished less than a year later, made the excitement even more intense. This first victory was proof that we would once again succeed, even if a hundred years were to pass.

On the podium and on every side of the square were thousands of national flags, each one seeming to smile at us. The faces of those of us who had emerged from the mountain beamed brightly, even those of two babes being carried by their mothers. Yes, we were the hundred people of different ages who in an unprecedented way had emerged into daylight from the bowel of the same mountain. On 21 March 2020 we had entered the mountain as 46 people and had emerged last year, on 21 March 2045, as 100. We had waited a quarter century and then been reborn, along with the fire of Newroz we had carried into the mountain with us and never let extinguish, on the contrary, enhancing it. Now we were conveying that fire to the hearts of many thousands of others as the light of victory. The answers to why and how we hadn't died in all those years were there in the songs of victory in that square. Kurdistan was finally free.

2020

As the taxi driver put our luggage in the boot, my phone began to ring. It was Çiya.

'Arzela!'

'Yes, sweetheart?'

'Where are you? Have you set off yet?'

'I'm on my way to the bus station. I'm still in Amed.'

'Please be careful, okay?'

'Don't worry. In a week's time I'll be with you. You take care too.'

'Okay Arzela, I'm sending you a kiss.'

'I'm sending one back, sweetheart.'

'Arzela! Don't for a moment forget that I love you. Okay?'

'What do you mean, my dear? How could I ever forget? Don't worry about me and look after yourself. I'll call you later.'

When the taxi arrived at the bus terminal, the coach was about to depart. I had only just made it. As the assistant driver stowed my bag, I climbed aboard. I had booked seat number 21, a window seat, and I was glad to see the one next to it was empty. It was a great advantage, when travelling on an old-fashioned road for the first time, to have a window seat and I was happy to be able to enjoy the view. Once everyone was settled, the vehicle set off.

At first, we travelled on roads I was familiar with, although everywhere seemed different. The Diyarbakır to Mardin road brought us to Kızıltepe. With the onset of spring, nature seemed revived and fresh, vibrant colours surrounded us. Despite the light rain, the sun did not neglect to show its smiling face from time to time. From Kızıltepe we turned onto the Cizre road and my excitement mounted. In two days' time it would be Newroz and the thought of spending it in Erbil made my heart beat like a bird's. As we passed through Cizre, I felt a pain in my heart as I recalled the lament for Taybet Ana,[6] whose corpse had lain for a week on the street, and the smile of Cemile, whose tiny body had to be kept for days in a freezer to prevent it decaying until the curfew ended.[7] The rain outside was accompanied by thunder, reflecting my mood.

We were approaching the Habur border post. I should call Çiya. He had not wanted me to travel alone and was sorry he couldn't accompany me on account of his work. His phone rang for what seemed like an age.

'Arzela, my dear, I'm sorry. I was in a meeting.'

'I wanted to hear your voice before I crossed the border.'

'Arzela, don't go! I have a bad feeling about this.'

'Please, we've discussed this. I will return safe and sound.'

'Ah, Arzela! Whatever I say will be in vain.'

'I love you too, darling. See you soon.'

As I hung up, we reached the checkpoint. After a long wait and search, we passed from Habur to the Halil İbrahim border gate. We waited a shorter time there and were soon on our way to Duhok. Oh, what death and bloodshed had taken place, and was continuing to, in these lands. Every inch of Kurdistan had been irrigated by Kurdish blood for centuries. Eventually we reached Mosul, meaning we didn't have much further to go. Çiya must be going mad right now, I thought to myself, but I couldn't do anything until I got to Erbil.

On the outskirts of Erbil, we stopped for another checkpoint and we were taken off the bus. I took a deep breath but the sharp smell of gunpowder filled my lungs and I gulped painfully. The sun was in that crimson contradiction between staying and going. As its red and orange rays spread over the sky, it seemed to smile sadly. Although there were signs of war everywhere, nature was grasping just as fiercely at life. When the checks were over, we climbed back onto the coach and proceeded into the city. The streets seemed to be both bustling and empty. From time to time, the sound of whistling filled my ears. I was sure the sound wasn't coming from inside the bus. It was familiar and the melody of the whistle took me back to my childhood. I looked up to the sky and smiled, silently murmuring, 'Thanks, little Arzela'. In my childhood, like all children in Kurdistan, I had felt as though the sky was saying 'Welcome' to me.

Finally we reached the bus station. After nine hours on the road, all my bones were creaking from lack of movement. I took my bag and began to wait. After a few minutes, two people approached me. I recognised one of them. It was Delil with his big friendly smile. I didn't recognise the woman with him. Like Delil, she was in her early twenties. We shook hands and hugged.

'At last, you've come, Arzela!' Delil said.

'Yes, finally,' I replied.

'Arzela, let me introduce you to my fiancée, Zilan.'

I saw Zilan glance coyly at Delil. It was the look of a woman in love. Delil took my bag and we began to walk. As I looked at the people around me, they all looked back. Some smiled at me and others appeared curious. We were in a bus station, I thought, they must see hundreds of strangers like me every day. It was only when we reached the vehicle waiting for us outside the bus station that I understood the attention I had attracted. On the opposite side of the street, hung a huge Newroz poster with my picture on it. I felt honoured to see my photo alongside such venerable names. We got in the vehicle and I looked around. Zilan and I sat in the back. Delil was in the front seat. He turned to me and said:

'Arzela, just so you know, we will first join the celebrations here tomorrow, then go to Kandil the day after.'

'Okay, that's fine with me.'

After driving for about fifteen minutes, we stopped at the beginning of a street filled with colourful lights. The Newroz fires that we had seen on the way were here also. People of all ages stood around these fires singing Kurdish songs with some performing *halay* folk dances. I had not seen such a flood of enthusiasm in years. When I saw again Zilan's coy glances, I remembered that I hadn't phoned Çiya, and panicked.

'Delil, I have to make a call.'

'Of course.'

As soon as Çiya heard my voice: 'Arzela! Where are you? I've been worried sick!'

'My dear, you know my phone doesn't work here. I'm fine. Don't worry. My friends met me a short while ago. My first task tomorrow morning will be to get myself a new phone.'

'You'll be the death of me, Arzela! Please don't neglect to call me. I love you my darling. See you soon.'

'I love you too, see you soon.'

After watching the festivities in the street for a while, we went to the house where we were to spend the night. The place belonged to a young couple with a child. They welcomed us warmly and invited us to sit at an already prepared floor table spread. We washed our hands and set ourselves down, chatting as we did so. The couple's names were Nubuhar and Demhat, and the child's name was Şoreş. Nubuhar was a nurse and Demhat was a doctor. While still engaged, they had been prosecuted for treating a wounded guerrilla and had had to flee to Erbil. Şoreş was only a year old, but tried to join in the conversation by waving his arms. Meanwhile, I learned that Zilan was a teacher, like Delil.

I was pretty tired and needed to be fresh the next day. So I called Çiya again, took a shower and as soon as I lay down on the mattress prepared for me, I fell asleep. I awoke early the next morning to the sound of marching music. I opened the window: what a magnificent sight it was! Women and children were dressed in multi-coloured clothes; the men were dignified in khaki. As I watched, I heard Nubuhar's voice:

'Good morning, Arzela.'

'Good morning.' I smiled.

'Arzela, your eyes are shining.'

'Yes, it's the first time I'll be at such a beautiful Newroz celebration.'

'You should see the celebrations tomorrow. Even the mountains will be dressed in the three colours.'

Everyone was awake by now. We prepared breakfast then got dressed. When I couldn't zip up my dress, Zilan came to my rescue. Then she gave me a pair of hairpins in the shape of a map of Kurdistan. I was so happy, I embraced her fiercely. I looked in the mirror and they looked so lovely I kissed Zilan on the cheek.

Everyone was smiling. Before we left the house, I called Çiya. As I spoke, Şoreş smiled next to me. I said to Çiya.

'Darling, do you still want a child?'

'Is that a serious question, Arzela?'

'OK, yes.'

'OK, yes?'

'Yes, alright.'

'Arzela, honey!'

'I have to go out now, they're waiting for me. When I return, we'll go to the doctor, sweetheart.'

The doctors had said I needed to have an operation in order to have children, but I had not reconciled myself to this. I don't know why, but the couple we were staying with and their child had triggered a maternal need in me.

Before going to the square where the celebrations were to take place, I bought a new phone and I sent Çiya a message. The scene in the square was magnificent. I looked around like a bewildered child. On seeing my own photograph on one of the enormous banners, I was overcome and started to cry. In the middle of Erbil, amongst the national flags, I was face to face with a huge banner with my name written on it in three colours. Underneath was a line from one of my verses:

'Hey, motherland of Kurdistan
We believe in you!'

What a great honour it was! As time moved, the square swelled with crowds and people began to sing and perform *halay*. Now it was my turn, and as I took my place on the stage I began to tremble. I could barely control my legs. I, who had performed in public hundreds of times, was as nervous as if it were my debut. As I arrived on stage, a tumultuous roar of applause broke out. After making a short introduction and extending greetings, I began to recite a poem to musical accompaniment.

'Look at what we have created with our hands
That which makes the fables of creation jealous
It is neither weariness, nor frustration
We are seizing time, despite tyrants

Carrying it to the light of tomorrow
Our heads held high, our eyes gleaming like the sun
We are the face of freedom and the belief
That imprints itself on the revolution
We will carry triumph from yesterday, to today and on to
    tomorrow
We are the earth and the sky
And they will hear, as we carry victory to tomorrow,
Our voice heralding the onset of Spring!'

I was on the podium for half an hour, amazed by how attentively the crowd accompanied me with each poem. I had never imagined my words would one day be known by heart by so many people. When I left the stage, I couldn't hold back the tears. Then Delil handed me the phone and I saw Çiya on the screen; he too had tears in his eyes. After my nerves had settled, I joined in the celebrations. By the time we returned to the house, it was past midnight. Şoreş had fallen asleep in his father's arms despite all the noise. I went to my bed and looked at my phone. Çiya had sent me dozens of messages. In the last one he had written:

'To the love of my life and my hope for a future family, I am so proud of you.'

After I had written him a long reply I fell into a tranquil sleep.

2046

I was one of the lucky ones who was able to wake on the morning of 23 January 2046. After decades of warfare and loss of life, the people of Kurdistan had declared their independence, simply announced it and let the world catch up to this fact. While we were in the bowel of the mountain the conflict had reached its peak, hundreds of thousands of people were being slaughtered outside, by the old empires of Turkey, Persia and America, in the last throes of their own imperial pretensions; whole Kurdish cities were being destroyed. Eventually, in the early 40s, the warlords' own economies collapsed and the entire Middle East began to reshape itself, a series of new states began to emerge, not defined by nineteenth-century Western mapmakers. Mesopotamia and Anatolia emerged and the fragments of old Kurdistan began to coalesce. After so many decades of savagery, even the Kurds didn't believe it was possible that an independent Kurdistan could sustain itself. But deep in the bowels of the mountain, we had proven to ourselves that a country could indeed exist, because we had created it; all we needed was to take what we had built in the stone vaults of that place and bring it into the light. Within a year, the whole country had declared it.

Despite the declaration of independence, our worries were not over. For whatever reason, none of us entirely believed that the unseen enemy, that had once enveloped our insides like a spider's web, could really be gone. Since time immemorial, they had thwarted us and we were convinced that, in some form, they would rise again.

It was now only a few weeks before the renewal of the Assembly and the presidential elections. Those of us who'd been underground had been invited to stand as candidates, but none of us had accepted. Many things had changed in our absence, right then, and we felt for us to be involved in the administration might do more harm than good.

There were three people contending for the presidency, one of them a woman, Hevi. Zınar and Zindan were the other two candidates. Zindan was also the current Speaker of the Assembly. From what I saw, he seemed too ambitious and could be dangerous for the new nation. Zınar was the head of a multi-national pharmaceutical company and a typical businessman. He had close commercial ties with countries that felt uncomfortable about a free Kurdistan. Hevi, by contrast, was an ecology expert who had brought herself up from nothing; she was also an active director of the organisation, World Without War. The population of the world had plummeted as a result of recent wars, natural disasters, and viruses that constantly mutated; and other risks persisted. World Without War was a body that created social awareness and organised campaigns among younger people. Although Hevi was the best candidate, the race was a close three-way split; the other two candidates appeared to have the same level of support, and according to some sources, Zınar felt he was going to win. As for Zindan, being the incumbent leader, he was also convinced he would triumph. Unfortunately, in spite of years of struggle, women were still a step behind men. But undeterred, Hevi campaigned all the harder. The majority of her team was made up of women who had worked selflessly for years for their country. Those of us who had emerged from the mountain declared our support for Hevi's campaign: having a woman like her running Kurdistan would be to everyone's benefit.

When the calendar rolled around to 1 February 2046, the news programmes announced that the country was dangerously low in stocks of vaccines and anti-viral medication. This was despite the fact that we were home to a huge pharmaceutical company, owned by Zinar, that distributed medicines worldwide. Zinar issued statements denying the situation had anything to do with his company, saying the problem was one of raw materials, a shortage that he would resolve immediately if he were elected president. Even a child could see his intentions.

A few weeks before the elections, hospitals began to fill up and an atmosphere of panic spread throughout the country. A significant segment of the population began to talk about voting for Zinar in order to resolve the crisis. But the supporters of Hevi and Zindan were not idle, and actively searched for a more immediate solution. Tragically, though, dozens of patients, mainly children, died on account of failing to receive the necessary treatment. Although people endeavoured to remain calm, the situation was like a powder keg.

Early one morning I had a visitor. It was Berfin. She sounded worried.

'Arzela, you need to come with me. Hevi wants to speak to you urgently.'

I quickly got ready and as we travelled out of the city, towards one of the old settlements, I could tell something was wrong. Normally, there would be no one out here, the area was only used for the most clandestine meetings. We stopped in front of one of the buildings. Three armed thirty-somethings – two of them women – greeted us and accompanied us through several tunnels until we reached Hevi's quarters. She was a good-looking woman of about 35. While normally she would always be smiling, today she frowned. She came over to me and grasped both my hands.

'Welcome, Arzela. Thanks for coming. I apologise for the early start, but the situation is critical.'

'I'm glad to be of assistance. What's the problem?'

'First, let's sit down.'

I could tell Hevi was nervous and with every passing second I became more curious.

'Dear Arzela, we have obtained intel from a reliable source, that Zinar has sat down with diploamtic representatives of ------, and is considering, shortly after being elected president, announcing a new security arrangement for Kurdistan, which would bring it under the protection of ------. If this happens, Arzela, the very freedom we have won will be signed away. Furthermore, who knows where this will lead – perhaps to a new conflict, one that ------ has been trying to provoke for so long.'

'How can things have gotten so bad? Doesn't he realise what this will cost?'

'Unfortunately, we've been aware of this for a long time. We declared independence precisely to stop him doing this at the next election. Otherwise, our hands are tied – we don't have sufficient proof.'

'Is Zindan aware of this?'

'Of course, I've invited him here. He will be here soon.'

She had barely finished her sentence when Zindan appeared at the door. After greeting us, he sat down.

'What's going on, Hevi?'

Once Hevi had gone through it all in detail, Zindan got out of his seat and started walking agitatedly up and down. I watched him. On several occasions our eyes met and he smiled. It was the kind of smile that made you realise the innocence behind it. But I sensed something strange in it as well. He halted, then walked towards Hevi and grasped her hands gently.

'Dear Hevi, let us unite our forces.'

'How?' She said, after a moment's hesitation.

'Let's announce that we will run on a joint ticket.'

'How, exactly? People can't vote for two candidates.'

'We will have one candidate, and that will be you.'

We all fell silent for a moment. I had always regarded Zindan as a typically ambitious politician, one I didn't think was capable of making such a sacrifice. Hevi looked at him and at me as if she were asking a question. Her hands were still between Zindan's palms. Zindan started to speak again.

'I realise you're shocked. I have always had my ambitions but, for me, the freedom of Kurdistan is the only one that matters. I've come to realise that you are perhaps the better candidate. We have to work together, otherwise we will all lose.'

A smile appeared on Hevi's face. She gave Zindan a friendly hug. She looked less worried.

'So what shall we do now, Zindan?'

'We will call up our teams without delay and explain the situation to them. I don't think anyone will disagree. Then we'll issue a press statement. There's no time to lose.'

Watching these two young people, a thought crossed my mind: while there were still people who could succeed first at being humans, life would continue and freedom could be constructed on the sound of laughter.

As evening approached, a meeting was convened and attended by a range of supporters, including those of us who had come from under the mountain. The situation was explained and, although there were one or two dissenting voices, the two campaigns agreed to fight the election together. A press statement was issued immediately after the meeting explaining that Zindan would run as vice president, under Hevi. There was no doubt that Zinar would not be pleased and would connive new strategies to overcome this. Hence, we had to do our utmost to ensure victory for Hevi. To this end, we all worked without sleep. Hevi and Zindan were in great danger on account of the decision they had taken, for Zinar's anger had become apparent.

The voting system was not as it used to be. In the old days, ballot papers would be put into ballot boxes and counted one by one. Now everything happened electronically. But we still had to be careful: technology may have progressed, but people hadn't, and malpractice was still rife. One thing about the new election process heartened me. Because the legacy of each election would affect them for longer, people aged between eighteen and twenty-five were considered to have more stake in the process so their votes were counted as double. Hevi thus had a great advantage as both her and Zindan's base lay partly in this segment of the population.

Eventually the eve of the election arrived. The following

day, that is 21 March 2046, ballots would be cast and the day of Newroz would see the first governor of Kurdistan announced. No one would dare celebrate until the votes had been cast and counted. Hardly any of us slept. Those of us who had emerged from the mountain spent that night together, our faces taut with anxieties we dared not give voice. But we still had hope: the Kurdistan that had suffered for thousands of years from suppression and betrayal would not abandon its freedom.

2020

We managed to sleep for a few hours and most of us woke up within a few minutes of each other. Şoreş's cute voice reverberated through the house. We needed to get up and go. Nubuhar came over to me.

'Arzela, put on warm clothes or pack them in your bag. The weather looks fine, but up there it can be frosty at night. We don't want you to get ill.'

We hurriedly ate breakfast then set out in two cars and a bus. It was a bright spring day and there was the smell of earth blown by a breeze that had also brought rain before dawn. We were heading for the Zagros mountains, to Kandil. It was not yet eight in the morning, but the sun was peeking above the hills. In the three vehicles, there were fifty of us in total. All the windows were open and the sound of Kurdish music filled the air. I had called Çiya a few times that morning, but had been unable to reach him. It was Wednesday and he must have left for work already. So I sent him a message, thinking he would get back to me. We were approaching Kandil now. As Zilan had said, even the mountains had been painted in three colours – red, white and green. The sight caused my heart to beat faster. Being so used to travelling, I never suffered from travel sickness, but since heading out that morning I had felt a queasiness in my stomach. I had put it down to excitement, but the feeling lingered. I had been on the road for nearly four days – perhaps it was that. It was strange that Çiya hadn't yet gotten back to me. I rang his workplace and when his secretary said he hadn't arrived yet and that they'd not managed to reach him, I began to feel anxious. Nubuhar saw I was worried and said, gripping my hand:

'Arzela, he's overslept. Don't worry, he will call you.' And I calmed down a little.

Eventually we reached Kandil. I was shocked to see the size of the crowds. I wondered if they all lived there, or whether they had come from elsewhere, like us. I asked Delil. He said that at least half of the people there had travelled there for the celebrations.

As I got out of the vehicle, I felt tiny raindrops touch my face. It felt like a silk scarf brushing against my skin. Taking in the mountain air, I realised there was a scent I didn't recognise. *This must be what paradise smells like*, I thought. For a moment I felt dizzy, the lack of oxygen, perhaps. Just then the phone rang: it was Çiya.

'Sweetheart, where are you?'

'I'm coming to you, Arzela.'

'What do you mean?'

'I'm on the road, there's not far to go. I cleared my desk yesterday and set out last night. Could I speak to Delil? I need to know the schedule so that I can join you.'

I handed the phone to Delil and I again felt dizzy. Then we mingled with the crowds. Sometimes we exchanged greetings, or ran into people we knew and embraced them. Although there weren't many children, most of the people there were under thirty. Colourful scarves and sashes, worn as belts, created a riot of colour. Everyone entering the area passed through a serious security check. The young people doing it were smiling and polite, apologising as they carried out their duties.

As the day wore on, I ran into people I had longed to meet for ages and had a brief chat with each of them. From time to time, I called Çiya and when I was unable to get through to him I began to understand *his* unease when *I* was on the road. Several times I heard the sound of gunfire and, although Delil and others reassured us there were no clashes on account of Newroz, I couldn't help but feel anxious. During the day I appeared on the stage with various other speakers. It was almost evening and the sky had turned a deep shade of red, the likes of which I had never seen before.

2046

It was time to vote. It was the first time we had ever seen a polling booth. We carried out the procedure one by one in the way we had been taught and then the waiting began. When the clocks showed it was midnight, the news announced that voting was now over and that we had to wait until an official time when the result would be announced. Hevi, Zindan and Zinar were being broadcast live from the same platform. When the camera zoomed in on Zınar's face, the look of hatred in his eyes filled the screen and made our flesh creep. During the tumultuous last weeks of the campaign, the situation with the pharmaceutical stocks had remained unresolved, with people continuing to die, albeit in reduced numbers. We'd been told that there wouldn't be long to wait. Just as voting had been carried out electronically, so too the count would be quick and automatic. The official time arrived and our anticipation reached fever pitch. We all stood staring at the live feed, projected onto the wall before us.

As we held our breath, it felt like the beating of our hearts was reverberating around the hall itself. The numbers started to be projected onto the wall. At the beginning it seemed close,

135

but before long Hevi began to pull ahead. Although the result was increasingly certain, we still had to wait for the official declaration before celebrating. As soon as it was announced that Hevi had won with 68% of the vote, Zinar's face appeared on the screen. He was casting venomous glances about him. I prayed for the hate in his face to diminish, before it dragged us all into a new fire.

With the result in, we headed back to the city to join the Newroz celebrations there. We reached the square at the same time as Hevi and Zindan and, through the crowds and security, shouted our congratulations. A little while later, through the throng, I noticed Zindan looking askance at Hevi. I shuddered and searched for a reason why he'd look at her like that. To me, she seemed to embody freedom itself. The sun was about to set and its last, lingering rays cast an enchanted light around her, bouncing off her hair. Despite light rain, the celebrations went on almost until dawn. By the time we returned home, the sun was about to rise again. I took a shower and went to bed, the image of Zindan's chilling look still haunting me.

Having fallen asleep in an anxious state, I awoke feeling drained. Switching on the wall-screen, I was relieved to see that things were normal. As I went to get make coffee, I saw the screen on my phone flashing. Hevi had sent a message about an hour before.

'Dear Arzela, forgive me messaging you rather than calling – I'm so tired. I would like to come and talk to you about an important matter. If you could let me know when would be convenient for you, I'd appreciate it.'

I called her straightaway and told her she could come whenever she wanted. Less than half an hour had passed when there was a knock at the door. I prepared coffee for the two of us. We sat down.

'Arzela, we appear to have found a solution to the medicine issue. We have a young team and I'm sure they will be successful with regard to the production side of things. But we need economic resources. I was thinking of inviting Zindan so that you could work with him to find a solution.'

I jumped to my feet. Without realising it, my voice rose: 'No, don't tell him anything!'

'Why not, Arzela? I need to tell him this, he's my vice president now. I have to share everything with him.'

'Leave the supply chain side to me, but please don't mention it to him. Not until we have taken concrete steps at least.'

'Arzela, could you please tell me what's upsetting you about this process?'

'I can't say, exactly, but there's something about him that troubles me. For now, please don't share with him any of your initial steps.'

Just at that moment there was a knock at the door and Zindan arrived. Hevi took what I had said into consideration and explained the reason she had invited him was for both of them to thank me. After a short time, Zindan left and the two of us were again alone.

'Arzela, please explain how you are going to resolve the supply chain side of things without Zindan?'

'My dearest Hevi, what I am about to tell you is a long-held secret. Many years ago, when my people first entered the mountains, we noticed something very strange about some of the tiny rocks embedded in the deepest seams of those caves. Occasionally, after turning off our torches some of the stones in the wall retained the light; only for a few seconds. We called these stones sivik stones; and it turns out they are precious, needed in the development of microprocessors. Everyone born in the mountain inherited an equal responsibility over these crystals. And no one outside of the community knows about them. Our people will happily share them with the Kurdish people, if they trust them.'

'Arzela, I don't know what to say!'

'Please don't talk like this. These crystals are not our personal property. The mountain gave birth to them and entrusted them to us. Now it is time to share them with the people of Kurdistan. If you can promise transparency and security, I will organise their delivery. Come here early tomorrow with the necessary protection and you will receive them. I think the crystals we have will be sufficient for your project.'

That evening, I explained the situation to my friends. They were all happy to share their allocations with the new government, knowing they were never an inheritance, more a guardianship. The next morning, Hevi arrived at the meeting place early and collected the crystals. Only once they had been converted to cash and the foundations of the new state-owned pharmaceutical factory had been laid, was a public announcement made. When Hevi told me about the way Zindan had reacted to this announcement, resigning his VP post and declaring they could no longer work together if he wasn't going to be consulted, my suspicions about him were confirmed. Zindan's intentions were not selfless. Following the announcement, the public panic that had been growing for months was replaced by calm and people began to smile again. In this way, public confidence in Hevi grew as she introduced other innovative measures for the country.

It was nearly the end of May and the pharmaceutical factory was about to open and begin production. In the meantime, efforts were being made to meet short-term demand through university laboratories. An announcement was made that the factory opening would take place in a few days time.

2020

The day was getting colder and I began to feel the wind through my thin jacket. I found Zilan in the crowds gathered outside the entrance to the mountain, and asked her to take me to the place where we had left our bags. We moved with difficulty through the crowd, running into Nubuhar who said she'd join us as Şoreş needed a change of clothes. Şoreş must have caught sight of his father as he started to cry 'Daddy, Daddy!', then we realised that Demhat and Delil were alongside us. We went together towards the entrance to the mountain. Once inside, what I saw amazed me. It was as if an entire city had been constructed inside the mountain. Everything needed to sustain life had been stored in different rooms and the appropriate conditions provided. On the way to our intended room, I caught the sound of water and started to follow it. I could not believe what I saw. A stream was flowing from high in the mountain, pouring into the roof of the main cavern then divided by fine channels and delivered to different tiers of that cavern, as well as passages running off it, where small gardens had been planted with all kinds of life. I couldn't believe my eyes. In front of me a small waterfall cascaded with a strange installation next to it. As I tried to comprehend what was happening, I realised Zilan was next to me.

'It's an electricity generator, Arzela. Sometimes it doesn't work for months because of the weather. Everything here has been designed with that in mind.'

'It's unbelievable, Zilan. All of it. I don't know what to say.'

We went back to our friends and continued on our way. There were clothes depositories, a clinic, food stores and so on. Everything was so well organised. In an ordinary city, above-ground, such order might be impossible to find. Most of the things there had been made from organic materials, like wood, and were hand-made. There were dozens of rooms in the mountain. Finally, we reached the room where our bags were. Inside, there were several bunk-beds with wooden cupboards standing beside them. There was also a large bookcase in the room, as there had been in most of the other rooms we'd passed. I could barely conceal my amazement, and those with me smiled at my surprise. On my way there, I had only imagined the most primitive of living conditions; I hadn't for a moment imagined such modern structures. Since entering the mountain, I had not failed to notice that it was fully illuminated. The electricity came from a natural source. When I asked my friends about this, they only smiled knowingly. 'It is the mountain's secret,' was all they would say.

We had put on our warmer clothes and were just about to go back outside when the sound of explosions tore through the mountain, followed by screaming. Nubuhar grabbed Şoreş and retreated back into the room where our belongings were, while the rest of us ran for the gates. Dozens of people were running towards us. The faces of some were gushing with blood. We heard people shouting about an operation. There were dozens of people with injuries and we didn't know who to help first. We had already reached the outer gate. It was a dreadful scene. There were thousands of people lying on the ground and bombs were still raining down. For a moment, I saw a familiar silhouette running towards me. There was dust and smoke everywhere and it was only when the figure was right in front of me that I realised it was Çiya and I let out a shriek. Just then, a bomb hit the ground near to us and I felt Çiya push me towards the gates. He remained where he was because a large chunk of rock fall had fallen between us and I could no longer see him. There was no point in shouting as the only audible sounds were of bombs and bullets. I didn't know what to do. I felt I was going mad. I felt something hot trickling between my legs and I tried to see what it was. I felt an intolerable pain from my hips to my toes. Just as I thought a bullet must have struck me, I passed out...

From time to time, I partially drifted into consciousness without realising where I was, thinking of Çiya being behind the rocks and then passing out again. When I eventually forced my eyes open, I heard a familiar voice saying, 'She's waking up, Arzela's waking up!'

Eventually I succeeded in opening my eyes. On feeling my hands held between warm palms, I assumed it was Çiya and tried to sit up but failed. There was a terrible contraction in my stomach. I looked down and saw bandages around my midriff and realised it was Demhat holding my hand.

'Isn't Çiya here? Didn't he come inside? Why isn't he with me? What happened, Demhat, why aren't you speaking?' I asked.

'Arzela, please be calm. There was a bombardment. We've been waiting for you to come to for days. You were seriously injured and we carried out a difficult operation. Please remain still, or your stitches will tear.'

'Tell me where Çiya is. What happened to all the people who were lying on the ground? Tell me they survived, please!'

'Arzela, I'm very sorry, but we couldn't help any of them because the entrances to the mountain were closed. I'm also sorry to say that we couldn't save your baby as the bullet hit you in the stomach. I'm very sorry.'

'What? Was I pregnant? How could that be?'

When Demhat realised I hadn't been aware I was pregnant, he felt guilty and passed my hands on to Zilan and left the room. I couldn't say anything. I had lost the man I loved, a miracle baby I hadn't even known about, and hundreds of my people – all in the same moment. In the face of such profound agony, the words dried up in my throat. I just wept silently. Zilan accompanied me. I turned to her:

'Delil, Şoreş and Nubuhar?' I was able to croak.

'Don't worry, they're alive. Delil was also wounded, but he will come to see you soon. Şoreş and his mother are very well. Nubuhar is trying to get him to sleep at the moment. He hasn't slept for days and is constantly crying.'

'Haven't you called for help?'

'Unfortunately, we haven't been able to do that. The bombardment has been going on for five days. The phones don't work and all the outer doors have closed. It seems we have no option but to wait for someone to find us.'

'Zilan, have the ones outside survived, do you think?'

'I would like to say yes, but it doesn't seem possible. I'm as heartbroken as you. But please think of yourself for the moment. You must get better, we need you. Now I will go and see Delil. I told him I would bring him to see you. He has been very worried about you. He won't relax until he sees you.'

Even before Zilan had gone out the door, my eyes had closed and I had fallen asleep.

2046

That morning I had woken up early, as usual. I had a coffee, got dressed and sat in my blue chair, and waited for Hevi to arrive. Today was the opening of the pharmaceutical factory and I had promised to accompany her. I saw her motorcade pull up and I left my apartment and headed for the lift. She looked noble and beautiful, as always.

'Good morning, Arzela.'

'Good morning, Hevi.'

'Arzela, I thought we could go to the hospital after the opening.'

'I would like that, as you know, but seeing me is not good for him. He has attacks for days afterwards.'

'I don't know why, but I thought this time it might be different, but it's up to you. And we could give him the good news about a free country. It might be good for him.'

'Okay, dear Hevi, if you want to, we'll go.'

I hadn't seen him for months. When I had been able to, I would go every week, to watch him from behind the glass, without him knowing, and silently recite poems and fables to him for hours on end. For he had always loved me doing that. I thought my voice might reach him in some way, so I went every week, without telling anyone.

We had reached the factory. Thousands of people were there to witness the opening and to applaud the success. Most of the important names in the government were there and were all smiling. But there was no sign of either Zindan or Zınar. It would have been surprising, of course, if they had been there, for they did not appreciate any of Hevi's success, on the contrary, it only seemed to incense them. Although Zinar was open about this, it was Zindan's attitude that was really dangerous. It was impossible to predict what he'd do next. Eventually all the speeches were over and the new factory officially started production. The factory had been equipped with the latest laboratories and had been built with protection against external attacks. We left and headed for the hospital. Several times I wanted to turn round but Hevi succeeded in convincing me. The hospital was like a hidden paradise behind high walls. It was one of the centres for rehabilitating Kurds who had been affected by warfare. We started to walk towards the area where he was being kept, and I began thinking about how I would put up with the screams he would let out the minute he saw me. When we arrived, he was sitting in the shade of a tree, playing with a pigeon he called Arzela. When he saw us, he stood up and the pigeon began walking towards me, before flying off to a nearby tree where it had a nest.

As I suspected, he started to scream as he walked towards me slowly. I stopped dead in my tracks; I didn't know what to do. He walked up to me and touched my hair and whispered, 'Arzela, my darling, so, you've finally come, eh?' I was just about to reply when he put a finger on my lips and again

143

caressed my hair. My whole body was shaking. Then he suddenly drew back and started the screaming again, which drove me to despair. Hevi quickly came over and shepherded me away.

'I'm sorry, Arzela. But at least today he came over to you. He will improve, believe me.'

I couldn't speak for sobbing and merely nodded to her.

Yes, he was one of the few people who survived that bombardment, my dear Çiya, but unfortunately he was profoundly traumatised and never really recovered. Indeed our very recovery from the mountain was thanks to what he told Hevi. After years of dealing with victims of war, Hevi managed to establish communication with Çiya and believed we might still be alive. After a long struggle, she convinced the then government to find the entrance to the mountain and, in this way, the rebirth from the mountain took place. But ever since, whenever Çiya set eyes on me he suffered serious trauma, being only able to recall the bombardment, and not me. But his behaviour today had been miraculous; it was the first time I had been that close to him. After we were rescued, no one could convince me he was alive. In the same way, when he first saw me, he thought I was a ghost. When Hevi dropped me off at my home that evening, I was tired. I fell into bed without taking off my clothes, and cried silently for hours before dropping off to sleep.

2020

It took me weeks to recover from the operation and even then the bleeding and pain persisted. Days, then weeks, then months passed, but no one came to rescue us. We had everything we needed to continue life in the mountain, but as time passed, we began to believe we would never get out and decided to continue in that way. We grew crops by the stream and endeavoured to replenish the food supplies. There were forty-six of us inside the mountain, then we learned that two women were pregnant. Moreover, after a few months three couples, including Delil and Zilan, decided to get married so before long weddings were held in the mountain. By now the mountain had become our world and life carried on. Our numbers increased and as the years passed, we began to feel as if we had always lived there. The children who were born there had no idea of the existence of an outside. When they reached a certain age, we decided, we would explain it to them. At first, we sought ways of getting out, but after a while we abandoned the idea and began to become attached to our little world. Years became decades and our number rose to 100. Our country was perfect, with no corruption, no cult of personalities, no politics as usual. We constructed our life in the mountain with affection.

Inside the mountain, Newroz was a time of mourning and would pass quietly. Twenty-five years went by and one morning we awoke to another Newroz. Since the loudest sounds in there were the voices of children, it would generally be quiet. However, that morning we woke to sounds coming from the skin of the mountain. A roar travelled up to us as if some giant was striking the outside of the mountain. We all panicked, ushering the children to the safest corner of the complex, and retrieving our weapons from their hiding places. These weapons were materials left over from the munitions rooms. As we readied ourselves, there was a sudden crash, followed by the sound of human voices. Dozens of voices were crying, 'Arzela' as one. We looked at each other, dumbfounded. Suddenly we saw strangely dressed people and the torches they held in their hands dazzled us. It was obvious that these people were looking for us and were not enemies, but we couldn't understand why they had waited twenty-five years to find us. Realising we were not under threat, we retrieved the children and those searching for us stood amazed. A short while later, we left the bowels of the mountain in unison. There was no sign of life outside, it was as if nature had gone into a deep sleep. We were put on flying vehicles and on the way we learned why we hadn't been found sooner. For a long time, the region had been bombed with chemical weapons and all life had been wiped out. Çiya, who I thought had died, and a few others, had in fact survived the raid on the mountain, and he talked deliriously about us. Eventually he persuaded the doctors to contact Hevi and when she visited him, he convinced her to send a team to find us. When no one came looking for us, we had sometimes wondered if the whole human race had been annihilated. But now our rebirth from the mountain had been realised and we had been rescued by a new autonomous Kurdish government...

2046

On hearing a furious knocking on my door, I jumped out of bed. On the doorstep stood Delil and Demhat.

'Arzela, we have to go immediately, the situation is really serious.'

'What is? What's going on?'

'Arzela, Hevi has been assassinated. At her home, this morning. A few of those who were born in the mountain have also disappeared. We must leave immediately.'

I couldn't think straight. 'Who would do such a thing?'

'The military it seems. Though they haven't announced anything yet. Either way, we must get to a safe area.'

As we got in the vehicle, I shouted: 'We're going to the hospital, I can't leave Çiya.'

They didn't object. When we got there, it was as if Çiya knew we were coming. He was packed and ready and came without a word. Within an hour, we had collected everyone apart from those who were missing, and left the city. On the way, I found out what had happened. During the night, most of the members of the Assembly, including Hevi, had been murdered in their sleep. A coup had been perpetrated and the rumours pointed to both Zınar and Zindan's involvement. Knowing the affection the people of Kurdistan had for the people of the mountain, they intended to silence us, too. After staying for a while in one of the abandoned townships outside the city, we decided unanimously to return to the mountain. There was no time to lose. It took us a few days to get there as we had to travel by night and go off-road many times to avoid the new checkpoints. When we finally reached the mountain, we tore at the boulders blocking the entrance with our own hands, the same boulders that had entombed us all those years ago, and locked ourselves in. Just at that moment, Çiya cried out and fainted. Delil and Demhat carried him to a room. Eventually he came round and as soon as he opened his eyes he hugged me, saying, 'Arzela, my darling, you're alive!'

'We're alive, my dear, we're alive,' I replied, hugging him back.

The children cuddled up to their mothers. Some were crying. We could say nothing to reassure them. A little while later we heard loud noises. It was obvious, I guess, that we'd come here. We were sure we were going to die. Huddling together, we held hands, as pieces of rock started to rain down on us. Rather than whimper, we sang our freedom song loudly all together, for even as we died we had a hope that one day, Kurdistan would be liberated from treachery and would be free forever.

As Çiya pressed his lips to my cheek, I whispered in his ear: 'My darling, we will be parents after all. Let's not keep our baby waiting.' He smiled and so did I. We clasped hands and fell silent... Sooner or later we would be reborn from another mountain in another Spring...

Notes

1. A Kurdish girl's name meaning snowdrop flower.

2. Survivors of Saddam Hussein's chemical attack on the city of Halabja on 16 March 1988, during the closing days of the Iran-Iraq War (an attack which killed between 3,200 and 5,000 people and injured between 7,000 and 10,000), reported detecting a sweet smell of apples as the chemicals spread.

3. On 12/13 July 1930, during the Ararat rebellion in Ağrı Province, the Turkish Land Forces on the orders of General İsmet İnönü (later to become President of Turkey), massacred between 5,000 and 15,000 Kurds in the Zilan Valley. Two army corps and 80 aircraft were used. According to the daily *Cumhuriyet* (16 July 1930), about 15,000 people were killed and Zilan River (leading into Lake Van) was clogged with dead bodies all the way down to its mouth.

4. In November 1960, a tragic fire in a cinema in Amuda, in the predominantly Kurdish governorate of Al-Hasakah in Syria, took the lives of 283 schoolchildren.

5. Amed is the Kurdish name for the city of Diyarbakır.

6. In the Silopi district of Şırnak (a district neighbouring Cizre), on 19 December 2015, an all-hours curfew was declared

by the Turkish authorities, for the purpose of conducting military operations against supposed members of the Kurdistan Workers' Party (PKK), a curfew that would go on for thirty-six days. On the fifth day of the curfew, a fifty-seven-year-old woman Taybet Inan (a.k.a. Taybet Ana) and her brother-in-law, Yusuf Inan (53), were shot dead and their bodies deliberately left in the street for seven days.

7. Cemile Çağırga was a ten-year-old Kurdish girl who was shot dead by Turkish forces while playing with friends in front of her family home in Cizre. During the two month curfew (14 December 2015 – 11 February 2016), the citizens of Cizre were unable to leave their homes, and the parents of Cemile Çağırga had no choice but to keep the body of their daughter in a freezer, famously photographed draped with a green cloth featuring Qur'anic script.

The Last Hope

Qadir Agid

Translated from the Kurmanji
by Kate Ferguson and Dîbar Çelik

'It is our duty to oppose those who violate our land, our blood, our honour; or at the very least not to offer them the hand of friendship.'

This phrase, emblazoned under a name and image suspended above the empty square, disappeared and reappeared at regular intervals. The man said to himself, 'I know this phrase, I've heard it before.'

Driverless cars – each identical in colour, sound and model – slithered through the emptiness like snakes. Propelled by magnetic thrust, they glided over the road, which was made of a single piece of stone so smooth you could see your reflection in it. Vibrant flowers adorned the roadsides, climbing around the doors and windows of the shops, spreading in a perfectly engineered fashion.

A car approached and flashed its lights blindingly before coming to a sudden stop. A beautiful, statuesque woman dressed in the latest fashions stepped out and walked over to where a young man with long hair and an earring stood waiting for her, exhausted. They laughed and embraced, love shining from their faces. They spoke fervently but he could not make out a single word they said. The car continued on its way, and a cool, pleasant scent woke him from his reverie.

He was startled by a sudden noise behind him. He turned to see a small girl who had fallen over. He moved to pick her up, but before he could reach her a robot swept her into its arms and stood silently, waiting for an old woman who was standing a little further behind, speaking with an illuminated figure. After the old woman folded up the hologram and put it in her pocket, the robot smiled and handed the girl to her, then walked alongside them.

The old woman was intrigued by the state of this innocent-looking man, by his clothes, his manners and the confusion written all over his face; he was clearly a stranger to these parts. Turning back, she went over to speak to him. But her soft, low voice cast a canopy of suspicion over his mind; he looked around with fear in his eyes and his only response was silence. In a ball of confusion, the old woman tumbled towards him.

'What is so terrifying that you are struck dumb? I just wanted to thank you,' she said.

'But I've done nothing worthy of thanks,' he replied.

His answer wrapped itself around the old woman's thoughts like a snake. Her eyes widened, she grabbed her granddaughter's hand and stepped back. 'Why are you angry? I just wanted to thank you.'

'I bear you no anger. I was simply trying to express my point of view.'

'But your voice is so loud!'

'And yours so very low – barely intelligible and suspicious.'

Once more, the old woman looked him over from head to foot. 'Your battledress is just like that of our forefathers from the last century,' she said. 'This is a face I have seen in many places before, perhaps even in pictures. The way you speak, your deep voice and your appearance are just like my grandfather. If you have no place to stay, there is a hostel for travellers and foreigners next to the Lovers' Statue. I can take you there if you like.'

His eyes were full of questions, but before he could ask any of them, the old woman continued, this time in barely more than a whisper: 'Fifty years ago, terrible suffering ransacked this country. Thousands were left without food, the trees withered, entire species perished, and the government could not keep up with the digging of graves and the burning of animals. This suffering lasted ten years; everyone witnessed the deaths of dozens of their dearest, had to close the eyes of their dead with their own hands. This tragic past and the images of death served as a warning for future generations; from then on, people's hearts were filled with mercy and compassion, the prisons stood empty, social discord evaporated, sinners confessed their sins, criminals their crimes, because after the–'

The woman's words were interrupted by the sound of uplifting music that suddenly filled his ears. The old woman and the robot looked up towards the sky, where a long car made of glass flew over their heads; they closed their eyes and began to pray. All the street lamps and shop lights went out, the only light came from inside the car. Through the glass could be seen dozens of electronic devices, and a few young women, like fairies in human form, gathered around a silver stretcher decorated with lace, colourful embroidery and photos of winged children.

'That woman is pregnant; they're on the way to the hospital. What you hear is the music of one life blossoming from another. Every medical condition has its own special music here,' the woman explained. 'Birth, poisoning, fever, depression... But I hadn't finished telling you the story of our soft voices. Illness took its fill of our loved ones, and it broke our hearts open, leaving us more honest, more attached to life, and more softly spoken. Year by year, this culture grew in us like a flower, and scattered its seeds among the generations that followed, and thus our voices are very soft. And this was also the reason–'

'It's late, it's late,' insisted the robot, then started walking away.

The old woman set off behind the robot at a brisk pace, before turning back to the man, 'You know, you are like a carbon copy of Qazî Muhammad. My uncle would always speak of him with great praise and often showed us pictures of him.'

'Well, I *am* Qa–' he began, but the distance between them had widened, and Qazî's sentence was left hanging in the air.

The shops, malls and markets built of glass left nothing unseen, everyone was visible and every person without exception wore a smile on their face, knowing that their lives were safe and secure.

A few steps on, he came to a large mall; inside, people reclined on rocking chairs, singing their dreams like lullabies with hands cupped over their ears. Their eyes were fixed on the glass ceiling above them, where scenes flashed by like a film. On the biggest pane, overlooking the road, was a screen showing an advert for a new novel, *The Land of the Atom*.

The Tabriz wind rustled the pages of Qazî's memory, triggering recollections of the bookshop Siruşt. Each time he was drawn back to this city, he would visit the shop, where he was befriended by dozens of books that still could not quench the thirst of his seven languages.

A hand shook his shoulder, a touch so slight he barely felt it, and two robots politely asked him to get into a car of black-tinted glass.

'Excuse us, but according to the information gathered from the mall's cameras, there seems to be a problem,' the robots began once the car had taken off. 'It appears you are a historical figure who died one hundred years ago. How is it possible that you are both alive and dead at the same time?'

'It's true, that's me, the person that you–'

'You have the right to remain silent until you have seen what's in your file.'

'Good. Then I will close my eyes until we get there. For one hundred years, my eyes have seen no sleep. It is all the fault of the Shah.'

The car stopped and the roof and side walls slid open, a glass staircase decked out with flowers hung from the sky. Qazî's head spun, afraid of falling. He summoned his courage and calmed himself: the annals of history would not remember him as a coward.

'Why are you walking the streets in the guise of an esteemed man of politics?' asked the white-haired judge from behind a one-legged table upon which sat an official-looking file. 'What is your purpose, sir?' With a nod of the judge's head, each of the robot-guards, who knelt on one knee like Samurai at his feet, withdrew and disappeared through the wall like rays of light.

'I have never worn another man's clothes,' replied Qazî. 'I am the Pêşewa, the Leader. I am Qazî, I am Muhammad. I am both alive and dead. But to explain it to you would be like a black rope, tightened once more around my neck.'

The judge stood up, revealing his tall stature; he threw himself into his arms and wept until Qazî's face grew wet with his tears.

'Even though I have never seen you before, my soul cried at the sight of you. Many photos of my grandfather and you, dressed in exactly these clothes, decorated our guest room. As soon as I saw you enter the room, I suspected it was you. I am the grandson of Hêmin,[1] your poet, the man who once wrote:

'The hand of oppression
At the end of the night
In Çar Çira Square
Sets up the scaffold of death.'

The judge's voice trembled. 'You smell of the history and tobacco of Mahabad. How is it that you are here, resurrected? I can no longer tell what is real.'

Overwhelmed by emotion, the judge sank down into the chair next to him. The family legends about the award ceremony at which Qazî had presented an honour to his grandfather, the great poet Hêmin Mukriyanî, came to him like fragments of a dream floating through his mind.

'I am both dead and alive and my story is both short and long. But, first, you tell me, what are you doing here?'

'After the rise of the Khomeini regime, my grandfather had reached the autumn of his life. Things were becoming harder and harder for those who were young and political; even the mildest court ruling against them could mean lifetime imprisonment,' the judge explained. 'And so we had to flee, as did my wife's family – she too shared many stories about you, to add to what we knew of you from those old photos. In the forty years that my grandfather lived after the Republic, he would regale our guests at any gathering with tales of the heroism of you and General Barzani.[2] He would say, "Our Pêşewa never surrendered to the enemy, but the collapse of the Azerbaijan People's Government,[3] and the betrayal of certain Kurdish tribes left him with no choice but to make this decision not to stand against the army of the Shah."

'It is true. Some Kurdish tribes turned against us,' responded Qazî. 'The Mangûr and Mamesh tribes were like woodworm, eating away at the trunk of the Kurds' tree; they collaborated with the central government against the Republic of Mahabad. And when Barzani had also surrounded Foc, which was about to wave the white flag, in the dark of night the Surchi tribe planted the dagger of treachery deep into the Kurds' back. Barzani had no choice but to withdraw to Mount Pires, and the next day the men of the Surchi, Barwarî Bala, Doski and Zibar tribes all attacked, forcing Barzani and his men to cross the Great Zab on rafts, which the tribes then burned, leaving no chance of return.'

'Our city is now a global example of progress, my Pêşewa. One of our neighbourhoods is entirely protected from the burning rays of the sun with an invisible shade, another is known as the neighbourhood of dreams, and another has become a hub of sentient robots who laugh, cry, and even write poetry. But the woodworm you spoke of continues to eat away at that trunk; and every day we open dozens of files of betrayal against Kurdish figures, leaders and organisations. The history of the Kurds has never changed its attire, and unpatriotic people appear at all times and in all places.

'You lost but one Kurdistan. Now, despite all of this progress, we lose a new Kurdistan every day, dashing the hopes of our people in the process. All of our leaders drink from the channels of an enemy, and flush away our rights without a thought. On top of that, 30 years ago, Kurdish soldiers in the Tammo and Azadî units made the fountains of our cities run cloudy, and sowed oppression on every street.'

'And what about Mîna Khanum...?' asked Qazî.

'Unfortunately, at the age of seventy, Mother Mîna was arrested and tortured, and after–'

'Did she surrender?'

'Never!'

To bring some relief to Qazî's suffering over Mahabad and Mîna, the judge, grandson of Hêmin, clicked a button and changed the colour of the room. On the walls appeared the snow-capped mountains of Qol Qolax, Xwezayî and Lendê Şêxan, as well as the different neighbourhoods of the city – Hecî

Hesen, and the Armenian and Jewish quarters. He turned off all the surveillance equipment and in his deep voice and villager's accent, asked Qazî to tell the story of his return.

'Yesterday, Mahabad lay drowsy, in total silence,' Qazî began. 'As I spoke my final words, the city drifted into sleep. I spilled the pages of my deeds at its feet like a handful of tears, my memories fell from the sky like raindrops, forming a lake in my mind, but the sun of truth dried it out. In the last moments, I bid farewell with my eyes to the minarets of the mosques, to the mulberry trees, to my first love and to the narrow streets. And when the rope of Mahabad kissed my throat, my soul rose upwards, like the leaves of a tree carried on the wind, a feather caught by the breeze; I saw the Iranian soldiers who, like spectres of the night, were scattered over the rooftops of Mahabad. On many of those rooftops, the Mahabad tobacco, which I once sold to buy arms for the Republic, was still spread out to dry in the sun. As I rose, my heart burst like a fireball over the streets of Mahabad, until I was little more than dust, like a lentil on a millstone. And when I saw my beloved, Mîna Khanum, pacing the courtyard below me, the veins to my heart were slit open. I knew she was unable to sleep, I was like a small child in my love for her, and I always–'

'But Pêşewa, you were in love!' the judge interrupted timidly. 'I mean, you had love in your heart!'

'I know what you mean. Mîna was my confidante – tall as the minaret of the Abbas Agha Mosque, her fingers more delicate than wax, she struck the hearts of young men like lightning, poetry flowed from her hair, nobody knew from which paradise this beauty had fallen. When I saw her that morning, my suffering came to an end and my soul passed through an opening in the sky to a place where it might one day unite with hers. There is no difference between the collapse of a republic and that of a heart.'

Qazî looked down at his ring and continued, 'After that, I

entered a long, dark, narrow passage, my heart was bursting, and I broke out in a sweat. But, at the end of the passage, a smiling angel was waiting for me and she wanted to help. "A day here," she explained, "lasts a hundred years of your earthly life. Upon your departure you were so preoccupied, so reluctant to abandon Mahabad that your arrival was late, so you will need to be patient. The Shah arrived before you did, and now he is facing his judgement. His sins are grave and he will not confess."

'I was shocked, my blood froze in my veins. The Shah had followed me even here.

'The kindly angel said to me, "I know you, you are Qazî Muhammad, the file we hold on you is clean. I want to help you; if you have any request, I will fulfil it."

'My head was still spinning through the dream of death, thoughts of Mîna and Mahabad. Not believing all this to be possible, I said instantly: "I want to return to the world below but with these new powers, I wish to know the situation of the city and of the Kurds."

'Upon this the angel replied, "I will send up your request and it is my hope that it will be accepted."

'I waited a long time for my request to be answered; no other thought or sensation occupied me until eventually I fell asleep. When I opened my eyes, I was descending through the skies, in the arms of the angel. On the way, the angel timidly told me that my request had been accepted and I had been granted permission to spend fifty years in Qamishlo.'

The next morning, the judge dressed Qazî in clothes equipped with hidden gadgets, and Qazî went down to the city of light under special protection.

In the graveyard, stood row upon row of black gravestones bearing red writing that gradually turned white, and upon which the names and pictures of martyrs appeared and disappeared in the same manner. A mother who was standing with her back to a faded gravestone was talking to herself.

Then suddenly the echoes of a martyr's voice filled Qazî's heart: 'Just as I was never listened to in my life, my family is not listened to in my death.'

'First tell me, why is your mother so sad?' Qazî asked the spirit.

'Because the anger of humankind is boiling over. My mother is sad because her wages are not enough to feed my children, because my two brothers have no work, and because my wife is ill.'

'But from what I can see, all the needs of life are met in this city.'

The martyr – his hands missing and half of his face gone – lifted his head and sat down next to his own grave. 'Don't believe them. My wounds were rubbed with salt and they still burn, my wife works from morning till night washing the clothes of the sentient robots, my brothers, penniless and out of work, help her, and my mother hands out roses to visitors to the city's rose garden.'

And then, to lift Qazî out of the wave of shame and unease, he smiled and said, 'I fought for twelve years in Til Hemis, Ash Shaddadi, Tell Tamer, Raqqa, and Deir ez-Zor. Bullets travelled through every part of my body, yet I was not killed. I lost an eye in an explosion in Kobane. At first, the soldiers and my commanders showed me great respect, but this dwindled day by day, and over time, Rizgar the Brave became Rizgo the Blind.'[4]

Reading Qazî's thoughts, Rizgo continued, 'I am all martyrs. I was caught in a volley of fire in the Sheikh Said Rebellion and in the Zilan Valley. I drowned in the Aegean in the Syrian civil war. I was burned alive in a refugee tent… In a forest on the road of the refugees, I was kidnapped and my organs were sold. In Serê Kaniyê, my mother took a stone from my grave and showed her support for me. In Mahabad I was hanged. I do not know where I was martyred. But after so much death, I carved the name of my son on the butt of my rifle, and hung it in pride of place in the guestroom.'

Qazî closed his eyes, thought for a moment, and pictured himself in front of the gates of a rose garden. Rizgo's mother, strands of her grey hair visible beneath her headscarf, handed him a rose. He wanted to offer her some comfort, but was too ashamed. He remembered the words of the Shah, who, in spite of all his cruelty, had said of Mîna Khanum, 'At the end of her life, take care of her.'

A girl in a short dress and a long-haired young man walked past; the girl took the flower that Rizgo's mother offered them, then tossed it behind her. Everyone they passed smiled in acknowledgement, but they barely gave anyone their attention in return.

Using a soft, low voice, as he had been advised to do by the judge, Qazî asked Rizgo's mother, 'Who are they? Why does everyone smile in fear at the sight of them?'

'There is no one in the city who doesn't know them. The boy is the son of Ismail the Devious and the girl the daughter of Imad the Cat. They say that 35 years ago, when the Rojava revolution began, many politicians and heads of parties that joined hands with the enemy sent their children away to distant countries. Once the revolution succeeded, their children returned with their fancy diplomas, having made a name for themselves and huge fortunes, while I became the mother of a nameless martyr, buried in an enormous graveyard... So it is with great pain that I return their smiles.'

She continued: 'Their fathers and grandfathers can't string two words of Kurdish together, have never joined a single demonstration, let alone fired a bullet or learned how to, in their entire lives. They couldn't separate two rams tangled in each other's horns if their lives depended on it. But they'd have you believe they were just like Qazî or Barzani! Qazî – whose oath was to the flag of Kurdistan, who for forty hours gave his statement in Kurdish in front of the military court for the cause of his nation. Or Barzani – who in his first battle, with seven revolutionaries, captured thirty officers at the police station of Xerzok.'

This time, in front of this old woman, Qazî's tears flowed freely and without shame. He wanted to kiss her hand, just as Barzani, weeping, had kissed all ten wounds of the revolutionary Khalil Khoshavi in the Russian hospital in Tabriz.

In the bookshop, Qazî found a familiar place of calm and peace. There was an electronic list of over a hundred thousand books but not one of them caught his attention. A young man, balding and wearing dark glasses, was sitting down, silent and motionless, a hand clasped against his chest. Qazî greeted him.

'My apologies, I was watching the novel *Mahabad Sold* in my glasses.'

'Mm hmm.'

'It's historical. It's about the republic of Mahabad and its collapse. I don't want to read novels, so I watch them,' said the young man.

Before Qazî could reply, the man continued. 'It says there was a wise general. He built a nation with the tobacco of Mahabad, but the Russians burned down the republic for a barrel of oil. The zeal of the Kurds had long been a thorn in their sides. But you know, Uncle, our situation is no better than that of the Mahabad of Qazî: we also had water, oil, agriculture, an army and a General, but our main ally abandoned us, our death warrant was signed, and in just a few days we performed funeral rites for three cities.'

'Indeed... The Kurdish cause contains thousands of knots, my son,' Qazî replied. 'If a thousand devils came together around one of those knots, they could not undo it. At that time, Sheikh Ahmed was in Barzan, Mahmud Hafid in Slemani, Ihsan Pasha in Agri, and Simko in Urmia; each was blinkered to their own cause, lending their ear to nobody else. And when the cause went up in flames, dreams as tall as the mountains of Kurdistan turned to ashes.'

'Yes, Uncle, isn't it the same here too? Can't you see with your own eyes? We have made such progress, we agree on almost everything. Yet still, for decades, dispute over the leadership has continued.'

Hearing this, Qazî's last hope died.

Turning his head to the sky, Qazî cried, 'My god, will the Shah's file never be closed? Will it ever be my turn to be judged?'

Notes

1. Hêmin Mukriyanî (1921–1986) was the national poet and secretary to the prime minister of the Republic of Mahabad, a self-declared Kurdish republic located in present-day Iran, of which Qazî Muhammad was president.

2. Mustafa Barzani (1903-1979) was a Kurdish military leader and leader of the Kurdistan Democratic Party (KDP). Following the collapse of Mahabad, he led fleeing Kurdish fighters through the mountains to the safe haven of soviet Azerbaijan.

3. The Azerbaijan People's Government was, like the Republic of Mahabad, a short-lived, unrecognised, secessionist state in northern Iran (Nov 1945-Dec 1946), centred around Tabriz, within northwestern Iran.

4. The name Rizgar literally translates as 'free,' while Rizgo is the diminutive.

The Snuffed-Out Candle

Jahangir Mahmoudveysi

*Translated from the Sorani
by Darya Najim & Khazan Jangiz*

'LEAVE IT, MY BOY, that's something else.'

'But Grandpa, what is all this dust sitting on these books?'

'I will tell you, but not yet; you're not ready.'

'Whether you like it or not, I have to know. I'm waiting for an answer. Tell me, what happened to you? Wait, where did you just go?'

He opened the small window, glanced at Mount Atashkadeh and sighed heavily. There was his grandfather, as he so often was, softly hoeing the soil under the pomegranate tree. The rays of the sun were calmly curled up around the branches of the tree. The red roses had given the garden a completely different hue.

'Grandpa Shoresh?'

'What is it, my son?'

'Look, I cleaned it up.'

'I told you to leave it alone, my son. Don't reopen my wounds.'

But Komar didn't listen. He stayed in the room and picked up the first volume of the book. Now, all of a sudden, he found himself in that Rebendan day.[1] There was no way out. He screamed for help but it was useless. The road ahead was a blur. The snow was swirling into his eyes and he couldn't see anything in front of him. His friends' situation was even worse. With every new footstep he came across the lifeless body of yet another comrade. To scream for help would be meaningless. Only patience and courage could help him now.

Komar found himself murmuring, 'I have to endure this. No, I won't do it. Even if I die, I will not eat the flesh of my friends.'

The hunger reminded him of the time he'd spent in prison during the reign of Reza Shah; that experience had left a bitter taste in his mouth. There had been no way out of the place. He was surrounded by locks and iron bars and the scorching heat of the sun made the metal sizzle. He would shout at the top of his lungs, but no one would answer. There were so many people in that place, including murderers. Every now and then the guards attacked and slaughtered prisoners. Their eyes would always turn red and blood would drip down their mouths. When he remembered all this, the winter cold felt easier.

'Oh my little Shoresh,[2] my one-year-old revolution, must you become an orphan? Who will raise you? Who will carry you piggyback on their shoulders and play games with you?

'Qazî, why did you do this to us? We left our lands, we were sure of victory. And then we got that monster, Reza Shah – where are you? Where did you come from? We planted basil but what we get are thorns.'

'Did you see, Alex, my comrade?

'All the places are being attacked. The dragons of Reza Shah are breathing their fire and whatever they come across, they burn to the ground.

'There is no way out of this nightmare, this mental agony. One by one, they are burning down all the houses in the village. The dismembered bodies of children, dogs, cats and birds are all mashed together. My own mother's hens and cockerels lie dead. Reza Shah's soldiers have let slip the sword of destruction and are feasting on their victory.

'The sky has turned red and Iran's four seasons have merged into one: the whiteness of snow, the green and yellow of summer and autumn leaves; the roses' red - they are all lost to us now.

'The rain has stopped falling and now blood pours down instead. I hear the clouds speak and listen to them in awe. "What have you done?" they boom. "What have you destroyed? Is this what humanity has come to? Even animals are above this! For how much longer is the world to be divided up like this, and the sun blocked out? The sun belongs to everyone, why are some people trying to block it out? We swear – as long as the world remains in this state – it will only be blood that we pour down!"

'The rain is lost to them. Love has been taken captive and, with the authorisation of the enemy, dragged all the way to Tehran. Everyone who remained was executed. Their bodies still hang in the qazwan trees.[3] Let's not hide from the fact: as Kurds, we couldn't be more proud of our trees, our mountains and this magical landscape. For years, we have shared our roads with the rest of nature, where else could we shelter? Every tree, every rock now has the photo of a martyr hanging from it; like the pendulum of a clock, tick-tock, for everyone to see.'

Komar was trembling with fear. A momentary opportunity presented itself and he bounded out of the room, shouting, 'Grandpa Shoresh, where are you?'

By this point, Komar looked like a ghost. He was shivering and you could hear his teeth chattering six houses away. All his shouting for Grandpa Shoresh had gone unanswered, and he had fallen asleep. If it had not been for that sleep, Komar would have died for real.

'Wake up, my boy,' a voice came. 'Why have you been screaming so much? What happened?'

'Who are you?'

All Komar heard were complaints. A voice screamed, 'Who are we?' A voice replied. 'How do you not know us?

'Have you never heard the name Dersim? Your name is 'Komar'?[4] Which republic are you? What about Halabja, Sinjar, Kobane, Afrin? Are none of these names familiar? We are the bones of those who were killed. Our assembly far outnumbers all other parties. There are so many of us, slaughtered, neither heaven nor hell can contain us. On the gates to each, a slogan has been daubed: *In accordance with your habit of wandering lost, justice dictates: you Kurds must wander forever.'*

'My dear friend, don't assume that we are the only ones. There are many more of us. Some of us are responsible for suffocating the rest of us. Let me spell it out for you. Some of us are children of the already powerful, living on in mansions and castles. The rest of us may as well go to hell. Those with power eat what they choose. Those without, are simply the ones *being* eaten.'

The skeleton continued, 'But now you are a stranger to us, your homeland has been freed. You have a Kurdistan. You are proud of it. A hundred years have passed, but for decades we shouted at the top of our lungs and never became whole. Each piece was taken captive by a different captor. Now, you're only a visitor who has found us caught between lost hours and a fatal nostalgia. Tell us, what is your country like? Is it as lost as ours?'

'I can't believe it,' Komar began. 'What are these people? What do all these skeletons mean? How many have you killed? What was the point? How sweet was the taste of power to have killed one another for it? I am ashamed for those of you who have been killed. I am ashamed for those you have killed.

'I, Komar, swear that I have never been, nor will ever be the accomplice to any killing,' Komar declared, 'Nothing is more valuable to me than freedom. I promise you, from now on, your new arrivals will not be as numerous as they have been. And when they come, they will make examples of you.'

'My friends, we who are but bones, do you see that even the future will not recognise us? We will remain strangers left to wander between four different worlds?'

'Komar, wake up. Wake up!' his mother shouted. 'My goodness, how deeply you sleep!'

'My beloved mother,' Komar muttered, 'hold my hand.'

'What is it, my boy, what's going on?' His mother was alarmed.

'My dear mama, this story breaks my heart. How did people live like that? Only ever knowing life in refuge. Only ever knowing death and slaughter; the poisoning of 5,000 people; 10,000 eyes; 10,000 hands; 10,000 feet – all gone in a heartbeat. In our world, even the locusts will be left in peace. You see what we have created here. As far as the eye can see, we have planted love; we have forbidden the sound of weapons; children live without a moment of pain. In this country, everyone moves freely, with no border to hinder their liberty. There are no border guards – how ridiculous they seem to us. The world belongs to everyone; the sun too, it belongs to all nature. No one goes in need. All rights are guaranteed.'

'Komar, come back! That room is too dingy. Look! The pomegranates are now fully grown. If we don't take them now, the winter cold will get them.'

'Mama, why are you talking about the winter cold? Winter cold! Our whole lives have been winter colds.'

'Hey listen up, tell your mother,' the book interjected. 'I have hidden myself away for years now, I have pretended not to know or care. I have coiled up in this corner, bent and twisted myself in this complicated house. My pages are endless. I'm like a cotton-cloud awaiting rain. I have become like the children of Sinjar, the sun's rays are burning me. My thirst is never quenched; I try licking rocks for water. I have become like the grandmother who put her head between the branches of an oak tree, only to hear the tree whisper: "Sweet mother, don't stay here. ISIS will come soon and burn us down like the other seventy-two times before. I have become like the guerrilla woman of Mount Qandil, whose lifeless body, in a nostalgic cry, spoke from the grave and said: "After I was killed, a group of honour-loving Kurdish men tore the collar of my shirt and ripped off my pants. One by one, they touched my dead breasts as they passed through, laughing. I knew every one of them.""

'Soran, Grandpa, hurry! Both of you,' the mother cried. 'I am losing Komar. His flame is flickering. What have you done? Why is our son coiled up like this? I told you it's your fault. It's his father's fault. That room! I told them to either lock its doors forever or demolish it!'

'My wife, what are you afraid of? I know the treatment for this. Allow me. If you can, bring me some candles. As long as there's a candle, the night will not be dark.'

'Komar, come out. The sky is clear. It is time for the birds to migrate. This country is not what it used to be. The deers and wild goats have come into the cities, unafraid that anyone will hunt them. There is no more traffic or smoke, the air is clear. There is no dirt like before. No one lives with the anxiety of unemployment, poverty, or an unpaid pension anymore. Equal rights are so guaranteed that freedom has become almost meaningless.

'Komar, my son, this is your father, I'm telling you to wake up. We would like you to be the one to light a hundred candles to celebrate your grandfather's birthday.'

Notes

1. The Kurdish month of Rebendan covers the last ten days of January and the first twenty days of February.
2. Shoresh, the boy's name also means 'revolution', which in the case of the Republic of Mahabad, lasted just under a year.
3. Qazwan, also *Pistacia atlantica*, is a species of pistachio tree, regarded by the Kurds, along with the oak, as one of their national trees. Coffee is also made from the qazwan tree.
4. 'Komar' means 'republic' in Kurdish.

Cleaners of the World

Hüseyin Karabey

Translated from the Turkish by Mustafa Gündoğdu

'THE TRUTH ISN'T AS simple as we'd like it to be. Everybody thinks we can choose our own truth, we can buy it.' She felt the serious expression on her face start to fade. She tried a smile instead but it didn't come out as naturally as she'd hoped. She started again: 'The truth isn't as simple as we'd like it to be...'

She was standing in front of the mirror, rehearsing the speech she was meant to deliver at today's meeting. At 45 years old, she still looked like she was in her 30s. 'You're not an emotional person,' people always told her, but today she needed to be. Somehow, everybody always took her to be calm and collected, perhaps even a little aloof. She never understood why they felt this, but for once she decided to try it their way, to be as they wanted her to be. There was a knock at the door and a brunette of similar age walked in.

'We have a problem, Greta.' Jiyan announced. 'We need to cancel everything.'

They had met nearly thirty years earlier during their school's 'Climate Strike' protests. Jiyan was fifteen at the time. She had offered her fellow protester a cookie and Greta had proceeded to stare at it for the longest time. Finally she took it. Greta's father, who had been watching her out of the corner of his eye, was astonished. Jiyan didn't understand the importance of what had just happened. And Greta didn't notice her father holding back the tears as she bit into the cookie. It would be a long time before either of them understood the real gravity of that moment. The cookie offered by Jiyan was the first morsel of food Greta had ever eaten outside of her home. After that, the two were inseparable. And many years later, their fates would entwine even further – not because of climate change or the global pandemic of 2020-21; not because of the endless atmospheric disasters triggered by the wildfires in Australia. What changed their destinies the second time, and bound them even closer, was a wave of racist attacks that began suddenly and swept through Europe in 2025. She remembered it like yesterday, the day Greta asked for help in return:

'Could they reach us if we went to Kurdistan?'

Jiyan didn't immediately understand the question. 'Who?'

'Those who don't want either of us here.'

She never wanted to come to Sweden. She didn't even want to carry on living after what she'd been through. At only twelve years old, her family and 50,000 others had to escape to the highest mountain in Shingal - one she had always seen from her family's orchard - following the ISIS attack of August 2015. Having long hair was precious to her, but her father insisted on shaving her head almost bald, and dressing her as a boy just in case. They had heard that women and girls left behind were forced to become sex slaves. No news came about her newly-married older sister and aunties, and when her father and three brothers went back to rescue them, she never saw them again. The rest of the family did their best to survive without them. The kids had to grow up overnight; no one ever played with their toys again. They stayed on that mountain for three months. ISIS surrounded the mountain and blockaded it, to starve those sheltering on it to death. The elderly and infants died first. The rest struggled to hold on. She tasted almost every type of weed growing on that mountainside and grew to know which ones made you sick and which sustained you for a while. She survived. When women guerrillas came to their rescue, they walked with them for fifteen days before they reached the border.

This time it was easier; they had food. As for their rescuers, they would never forget them. Once, Jiyan was caught staring at one of their guns. The guerrilla, whose name was Rosa, handed it to her, but Jiyan couldn't bring herself to take it. She had seen too many people torn apart by the fire that came out of barrels like that. In that moment, she vowed never to touch a gun. They were just cold lumps of metal that brought death. She had seen enough of that. Sensing the girl's apprehension, Rosa bent down and stroked Jiyan's hair. One day, she told her, if she ever got bored of life, she could come back to the mountains and live with them, and never have to touch a gun if she didn't want to. She would be free in the mountains, she told her.

Soon after, they became separated from Rosa and the other guerrillas. First, they were moved to Erbil with the remainder of their families and one injured guerrilla. Then, they were sent to Sweden. On the plane to Sweden, Jiyan held the hand of Sozdar, the injured guerrilla who'd lost a leg to a landmine, for the entire flight. This was their first time on a plane; they were nervous.

On their arrival, snow and cold greeted them. In this strange, unfamiliar country, they made their little home, and for a long time Jiyan refused to go outside. Eventually, she started to venture out, going to school where she didn't understand a word that was said. Everyone at school was nice to her, but the look in their eyes made her feel she didn't really belong. Then, on the day she met Greta, something strange happened. Greta looked at her differently. In fact, she could barely look at Jiyan at all. It was like (not quite) looking in the mirror. From then on, they felt very close to each other, though they never spoke. Greta was refusing to speak generally, at the time, and Jiyan couldn't talk even if she wanted to. No one heard a word from Jiyan's lips until she had fully mastered the Swedish language. Then, one day she saw a banner in Greta's hand and, with perfect pronunciation, she asked:

'Where do you go every Friday?'

Her schoolmates were stunned, but Greta was not surprised. She looked at Jiyan. 'To save our future,' she said. 'Would you like to come?'

Friends and teachers listened in astonishment at the dialogue between these two silent girls. Since that day, both Greta and Jiyan held sit-in protests in front of the Swedish parliament, becoming figureheads of the Extinction Rebellion Movement without even knowing it.

Sitting in protest in front of the Swedish parliament with a banner in her hand, Jiyan felt good. She loved the solitude, and in those early days, theirs was a meaningful loneliness. No one understood what they were doing. But as more and more children joined them, people started following them in the news and online to understand what was happening.

Greta's brain worked differently to others. Nothing she experienced or noticed went unprocessed. Everything is black and white, she explained, when you have Asperger's syndrome, especially when it comes to existential matters. There was never the slightest contradiction between what she said and what she did. She has never told a single lie in her life. In fact, it took her years to comprehend what lying was. She only spoke when absolutely necessary, and when she did, it was only to her mother, father, or sister. But when the Extinction Rebellion began, she had to talk a lot more.

She never liked talking. According to her, humanity invented speech to further the purpose of lying. That's why she preferred to talk less and do more. But people always wanted her to talk. No one knew how she did it, but she always gave the shortest, most effective speeches.

The climate movement, which won huge support around the globe in the space of just a few years, became an open target. Those who'd grown rich from oil wouldn't give up their gains so easily. They would eliminate anyone who tried to thwart them. Even though these were white kids, from well-educated, comfortable backgrounds, they wouldn't hesitate to use any form of violence or propaganda against them. Just like all those dark-haired non-Christians who migrated to Europe centuries ago became the first targets, Jiyan was dark-haired and Yazidi…

'Do you think there is a connection between what happened to you in Shingal and global warming?' Greta asked Jiyan one day.

It made Jiyan think, in a way she'd never thought before. She didn't want to remember anything about her past, before she came to Sweden, but in her dreams she couldn't escape that reality so easily. She never stopped seeing those mountains. Never stopped tasting the weeds she ate to survive. Sozdar, the injured guerrilla whose hand she held, told her about the mountains the whole journey back. As she talked of Mount Gabar, Cudi, Metina, and the mountain ranges of Zagros, Taurus and, of course, Qandil, the soldier smiled through her tears. Jiyan would never forget the look on Sozdar's face as she spoke. As she peered through the tiny window at the Alps below, Jiyan asked her: 'Why has this happened to us?'

Not knowing how to answer this question distressed Sozdar, so instead of trying to, she simply squeezed Jiyan's hand tightly. Then she whispered: 'I don't know.'

Jiyan didn't know either. These questions had no answers.

Nor could she answer Greta's question that day about how their stories were connected. Instead they stared at each other for a moment. Jiyan was the first to look away. Greta's question had forced her to think about her past for the first time in five years. They were now seventeen.

Jiyan walked in and looked at Greta who was still rehearsing her speech in front of the mirror. Instinctively, she fixed the collar of Greta's dress and smoothed her hair.

'It turns out our nano-drones can be spotted and disabled,' Jiyan said. Greta remained calm.

Arriving at this day had not been easy. Thirty years they had been together, many of them in the mountains of Kurdistan, taking refuge after the brutal attacks on climate protestors and the lynching of refugees that followed. They never stayed in one place very long.

The local movements that had taken care of them when they first arrived were convinced that their paths to freedom were one and the same. Internal debates within the climate movement and the relentless efforts to destroy them led to the formation of a new structure, based on Eco-Marxist resistance units.

For the last five years, they had been preparing for this moment: organised as an independent confederation, they would make one last strike, one Final Rebellion. The speech that Greta was about to make would be hacked into every TV and internet channel across the world, and broadcast live. When she finished it, Greta would press a button and the greatest battle would begin.

They walked into the communication room where the executive council of the Final Rebellion was about to convene. The council consisted of twenty temporary members and five permanent ones. Actions, like the forthcoming attack, were all decided by them. Below this council, sat an assembly of local government representatives. This consisted of spokespersons selected from resistance units around the world. There was no fixed size for this assembly but for the last two years it had boasted around 2,000 councillors. In fact, this assembly represented the engine house of the whole movement, the heart of its power. It answered to a further 30 million members around the world. Its work was simple. All they did to change the world was gather knowledge and develop new actions in the light of it. Today's meeting was taking place on the eve of the great action. You could tell it was a special occasion: everyone had their quantum devices with them. These were impossible to wiretap, or track locationally. A young member of the movement, whose father was a director of the Indian space centre, had invented the device. He had wanted to follow in his father's footsteps but for proposing the development of this device to his fellow researchers at the Quantum Communication group at Beijing University's Technopark, he had been expelled. Little did they know he already had a working prototype and plans for production ready to go when they threw him out. The first versions of the device had come out ten years ago. They were now onto the fifth generation of them and no one else could keep up. Jiyan set the device to the latest agreed frequency. Other attendees had already started to crowd into the twenty-five small screens arrayed across the traditional intercom system before them. Greta and Jiyan sat down next to each other and waited for the meeting to begin. Greta clutched at her necklace, reminding Jiyan of Greta's father, whose photo was clasped inside.

Greta's father had asked Jiyan to promise that she would never leave his daughter's side. Anyone who paid any attention to Greta would quickly see she didn't need anyone else. But in her father's eyes, she would always be just a child, someone who needed protection, even if she was now co-chair of the Final Rebellion Movement, with millions of people around the world hanging on her every word. At first, her father didn't want her to come to Kurdistan with Jiyan, but it was impossible to ignore the personal danger she faced in Sweden. He knew that she would never give up the cause, so he wanted Jiyan to be next to her.

They reached Kurdistan after many weeks of travelling. Kurdistan was not yet a country, merely a geographic concept. It was still divided into four pieces. The arms manufacturers and energy conglomerates didn't want a nation of 30 million people to be suddenly united. Stability was the last thing they wanted in this region. The energy resources buried beneath this landscape was a curse on it, rather than a blessing. And it didn't look like they would run out any time soon. Neither an independent Palestine, nor a free Kurdistan, nor a federation of Mesopotamia standing on its own two feet were desirable. All they wanted for the region was a perpetual state of medium-sized wars – with wars, they could test out their new weapons, deploy artificial 'crisis methods' to manipulate the oil price, and most importantly, block the mass migrations from Asia and Africa into Europe by land that followed the great Famine Rebellions.

That's why the Kurds have never been able to create an independent country, even though they've been allowed to form semi-autonomous territories within the four countries that occupy them. The model for the international solidarity movement and collective government that emerged in Rojava during the Syrian Civil War continued to survive in dozens of isolated pockets across the four countries, usually in hard-to-reach mountainous areas. These territories, which were defended collectively, became not only safe havens for freedom fighters but also for minorities marginalised by the system, refugees and climate activists who felt their lives were now in danger. The Europeans who didn't want to be part of the second wave of 'democratic fascism' in Europe had escaped and sought refuge here as well. Greta and Jiyan had come to these mountains with another 35 senior members of the climate movement. The Collective Administration had listened to their demands and agreed to provide all the support they needed. They were also promised protection. In return, Greta, Jiyan and their colleagues shared their knowledge and skills with the guardians of the Collective Administration. Among the activists, a new generation of hackers brought with them mobile emitters that could detect and shut down all kinds of military drone activity. However advanced drone technology had become, with surveillance vehicles now being as small as large bumblebees, the hackers could always spot them from the formations they flew in – suspiciously well-spaced, symmetrical and regimented. They never moved like the insects they pretended to be. This detection allowed them to create a fragile no-fly zone, free from the surveillance drones, although they were still subject to the occasional fly-by by manned fighter jets.

Such partnerships between the Collective Administration and the tech-savvy climate activists allowed a better understanding between them to grow. The eco-Marxist movement never gave itself a particular name, the way it never needed a single leader. No side demanded any compromise from the other. Everybody continued to work in the areas where their expertise lay. They answered to the Local Representative Assembly which oversaw the movement's coordination. Now, the most important organ of this assembly, the executive council, was about to start a historic meeting. After all the connections were established, voices started to rise from holographic screens around the room. The computer coordinating the meeting pinged. It was time to start.

Yewande, the eldest member of the African delegation, opened the meeting. He was fifty years old and had cut his teeth in grassroots Nigerian struggles against the big oil companies. Yewande had lost his mother to complications in labour, which was where his name came from: it meant 'Mummy has returned'. Yewande presented to the council an update from the team that was going to conduct the attack.

It had become obvious their planned drone attack on the refineries wouldn't work. Greta was not angry but determined.

'Let's activate Plan B then,' she told the other attendees.

Jiyan stared at Greta in surprise. She hadn't even known there was a Plan B. In fact, only three of the 25 present knew anything about it.

Three months earlier, a video had been sent to the CEOs of all the main oil conglomerates as well as all major news media outlets. In it, they issued a brief warning: if oil production didn't stop immediately and unconditionally, they would render all the world's reserves immediately unusable. This was a reality, not a threat. In the same video, they showed how it had been them that had made the stockpile of crude oil in Kirkuk unusable, the previous month. In microscopic close-up, the video showed 'bacto-bots', cyanobacteria synthetically engineered by the activists from naturally-occurring oil-eating bacteria, rendering the oil they swam though unusable. As the efficiency rate of the contaminated reserves fell, the oil ceased to be suitable for processing whilst simultaneously reducing the carbon in the atmosphere around it, as it lay unused – thanks to the photosynthesis of the cyanobacteria. The most exciting part was that these 'bacto-bots' worked so quickly that once contaminated, any reserve, no matter how large, became useless within twenty-four hours.

Jiyan had always assumed that the last throw of the dice would be the deployment of these 'bacto-bots' through their own fleet of nanodrones but she had no idea what Greta intended now. Similar grumblings began to ripple round the meeting. What was this Plan B? And why had they not been consulted till now? The questions poured in…

Jiyan looked at Greta curiously, waiting for an explanation. Greta, with her usual calm, began to explain herself.

'Dear Members, as you know, following a discussion and vote by the council, I was given permission by the council to select five members of our science committee to devise the whole plan in secrecy. I realised then that not having a back-up was itself a weakness and might undermine the whole movement. I made a prediction: that our first plan wouldn't work. Now I know how accurate this prediction was.'

The computer suddenly pinged several times indicating a barrage of questions coming in from the other participants. The question requests appeared on a list on the screen, in order. There were twenty in total. Greta smiled to herself, privately guessing what the questions would be.

'Yes, you're right. Let me explain.'

It all began twenty years ago, back when they had no such methods of resistance in mind. They would be out on the streets every day, somewhere in the world, but all they really had at their disposal was silence; sit-ins. But even in silence, they couldn't be stopped from multiplying, rapidly.

These children – who swore to keep fighting until real change took place – were regarded by many governments as a global threat. They needed to be silenced as quickly as possible, but everything was so difficult, with kids. For once, they genuinely posed a new kind of threat. Many of them were the establishment's own children!

How could they brandish their own children 'terrorists' simply for pointing out that the world is going through its sixth mass extinction event? First, the protesters were met by media silence (after initially securing widespread coverage). Then, not to be thwarted, they took to social media and other online platforms, only to be blocked by them in turn. After that, they developed a completely new form of communication, using low voltage, hard-to-trace signals through the existing electricity supply, and organised through that.

Declaring Fridays (when most Climate Strikes took place) 'a working-from-home day' failed to deflate the movement. And when the ash from the annual wildfires sweeping across Australia and California began to fall as acid rain on Europe, parents stopped sending their children to school altogether. But even this fragmentation of the youth didn't stop the movement from growing stronger.

But the thing that really put a target on their back was different. It transpired that recently discovered fossil fuel reserves would keep the industry going for at least another century, much longer than previously expected. In order to extract these new resources at reasonable costs, the oil corporations, in partnership with world governments, consciously planned for global temperature increases in the hope of controlling the response. The activists exposed these plans, and no one could forget how sick they felt when they saw the lengths to which these plans went. The energy sector had set everything in motion already: the North and South Poles would be divided up between the world's largest governments, and then managed by them exclusively.

The first set of leaked documents came from Arundati who was only sixteen when she discovered them. She was born in Boston, though her parents were from India; they had met at Harvard as students, and decided to get married despite their families back home being from different castes. They were two of the sharpest brains in India but they knew they would never be able to move back there. Perhaps for this reason they took their daughter's name from a star found seventy-two light years away from home. 'Arundati' also meant 'unstoppable', 'unpreventable'.

Arundati had been involved in the climate movement for the last three years. At first, her parents had regarded her activities as perfectly innocent and legitimate, but then one day she turned to her father and said:

'You are one of them, aren't you, Dad?'

Her father didn't answer, but from then on he tried in vain to stop Arundati from participating in the movement. Nothing could stop her though. Day by day her doubts about her father grew. After all, he was the chief engineer of one of the largest oil companies at the time. The set of documents she chanced upon on her father's computer proved to be the beginning of the radicalisation of the entire movement.

The documents related to the unexpected discovery of vast new oil fields. These reserves, which were currently too expensive to extract, had been found beneath the two poles and those parts of the continental shelf that had sunk deep beneath the oceans millions of years ago. At the end of one of the documents was a solution to two of the reserves' cost problems. The reason why the North and South poles were so expensive to drill was the challenge of drilling through permafrost, and the cost of keeping the crude oil from freezing. But if global temperatures could be allowed to increase, through greenhouse gas emissions, the problem of the permafrost and sub-zero temperatures could be eliminated. In short, global warming was no longer an accident but the result of a deliberate continued intervention, the main aim of which was to melt glaciers. The oil and natural gas deposits in these areas made up three quarters of the entire planet's reserves. The only thing standing in the way of affordable extraction were the glaciers.

The document leak triggered a huge debate within the movement. At first, activists could barely believe it, but then other teenagers whose parents occupied important positions started to leak similar evidence.

They now saw that they would soon be caught up in the most unimaginable horrors: flooding, forest fires, extreme weather events, ruined harvests and the inevitable collapse of social order.

Some agreed with Jiyan and Greta that the movement should be prepared to do anything to stop it, but many others couldn't bring themselves to endorse any act of violence, even bloodless violence, as it went against the philosophy of the entire movement. No one *wanted* violence, of course. The oldest member of the group was just twenty-three and their numbers were growing fast. Before long, they started to influence consumer habits. There were even rumours that a handful of airline companies had gone bust because of the pressure young people had put on their parents not to use planes. But none of this was enough. If climate change was to be halted, altogether different measures needed to be taken against the conglomerates.

As their tactics grew more radical, disrupting major sporting events, blocking motorways and supply chains, defacing artworks, they opened themselves up to first verbal and then physical attacks. Despite the daily escalation of violence towards them, they knew that if they ever responded in kind, they would instantly be labelled a terrorist organisation. They abhorred violence, and talked at length among themselves about whether violence against violence ever worked. They even initiated discussions on what violence was. They all agreed on the following definition:

'Violence is any kind of action or attitude that results in (or is likely to result in) the causing of hurt or injury to another living creature; it includes threats, coercion and any action that results in the arbitrary deprivation of freedom. Violence can take place in personal or public space.'

This definition of violence included many of the actions taken against them. Thus, they vowed not to commit any act against others (even those they saw as their enemies) that they wouldn't wish to be committed against them. It was against their nature; their enemies were well versed in the language of violence, but to them it was anathema. The generation of 1968 had made this mistake before them. The same mistake was expected of this movement now. At first, the students of '68 who had taken to the streets demanding greater equality and freedom made a great impact. The authorities at the time couldn't find a way to deal with such peaceful demonstrations. All they knew was that somehow they needed to make the youth speak the language of violence, and eventually they succeeded. Every movement since has been met with violence and been forced to talk its language, whether it began peacefully or otherwise, until walls of fear built up in the eyes of the general public. The cycle has never been broken.

All they had to do was stick to what they knew best. Their actions would continue to be non-violent ones, armed only with knowledge. They would target the lifeblood of the system, rather than spill the blood of humans. But they would be prepared for the worst. And to make those preparations they had to leave Europe. Chaos was going to hit Europe first. That's why Greta asked Jiyan about the far-flung mountains of Kurdistan. Their initial destination wouldn't be too remote. But in the end, they had to leave sooner than expected, in a small party made up of Jiyan, Greta, the wounded guerrilla Sozdar and around thirty others from various countries.

Jiyan hadn't been separated from Greta since the day they left. And now she sat beside her, eagerly waiting her explanation.

'We devised a Plan B, and in fact we've already started to implement it. Only the five permanent members of this council knew any of the details.'

Jiyan was transfixed. How had Greta managed to devise all this under her nose without her knowing? Greta continued to talk calmly.

'In our reckoning, human beings are creatures as fond of

selfishness as they are of sharing, as capable of cruelty as they are of mercy, as likely to enslave others as they are to respect their freedom. They host all of these tendencies. They cannot relinquish the idea of the self even at the cost of extinction. And as you can see, we are not the only ones who have clung onto their beliefs and their existence. I am sure our enemies won't give up either. That's why I decided we shouldn't leave them any choice. Our original plan – to hit the refineries, of which there are a relatively small number around the world, with our fleet of nanodrones – was always a decoy, a distraction to draw fire and attention from the real attack. The real plan, Plan B, was to use a new kind of drone, developed in secret by our team; one that studies and learns from the flight patterns of nature's own insects, and even flies with organic insect swarms for cover. Rather than the refineries, where the full might of the oil corps' military defences will be waiting for us, these hive-drones will target rigs – on and off shore, fracking rigs, drill ships – as well as pipeline terminals, of which there are many thousands. These hive-drones will also be accompanied by a fleet of nano-ants, earth-working drones capable of also perforating rock and even steel. The technology had already been developed in private by the oil corps, for repair work.'

Greta paused to take a sip of water and smile. 'We merely borrowed and tweaked it; they dig their way in, and then seal up the hole after them. Nano-ants are capable of excavating through five metres of soil, or 5mm of steel, a day. We only needed four weeks for them to dig their way from the perimeters of these sites to the central pipelines. Three months ago, when we sent out our video warning, that wasn't the only thing we delivered. We also sent this two-fold swarm, hive-drones and ant-drones, millions of them, complete with their bacto-bot payloads, to over 1000 rigs and pipeline terminals around the world.'

Greta's explanation was accompanied by a perfectly animated illustration of the plan that kept everyone spellbound. She wasn't finished but she needed to catch her breath, and the meeting computer sensed this and allowed for one short question. Yewande's question was indeed short.

'Are you telling us all these reserves have been contaminated already?'

'Yes,' Greta responded.

'So there is no button to press anymore?'

'No' Greta said.

'Why are we even here, then?' Yewande asked. 'You've acted without us.'

Greta had no answer to this yet, but Jiyan could see a tentative smile on her face. A heavy silence hung over the room.

Yewande repeated: 'Why are we gathered? What do you expect from us?'

'You're right, there is nothing much left to do. I thought maybe we could celebrate the first step of our victory after thirty years of struggle.'

There was silence. Everyone seemed to be frozen and just stared at each other. Yewande was the first to break the silence, raising her fist she shouted the Kurdish word that had become the council's battle-cry: 'Azadî!'. At this, everybody turned their screen mode to 'flashing' to show their joy. The room was suddenly filled with a dance of colours, a soundtrack kicked in, played by the meeting computer; people started to break off into holographic pairs and conversation spread. Greta reached for her necklace and looked at Jiyan. This time their eyes locked. Jiyan couldn't help herself and threw her arms around her.

Perhaps this raucous jubilation, this cacophony of relief would have gone on for much longer, if the meeting computer hadn't immediately sounded a shrill alarm. The central computer cut all other audio to inform each of them in a grave tone that the meeting had to be terminated, and that everyone had three minutes to reach their bunkers: a drone attack had been detected.

No one panicked. Their meeting hadn't been hacked, but there was a limit to how long they could use their quantum devices before their locations were detected. Once again, a council meeting would end with everyone making their way to a secret bunker: where no doubt they would have to hide for many days. After all, this wasn't the first drone attack they'd faced, nor would it be the last, in the chaos that would follow.

Rising Like Water

Ömer Dilsoz

Translated from the Kurmanji
by Rojin Shekh-Hamo

When she reached the top of the hill, she didn't hesitate to take the road that led to the mountains. Neither the path to the coast, nor the path to the plains appealed to her. Her legs propelled her up and up the mountain road. No doubt, there was something inside her that had made the decision long ago: her path was upwards.

Coming to a great, ancient walnut tree, at the edge of a clear spring, she stopped, exhausted. She needed to take a sip and have a rest.

He let out a sigh. All four of his friends were listening, eager for the story to unfold. One of them said, 'So? What happened next?' Another said, 'I'm genuinely curious: where is this dream going?' A third added, 'Seriously! What is this about?' The fourth complained, 'Have we come here to listen to stories?!'

Zanyar murmured phrases to himself: 'experience' and 'proof besides'... but his voice didn't reach his friends. He was gritting his teeth so hard, he nearly choked on his words, so tried to rearrange them slowly again on his tongue. He was in mind to finish the story, but then he said nothing at all. Instead, he simply clutched his right wrist and scratched it. As if to say: here is my wordless proof.

For ten uneventful years, this handful of friends had been on a long journey together to reach this destination: Bêstûn, 'the columnless, bottomless cave'.

For the last few days, they had been camping in the gorges and canyons around the Spilk mountain ridge, until eventually the signs and traces they followed led them to their destination. The leader of their group was Zanyar. It was he who had first proposed the idea to visit Bêstûn, years before, on social media, to conduct some research on it.

Eventually four like-minded researchers had answered Zanyar's call, all with their own interest in the cave.

There, at the entrance to the cave, they sat putting the world to rights. One word followed another, and from questions of homeland, freedom, war and faith, they eventually moved to mythological and eschatological issues. But while they rattled through these topics, one question had them stumped: the future. What future world could they imagine for their people; what would it look like? For them, the aspirations of history clashed against the reality of life, and got stuck there. Neither the prophecies of the fortune tellers, nor the predictions of the best academics could offer a plain and a straightforward path to what reality had in store for them. Reality was like the Bêstûn cave itself, solid but bottomless.

They argued, they talked, they offered feedback on each other's theories. One said, 'A war between the solar systems will start soon. Distant aliens must have been observing our behaviour for decades and soon they will reveal themselves to us.' Another replied, 'What nonsense! The truth is simple. We all live up to a certain age, and then we leave this world. That's all there is to it. A third disagreed, 'No, I believe there must be some meaning behind it all. Our ancestors sacrificed so much for so many years, it's no exaggeration to say they've watered every inch of this land with their blood. What's the matter with you? The fact of the matter is we, as Kurds, were born in the battlefield of existence but at the end of it all, there must be...' he swallowed his words and fell silent. He couldn't find the right words for the current situation.

Zanyar drew the conversation to a close: 'I think we have all been flattened by our history. For how many centuries have great wars and massacres befallen us, as a people? How many homes have been ravaged? How many children have been sacrificed? Fathers have buried sons. Mothers have planted memorial trees on their daughters' graves, adorning them with bridal gowns and jewellery designed for other uses. This world didn't allow us to cast our grains in the open air... instead other nations have cracked their walnuts on our hearts, then passed the kernel out among themselves.'

'It's true,' his colleague chipped in. 'They've torn us apart.'

The word 'torn' silenced everyone. So Zanyar added a note of optimism to the proceedings: 'Anyway, it's been ten years... and there's been no war. No movement. Perhaps the spirit of resistance has gone. Everyone is quiet. Each stands still beside the next as if time itself has stopped.'

The heavily-moustached colleague, who gave the impression of being as wise as he was old, said, 'If you want the truth, I see it like this... everything has stopped. The future has been cancelled. When society doesn't go through instabilities and upheavals, progress doesn't take place either. My point is... what I mean to say...' He tried to change the way he was talking. 'How much progress has any nation made in the past few years?'

'Your aim is *progress*?' Zanyar's question brought the tone down again for a moment.

'What I mean is... it's been a decade and a half now, and what has improved in real terms, in the fields of science or technology? Has there really been anything *that* new?'

Nobody spoke. The colleague concluded his point, 'I mean... pay attention to this. Once every six months or so, you notice some new device is released into the market, promising to be yet another 'game-changer'. But if you really look it, all they offer are new developments on old features that have been available for decades, reinforcing the status quo. We're the same, as human beings, we've also stopped improving – in our functions or rationality; we just reinforce the status quo. We need a new impulse to reinvigorate us, to make us jump, out of necessity, to a new level. Like a new energy intake... maybe...'

'*Maybe!!*'... this felt like a new word for Zanyar. His questioning use of it left his four friends on the edge of their seats, as if they all asked, 'Go on?' 'You're right,' Zanyar said eventually. 'I respect your opinion. What you're saying is true. It's been ten years, not only here, but everywhere; the world seems to be in stalemate. Perhaps we have indeed reached a plateau and stayed there; the end of history. For there are only finite resources at hand to take advantage of... but no, no, I don't like this notion of *progress* being like *growth*, that we must expand all the time, and profit more and more from everything – otherwise it's of no benefit to us. In that reckoning, the last ten years have not been a standstill but a decline... I prefer to see these ten years as a time of preparedness for a new stage, a new epoch... you're right, we do need a new word.'

Their female comrade echoed Zanyar's thoughts, 'Exactly. The words we use also shape the sides and aspects of the society we live in. It's better for us to stick to new words.'

The heavily-moustached comrade said, 'For example, from now on we can stop talking about "leaders."'

As if to say, *What the hell was that?* all eyes stared at his mouth. They awaited an explanation. Then he started with a simple phrase: 'A Mission. That's what is needed. The Torah told the Jews, "You are the chosen ones. God has made a covenant with you." With this power, the Jews were set free.

Despite everything that beset them, they remained strong and defiant. They drew strength from the covenant that had been made with them, and never gave up. Likewise, Isa… Jesus was crucified, but not before he set a new covenant with his people: "the Truth will set you free", which so empowered his followers they rose and never fell.

'Ultimately, my mission is… to tell you… that all the years we spent saying, "If we only had a great leader too" and all the time we wasted waiting for that person, we threw hope behind the bars of history. And it remained behind those bars for so long because of that one "if". It wouldn't work with "if"s. We should have changed the words we used. We should have said, "From us, a great leader has indeed risen" … or rather, "From us they rise, great leaders, flowing, cascading, intensifying wave after wave… like water."'

Zanyar again clutched his right wrist and scratched it a little. As if to say, 'My evidence!' then replied to his friend with a laugh, 'You can put me down for the next six years.'

The eyes of his four friends remained on his mouth. They were curious as to why Zanyar would be so specific. Why six years? The screens all showed the year was 2040. Silence had prevailed over Kurdistan for a decade. That day, and for the next six years, Zanyar and his friends worked to create a new movement inspired by the cave of Bêstûn. 'We need a new vocabulary, a new expression, a new way of thinking, a new aesthetic, a new word,' and they said, 'We are the leaders, the favoured ones! We have a mind and a purpose!'

Then they got up! Like prophets who had just received a holy revelation from their god. They set out with a keen and severe diligence into the crowds to spread their cause. They became like water and flowed. They became waves, then rippled. They turned into all the forms. They suited every manner and shape. But most like water, softly and sympathetically they advanced.

Organising through social media platforms, they adopted a mantra, 'From us they rise, great leaders flowing like water, intensifying wave after wave.'

This new configuration of words spread swiftly because they were also represented in actions. They reached out to expert scholars and made a pledge to worship only knowledge and science. They built a laboratory, established a university, and in the name of research in the pursuit of a new kind of power, they worked around the clock.

First Zanyar and his four friends threw themselves into studying the mindset and memory of their homeland. They interrogated every word and every understanding of this land. They questioned everything, from first principles. They delved into the roots of the roots.

They built on the latest cutting-edge research, drawing in scholars and experts, from every discipline. They spread their knowledge on the threshing floor of their collective brain. Every detail was important to them. Then they became water, and turned into every shape and form.

It was their most significant project: to harness the full potential of solar power and free the world of mining, drilling, fossil fuels, and other 'legacy' energy sources. They believed that, by harnessing the sun's energy, they could create a whole new world. According to their ideology: travel from one place to another should only be allowed with the use of solar power. Their sights were set firmly on this new world.

Zanyar and his friends started to go to football matches to spread their ideas among the different factions of the fans. In student societies, in worker associations and in trade unions … they had eyes everywhere.

Their demand was humble. They said, 'Listen to us. Let your eyes be on us too. Tomorrow, we will take a big step forward for the world of science. Just as, not so long ago, a scientist named Nikola Tesla wanted to control lightning to provide the world with energy, we too want to shine a new light on humanity, with the energy of the sun. After all, our country is one of the sunniest spots on the planet. Enough already of fossil fuels! These belching factories and nuclear plants have made our lives hell, made our planet rotten.'

Many people quietly ridiculed the rise of this movement. They became the target of both comedians and politicians. They underestimated them.

They were prepared for this, however. They didn't care if others dismissed them. They were busy with their work. By now, they had convinced themselves they were the 'favoured ones' and that their invention would be developed by their own hands. Their minds would take them forward. There was no time for 'ifs' and 'maybes' anymore. They had taken a certain path and even if they failed a thousand times, they would rise again and try a thousand and one more times.

Now there was just one question: how could they use solar power more efficiently? Obviously, solar power institutions already existed all around the world. In fact, whole cities were already entirely dependent on solar power. Many vehicles and airplanes were powered by solar power. This idea had been around for a long time. It was already a very well-developed technology... So? Were they deaf to all this? Of course not; they were well versed in all these developments. But they aimed for something else.

This handful of Kurdish friends, who according to many were hopeless optimists, naive dreamers, were after a different kind of breakthrough, a new way of thinking. Something no one had tried till now...

So, after six years...

With the screens all showing the centenary year, Zanyar and his four friends found themselves back in the cave of Bêstûn. This time they had enough to talk about for days.

They were tired, understandably, after six hard years. They

had made progress, but it was still too early to see many tangible results. Yes, they were able to extend the efficiency and charging power of solar cells. And they had conducted many new experiments on the solar generators. But they were still far away from their stated aims. It was still too early for a breakthrough, or to be able to give current technology the boost it needed. Their achievements so far were a drop in the ocean.

That evening, after dinner, they gathered once more around the fire at the front of the cave. They loved doing this. Conversation around the fire was the best.

Zanyar scratched his right wrist, as usual, but this time he said in a calm and confident voice, 'It's time.' All eyes turned to him. 'I asked you to wait for me for six years. Now I will tell you what happened to me. I believe after hearing about that 'experience', our minds will be a little clearer about our next course of action.'

Everyone stared at him in anticipation. They had no idea what 'experience' he was referring to. He had spoken about it before like he might talk about a short story he'd read, or a dream he'd like to relate! But what was he about to say now?

His friends leaned forward.

Zanyar said, 'Look at my wrist.' He pulled back the sleeve on his right arm. Like the seal of a blazing emblem, a small mark the shape of the sun could be seen on the back of his wrist. His friends stared at the tattoo with amazed eyes. Through his nervousness, he said, 'Be patient, I will explain.'

Zanyar prepared himself as if he were about to set out on an arduous journey.

'Six years ago, today... back when we first came to this place... I, like every other Kurd I knew, was a little heartbroken, a little depressed, a little ashamed. Life and I had had our ups and downs. But now, as you see, I have my mission. All of us are from a community that enjoys very few advantages. To fill that gap, we nurture momentous and distant dreams. I'm no different.

'So, I've always had an interest in parapsychology and supernatural phenomena. Stars, galaxies, and discourses in these fields have always attracted my attention, even though I never actually believed in any of it. And now here we are. Life is so strange! It catches you by surprise in so many different ways. If it wasn't for this moment, this evidence, I myself would never have believed the things that happened to me. It was all impossible!

'Since there is evidence, I will report the incident just as it "happened" as if it were "your truth", my precious friends, and not just my own.

'Let me say it like this: in this infinite universe, you should believe that everything is possible. My reality – or should I say *our* reality – is just one of those "possible impossibilities", and it lasts but a fraction of a fraction of a second. Like a drop in the ocean.

'I don't know which time parallel we live in. I will never know with which spokes the wheels are moving. Maybe I should say there is no "time" in any one moment, and I'm sure my words won't be considered as an exaggeration. Dear friends! This fire is real, isn't it? This cave and that sky where the silver stars sparkle... Yes! If we can see them now and if we are here now, then they're as real as we are. But the question is how real are we? I believe we don't have the answer to this question.

'I would say, "that day" I saw it, even though I never believed it. I saw it with the eyes in my head and with conviction in my heart. Even though I still didn't believe it, I saw it through the eyes of a young woman...

'I was working for NASA at the time, I had been working there for a while in fact. But how did they take me to that place, and why did I arrive there in the figure of a woman? That is not the question... The question was: what was going on at NASA? They had a crisis. Certain things were happening that couldn't be explained. But according to them, they found the culprit. It was like a gateway to the most distant stars. They found a portal, an entrance. That gate, according to them, is located in the cave of Bêstûn. That's why I brought you here...

'Wait, please. Bear with me. Let me tell the whole story. You have to be patient till the end.

'They called me "Kurdika". Their voices were intense and discordant. They needed to make a decision immediately, in order to discover where this culprit came from and what it was. They had to send some people. But who? The professors of NASA weighed their options, going round and round in circles and failed to reach a consensus. The risks in any mission, and the stakes, were so high. They needed a guinea pig. For this they needed a dog, a monkey, and a human. In addition to this, NASA had to implement the mission in total secrecy. They couldn't use someone from the outside. Though homeless people – of which there were hundreds on any street – were considered.

'In our department, as well as myself, there were Turkish, Persian, Arabic, African, and Asian assistants. Not to mention, of course, Europeans, Americans, Russians, Japanese, and Chinese people and many other nationalities...

'Their decision was made quickly: the name "Kurdika" was heard on everyone's lips. At first, I was honoured. Out of all these religions and nationalities, I thought, they chose *me*. Later, I realised there was no reason to feel proud. Being a Kurd, if something were to happen to me, I wouldn't have refuge; no one would have my back. I have no fellow countrymen. They could use me like a guinea pig.

'I was expecting them to put me, the dog, and the monkey on a rocket and fire us off into space, but no... quite the opposite! We were taken underground. They put us in an elevator, I couldn't tell you how many floors down we went.

'We reached a room that contained within it a kind of pond. A clear, green pond. I didn't know what the connection was, but a sudden thirst for water tore at my soul. I can't explain why I had this feeling. Then I noticed the professors had left me at the water's edge, and returned to their glass-walled offices, to sit in front of their computers. I knew they could now see me; I could hear their voices through the speakers. Gently, one voice told me: 'Dip your hands into the water, fill your mouth and splash your face. Just like when you pat a face...' I didn't need much persuading to do it, and then I passed out.

'Suddenly I was in a different world. I found myself at the top of a hill, at a triple crossroads. My feet were already choosing the path up to the mountains. Then I stood under a walnut tree at the edge of a clear spring. I was suddenly relieved and said to myself; 'So that's it, then. A quick, safe test run. Now I'll splash water on my face again and return to that underground pond at NASA.

'But when I splashed water on my face, I was still there, on the foothills of a mountain, that wild place under a walnut tree... I quenched my thirst with the water. As if I was in an ancient tale, my mind and my heart shook against each other, neither one listening to the other. Everything was distorted.

'I looked down at my reflection in the water. A beautiful young woman with luscious hair and braids looked up at me. It was only left for the man inside of me to fall in love with the woman that I now embodied. I couldn't grasp how nonsensical my situation was.

'I went towards the mountains and said to myself, "Just cross that border, pass that summit and you will find an exit." Then I checked myself, "Forget it, man, it's just a dream. Soon you will be awake and everything will be back to normal." The thought relieved me, up to a point.

'In no time, I had reached the top of the mountain. Behind me, now, was the steep slope down, in front of me, on the summit, an arbour. I walked towards it. Upon reaching it, an old man appeared beside me, speaking my language: "My daughter, after three valleys, you will reach a country. There…" he repeated his words seven times but could not complete them. Then he said, "For me to finish this sentence, I have a condition you must fulfill." I said go ahead. "With me," he said, "I carry a keen power. A silver bracelet. Whoever wears it on their wrist will see people bowing before them. But my condition is I have to stamp you with the seal of the sun. I said nothing, stretching out my hand, and he was already lifting his branding iron that flamed like a burning ember to stamp my right arm… and here it is!'

Once more, Zanyar showed his friends the seal on the back of his wrist. They sat quietly, their eyes wide open, not knowing what to say. Believing him was one thing, not believing him would be something else altogether. Was it possible Zanyar, in order to cast a spell over his friends, had made all this up? If so, why wait six years then tell it? Since he'd shown it to them back then, why not share the story at the time?

As his friends stared at him, Zanyar could tell what they were thinking and smiled: 'I know it's really difficult. Not only for you, but for me too. It's really difficult to believe I had this experience. I'm still struggling with it myself, so I have no right to ask you to struggle with it too.

'As for why I didn't tell you six years ago: two reasons. First, if I told you earlier, this work of ours for the past six years would never have happened. Because no one would trust and work with someone with such an absurd story. Second, you needed to know me not by my story, but by my work and personality. Now look at me and tell me: over these six years of work, which Zanyar did you know?'

One said: 'You're a man of your word, Zanyar.' Another: 'A gentleman and a scholar.' 'A man of good faith,' said the third. And finally, 'What can I say; you have illuminated our path.'

'In that case, let us now resume our path?' Zanyar said, throwing a thick log onto the fire. The blaze from the flames shone in his eyes like hope itself.

'...When I first arrived at that mountainside, it was dawn. The first thing I focussed on was the sky of that world; three moons hung in the firmament and one sun. The North star was still there, but the Shepherds' Star was to the south, the Morning Star to the west. As if the world had been turned upside down, and become its mirror image. Then I noticed that the sun was rising from the west below us.

'I had no idea what had become of the dog and monkey. They had been talked about at length at NASA, but it seemed neither of them had been chosen. Only I had been led to that underground pond. Finally, I was standing in front of that gateway to a new country. After all these years! How that door opened and that old man came to greet me, I will never know.

'How can I describe it? I saw wonders – with my own eyes, and in disbelief. Finally, I had truly become Kurdika, and would stay that way. The girl from the stars. In a place they called Rojbeyanê, the land of the sun. The coming of Kurdika brought great prosperity to their world. Rain poured over the land. Their orchards and gardens became fruitful again.

'The terrain was similar to the rural region of Kermanshan, in front of the mountain range. Their lifestyle was similar to that of ours a hundred years ago. They spoke Kurdish fluently. They protected their sovereignty with towers and forts. Too often, raiders and pirates had brought destruction to their doorstep...

'Comrades, whether you believe me or not, I lived there so long that I no longer believed in my life here in this world. I used to think the world was just this place. Now I know their small, warm country is much better than our huge, cold one. Now listen to this next wonder. I fell in love with a man called Sêvdîn. We married and had three boys and two girls...

'Then, one day, I happened to be visiting the great castle of that country, and wandering through its courtyards and gardens, when something caught my attention. I found myself walking towards it. A pond, thronged on all sides by flowers. A pleasant and familiar scent, even though it didn't belong to that world, drifted into my senses. I bent down to smell one of the flowers, and my head span. I felt dizzy. Thereupon, I splashed some water on my face and found myself back beside the pond in that underground room at NASA. I splashed water on my face again and found myself here; in the cave of Bêstûn... That was six years ago. I returned again to my life and my work, and adjusted back to my own era.'

It's not clear if Zanyar's friends ever believed his account even with the 'evidence' on the back of his wrist. But from that day on, they created a great banner for their movement, a symbol that showed the world the seal that had been stamped on their friend. It was only later that they realised this emblem was the flag of Kurdistan itself. And it wasn't until later still that they realised their path was leading their country into a whole new era.

And so, 300 years after the epic poems of Ehmedê Xanî,[1] the words 'If only' ascended in the speech of the Kurds. Kurds themselves became the bearers of their own burden. One hundred years after the establishment of the Republic of Mahabad, Zanyar and his friends gave a new beginning to the way all humanity thought. And in the year 2146, on the 200th anniversary of Mahabad, in Çar Çira Square, in front of a university founded by Zanyar and his four colleagues, a statue of Qazî Muhammad was installed, under the flag of independent Kurdistan.

Note

1. Ehmedê Xanî (1651-1707), author of the epic love poem, *Mem and Zin*, considered to be one of the most important literary discourses on Kurdish nationalism: The 'if only's might refer to specific lines: 'If only we had a king then the Ottomans would not dominate us.' 'If only there were unity among us, and we would obey one another, then all of the Ottomans and Arabs and Iranians would become our servants, we would reach perfection and we would become productive in knowledge and wisdom.'

The Age of the Iron Locusts

Yıldız Çakar

Translated from the Kurmanji
by Harriet Paintin

From Above

'DEAR LISTENERS, IT'S THE 14th March 2046. You're listening to Mahabad Radio, welcome to *The Oak Tree,* my name's Ava Bahramî. Good morning everyone. Before we get started with the show, which will explore the history and culture of the lands of the sun and moon, I'll pass you over to my colleague, Ezra, for today's news. After that, it's straight back to me for a very special surprise! OK, Ezra, over to you!'

'This is Ezra Xorasani; the time is 11.01am, here are today's headlines live from the studio. Chaos continues to escalate across the globe, as the fallout from the collapse of the Great State can be felt with each new conflict. New clashes are being reported in multiple cities, as tensions escalate. Casualties are thought to be high, although numbers cannot be estimated due to the military bans on journalists in many territories. Elsewhere, the so-called Great Devaluation continues to have its impact, sowing poverty like a virus through most of the world's economies… Dear Listeners, leading scientists have gone into hiding and issued a message for the rest of the world. In this

204

statement, they call attention to a new pathogen, a pandemic that is gathering apace, crossing borders and killing thousands.

'In their message, they argue, "These illnesses are being manufactured in laboratories under the pretence of research, and then 'accidentally' [in quotation marks] released into the community. It has happened too many times this century for it to still be an accident." They are describing it as the Great Weapon of the Twenty-first Century…

'Meanwhile, the battle over water continues. Laurasian forces have targeted reservoirs across Gondwana for the forth consecutive night. The Gondwanan president has declared war in the name of defending their water supply, and has committed their entire army to defend their water sources.'

After three intense months, the heat of the sun was slowly spreading across the valleys and mountains, its warm hands stroking nature's head, the way a mother caresses her child's. As the dark clouds retreated, light was finally rousing the land. On the peaks, snow was slowly thawing and the melt-water finding its way into small streams reaching down to the heart of the earth, journeying from the higher ground like caravans, weaving their patterns, their black threads against a white background. After three months hiding under tree bark, insects were starting to emerge from their crevices, writhing upwards against the weight of winter, while leaves adorned the branches with life, reaching up towards the sky.

On that particular morning, the spring wind and the gentle voice of water trickling through the streams blended with the sound of my pocket radio. I had no patience for the news. Amongst all that beauty, I couldn't stand to hear of war. All that was a world away. Fortunately, waves of music soon replaced the bulletin and poured out of the little plastic box, cascading out onto the road I was walking down, as if crashing against rocks.

Mamle's[1] voice flowed out, falling on and weaving amongst the daisies that hugged the highlands like a dress. Flowers of seven colours stretched up from the lowlands and valleys, like bolts of bright velvet rolled up against the hills. His voice caressed the roses and sweetbriar, kissed the dancing backs of yellow bees, the flying birds, the crawling insects, even the black-eyed fox.

Through the melody, all of nature's creatures seemed to come together, in unison. Nothing was missing, all was at peace and in its rightful place in the order of things. Even those creatures that couldn't bear offspring themselves helped in the perpetuation of life, feeding and nourishing others. There was constant movement, as ants crawled through the earth underfoot, writhing and slithering like foxes bounding between the dapples of sun and warm soil. Everything was calm and complete, flowing like sweet syrup between the layers of a pastry. In front of me stood an oak tree, in whose branches butterflies with wide, round spots and delicately laced antennae hid themselves. With the swell and ebb of Mamle's melody, they opened and closed their wings, and thought themselves more beautiful than the fluttering flowers, more powerful than the trees. That's why, like innocent leaves of colours, they hung around the oak trees, like hunters. Hunters of the wind...

Walking amongst such greenery was like opening a door to another era. The oak's branches made me think of my grandma's open arms. In a short space of time this tree had grown so tall, her branches spanning outwards like dozens of hands covering the sky. Gently, I took off my cloak and respectfully placed it on the ground... Slowly, I approached the base of the tree and hung my radio on the highest branch I could reach. A wave of contented tiredness swept over me and I craved to lie down and sleep in her shade, if only for half an hour... Nothing bad could possibly happen if I did. I sat down beside her trunk and rested my head at her base. This oak's roots had been my pillow for years now... bulging with all their intoxicating lusciousness. The tree knew me inside and out... As the afternoon slipped into evening, I noticed two round eyes blinking from one of the tree's higher crevices. When I tried to look closer, a white owl suddenly flew out, flapping its wings in my face as it took off. In almost every branch there seemed to be a bird's nest and in every tree hole thousands of insects crawled – these were her children. The tree was their protector, but they were also protecting her.

My grandma always used to say to me: 'Every part of the land, every mountain, belongs to someone. They own whatever is on it, and whatever is below it. Apart from them, nobody else can live there.' She would take my hand in hers and continue, 'Although they may build many nests on the land, their trees will never take root.'

Before my grandma passed away she whispered in my ear, then took a seed wrapped in a green headscarf from under her pillow, and pressed it into my hand. Since that moment, my hand has felt a strong connection to the turpentine tree. I have crossed mountains and valleys, planting these trees wherever I go. Using a small spade I carry with me I dig into the soil, plant the seed and gently cover it. This earth is not the same earth as that which covers the faces of dead people. It is a living substance which has witnessed storms, wars, and genocides. But each time it is reborn.

And as each tree grew, she would make friends with the sunbeams above-ground, while stringing chains and tying knots below. A fine, yet strong lace, binding herself to that distant fire that burns within all life, knowing that whatever fire should burn her, a new tree would be seeded in her ashes, wherever an axe might strike her, out of the wound, a new limb would grow.

As I rested against the tree, the spring wind caressed my face, and my eyelids grew heavy. This breeze, so familiar to me, brought back a memory as vivid as if it were yesterday: I was carrying baskets of grapes to attach to the back of the motorbike; Grandma was sitting quietly next to the door, in a wooden chair with her back to me. Suddenly, out of nowhere a feeling of panic gripped me. I quickly dumped the rest of the baskets by the bike and ran to her. Her head had slumped on her chest, and I slowly took her hand in mine as I whispered softly: 'Grandma, wake up. I'll take you to your room.' She slowly opened her eyes, and peered at me sleepily. Squeezing my hand, she lifted her head and focused her gaze on something over my shoulder. I tried to follow where she was looking, but before I had fully turned my head, she shook herself and spoke with a heavy voice. 'Ah, my grandson... You know, those trees and bushes, the forest and the mountains – a long time ago, all of them were burned. Not a single tree was left standing, nor a single animal allowed to live. All of this greenery – they burned it to the ground. But, grandson, the land knows its true owners. For years, the land lay bare. We didn't plant or harvest anything. No rain fell, nor a single snowflake. In their place, bombs dropped like rain. But after seven years of this, suddenly one spring morning we saw that everywhere was green. The oak trees towered over us once again. This was no miracle; it is our truth, the land's truth. Grandson, I witnessed with my own eyes how nature can be reborn from the ashes.'

When Grandma talked about the land it was like she was describing her beloved. In my family, Grandma was held in higher regard than any other, even the older men. She was illiterate and had never been to school, but her wisdom seemed unsurpassable. She knew all there was to know about plants and healing, and as a midwife she had delivered hundreds of children. Whenever anyone fell sick, they came to her for help. She knew which herb to use for any ailment.

As for me? Well, at that time, I was obsessed with frogs down by the river. So much so, I was always collecting them, playing with them, passing them between my hands. But one day I suddenly saw spots breaking out everywhere on my body – my mouth, face and hands became overwhelmed with these spots! Whoever saw me would instantly flinch, let out an 'Eeeyew', shut their eyes and hurry away. And so for a day or two, my grandma would climb high into the mountains to collect a handful of herbs. She would grind them together in a pestle and mortar, mixing them with the thick cream that forms in the tankards of rich buffalo milk. For two days, she fed me this medicine, and on the third day the spots completely disappeared. She may as well have stood over me, waved her hands and said 'Abracadabra!' When the bellies of sick children swelled with oedema, or when rheumatism or the cold set into the joints of the elderly, she would spend her evening placing bricks in the fire to put under their mattresses. I still remember when Uncle Eyaz fell ill, with an infection so bad his flesh turned black, she said, 'I need to burn the wound to stop it spreading over his body.' So she wrung out a cloth, constructed a fire and carefully placed the cloth on top, before lighting the fire to burn, very gently. The smell of burning fabric filled the air, and with great care, she brought the cloth's embers to the tip of his finger. Then the screaming started, only it wasn't Uncle Eyaz who was screaming, it was me! And the crackling, burning flesh was my finger!

I jumped. My finger had been burnt. It was as if a small ball of fire was stuck to my fingertip. My whole body was shaking, and a chill descended on me. I sat up. The soft fragrances of spring seemed to have passed, as if the beginning of autumn had fallen on me and my tree. The piece of string that I had attached to the radio years before, as a kind of handle, swung from the tree branch in a strange wind that came from nowhere. Suddenly an unfamiliar voice began emanating from the speaker. I tried to stand up and reach for the buttons and dial of my radio, but I couldn't move.

My eyelids felt heavy. The pain in my finger was slowly spreading through my body, as if a black-tipped knife was moving inside me, cutting through anything in its path. I suddenly wanted to get closer to the tree and embrace it; only this could relieve the pain coursing through me. I moved closer and rested my back against the tree. I couldn't breathe, the pain was like a tight fist around my heart. I had no strength left. The only thing I could do was to let myself drift away into the sleep that was taking me…

'Oi! Open your eyes…'

'I said, Oi! Wake up!…'

'I said, Get up!…'

Suddenly I jolted awake. An attractive woman stood over me.

'My name is Septa.'

'Septa?'

'Musa! It's Judgement Day, we need to go.'

'What? What judgement day? How do you know my name? Who are you? What are you talking about?!'

A woman had come from nowhere, to disturb my sleep, and now she had the audacity to tease me with this nonsense about Judgement Day? Who did she think she was?! Damn her! Judgement Day, that was the last thing I needed. I had no energy to talk. I thought to myself, *If I just open and close my eyes a few more times, maybe I'll wake up from this peculiar dream and that woman will not be there anymore.* I quickly blinked. She was still there. This time, I slowly closed and opened my eyes. Still the woman was standing over me with a stern expression on her face. I edged a little further from her towards the tree. I was trying to find my voice when she spoke again, sharply.

'Get up, now! You can hear them, can't you? Be quick!'

I couldn't utter a word. She leaned over me and looked deep into my eyes. Then, she took my hand in hers and pulled me up sharply. I couldn't believe what was happening. What road was she now taking me down? The sounds of the wind moving through leaves and branches, the rustling of the undergrowth, birdsong, all these noises suddenly disappeared.

As we walked, I looked around us. With every passing second, everything was changing. Wherever our footsteps fell, the land grew arid. It was as if with each step, we passed from dream to nightmare and back again. The steams dried up before my eyes, daffodils were wilting into the ground. The crowns of the oak trees had all been decapitated, the insects in the trees showered down in plumes, dead as the dust. The yellows of bees and reds of flowers became the glow of embers. My radio, like an elegant white mare with broken legs, sizzled in distress. It was a sound that seemed to come from far off. I felt like a single strand of straw, cast on the empty earth. We were walking quickly, so fast you'd think a seven-headed beast was at our heels! As we turned towards the mountain, everything momentarily became lighter. Then a black fog enveloped us. I could barely see my hands in front of my face. Nor could I hear the sounds of our hurried footsteps, or feel the ground beneath my feet. I just blindly kept on running, almost involuntarily. Where I was headed, I didn't know. In that dark fog, I could have believed we weren't moving at all.

'Heyyy, where are we going?'

'Shhh! Don't make a sound.'

'Why?'

'I said don't make a sound! Be quiet!'

My question was still in my mouth when suddenly we stumbled out of the fog, onto the top of a high, rocky outcrop... To the east, the sky was filled with darkness. It looked like a vast door had opened among the clouds, and from this open portal, small dots were falling one after the other. No, this wasn't like a door! It was like a black wound in the sky, with something like black blood dripping from it. At first I had no idea what it was; those black dots were not just falling downwards but coming towards us, and slowly, ever so slowly, they were getting bigger. Like a flock of birds flying straight towards us. But not birds, not even eagles exactly, nor a seven-headed beast. I froze. The blood drained from my face and I felt like an empty husk just before it's scattered by the wind. Powerless.

'I'm Septa!'

'What?'

'Listen, Musa, I know that you don't understand what I've been saying, I know you don't know what's going on. But we should try to hurry. The Iron Locusts from the East are looking in our direction. If they reach the Women's Village, it doesn't only mean the end for the Land of Sun, it will be the end of the world.'

'How?'

'Musa, look at the sky. It's being swallowed by darkness. Don't you see it?'

'I can't make it out.'

'That is the Dark Mind, Musa! Look around you.'

I looked around. I was no longer the person I had been just a few moments ago, sleeping under the oak tree with my one-eyed radio, surrounded by the calm beauty of the forest, with the sound of Mamle gently blending with the sounds of nature. Now...? It felt as if I had woken up from a dream and plunged again, even deeper into a nightmare. If this is reality, I thought to myself, let me go back to my dream.

'I just want to go back to where you found me, if that's ok?' I said. 'All I want is to go back to my oak tree, do you hear me?'

'Musa, look at that hill!'

Ignoring my pleading, the woman pointed towards the rounded hill where my oak tree lived. Together we headed towards it. On arriving, I immediately saw that my tree had died. Only the skeleton of it remained. My one-eyed radio was still hung from one of the branches, like a piece of ripped fabric blowing in the wind. How could this be?

'Do you see, Musa? The oak tree, do you see?'

A sob died in my throat. How could this have happened? My grandma had told me the legend of the oak tree. Throughout my life, I had planted thousands of them with my own hands. Sometimes, when I bumped into someone from the Women's Village, they would laugh and say, 'Musa, you should have seen how many berries we've collected from your oak trees!' Every time, I would take it as a joke and reply, 'The trees aren't mine! They belong to whoever's looking after them.'

But today my grandma's legend seemed obsolete: 'Each part of the tree is medicine for some ailment or other; every branch is blessed,' she used to say. 'Nothing can take the soul of the oak tree: not fire, water, dust, nor wind.' Yes Grandma, but what about now? Life had become as empty as her words. Everything became black, everything.

'Musa, you have to help me. Come with me as far as the Women's Village. It's not late yet. If we're able to reach it, we'll also be able to return, alright?'

'Me? What can I do?'

Ignoring my question, the woman muttered under her breath: 'The real fight hasn't started yet. We need to climb the Zengê mountain before the tanks come.' She was talking so quietly that I wondered if she could even hear herself.

'Did you say tanks?!'

She didn't answer me. She didn't even look up. She appeared to be mumbling to herself. Again I turned to her and demanded:

'Did you say tanks?!'

As if waking suddenly from a deep sleep, she opened her eyes wide and looked at me with her full attention.

'Those are not crows or eagles,' she said. 'Their bodies looked scaly and black as iron. Their minds are far more conniving than machines. Firstly, they want the water and wheat.'

'Water and wheat?'

'Yes. Today, water and wheat. Tomorrow, they will move on to land and peace. In the Land of the Sun, your fire is warm, your wind is soft, your water is sweet and your land is green. That's why the Locusts want your bread. They are hungry!'

'Why are they hungry?'

'On the other side of the world, there is nothing left except industry and technology. Over there, everything has become illusion. Nobody sleeps gently under a tree to the sound of water, like you do, Musa. Now the sound of water only comes from pushing a button, dreams only come from pushing a button. You can't achieve anything except by pushing a button over there.'

While the woman was talking, a dark shadow suddenly passed overhead. Looking up, I was struck by an immense feeling of grief for my age. I knew then that time was out of joint. I felt overwhelmed by this immense empty shadow. The woman reached out her hand. I don't know how, but slowly and very tentatively I took it. Like terrified runaway children, we began walking quickly. No, we weren't walking – she was pulling me. From when we stood under the tree till now, she had been dragging me by the hand. I had never held a woman's hand so tightly in my life.

Then she released her hand and pointed.

'Musa, you see the mountain over there. There is a road going up it. That's our route. From a distance, it looks like the mountain has only one path up the middle of its brow, like a Cyclops's eye staring at us. But the mountain has many paths, and a myriad of eyes, their edges catching glints of the sun. We have to find the right one among so many, only it will take us to Women's Village. Do you understand, Musa? That's where we're headed.'

I don't know why the woman showed me all this. She continued talking, as if to herself, when suddenly, from the emptiness within me, came a voice. It filled me with such horror that I became desperate to shut my ears and throw myself into the emptiness. The shadow over our heads was growing larger and larger. My eyes, timid like a young child's, met the eye of the mountain. I snatched my hand from hers and ran quickly, up towards the summit where there was still sunlight. The woman was now far behind and below me. A sob stuck in my throat, trapped like water behind a dam.

Who can say that the trees are not like our children? Ever since my grandma put that seed in my hand, I have been holding onto the idea of it. It wasn't just a tree, it was a thought that I watered every morning. Even if she wasn't thirsty, still I gave her water. I filled my hands at Kaniya Xanike spring and gently let it trickle down into her soil. Sometimes the village women laughed at me and said, 'The roots of the tree reach down to a well of water, you don't need to give it handfuls of water like that.' They didn't know that I wasn't giving that water out of necessity, but out of love.

Suddenly the world became dark. I span around fearfully to look behind me. The woman wasn't there.

I was back under the oak tree, my tree, the one that had become a skeleton of her former self. My chest surged with a cry for help: I had to do something. I wiped my eyes with my dark green sleeve. I walked two steps towards the tree, put my arms around her and lay my face against her trunk. The dam in my throat opened, and I wept. The sound of my crying opened the mountain's cracks and the mountain cried with me.

And suddenly, a voice came from my radio:

'Dear Listeners, today, the 22nd of December 1945, is a historic day. All across the land, the Children of the Sun are walking towards Çar Çira Square. The city is heaving with people; thousands have come from every neighbourhood, from every village: men, women, young and old, are marching and chanting 'Long live the Land of Sun!' People are ululating with happiness, holding hands, children are performing traditional circle dances, like rivers reaching the sea, they stream into Çar Çira. You have to see it to believe, dear Listeners. From a small window, I pose today's topics to you. But to start us off, let me recite today's poem...' The presenter's voice was interrupted by the susurration of static. Zzzzzzzz. '... Each one of us is a country. We cannot be divided by four. The country of the day is one country. It cannot be divided by four...'

What is this radio presenter going on about? I thought. Of all the voices that could reach me through the cracks in reality! My father had bought this radio when I was a kid, in Zaxo, from a blind man in a tiny shop. The old man gestured towards the single speaker, resembling a wide-open unblinking eye, and said, 'This is not only a radio, it is an eye of God.' From that day till now, I've carried it wherever I go, up mountains and down valleys. It is not only my travelling companion, it sees everything I see, hears everything I hear. It removes borders from between people, and makes the foreign sound familiar, the familiar sound foreign. With it by my side, isn't God everywhere in the world! Ha! If my grandma had ever heard me saying that, she would have slapped me and said, 'How can you put the radio in God's place? You Infidel!' It's a good thing only I can hear that thought now, just as only I can hear the sound of my radio! In truth, I adored it: it was the kind of sound that made your heart feel at rest. The kind of sound that took me back to nights filled with storytellers and singers.

And now?

Now its eye was not like its eye from before, nor its voice, nor its news. It was as if another soul had possessed my radio. I stepped away from my tree, or what was left of it, and turned to look at the sky. The sky had become like an empty wilderness, like the great barren ocean you see at the heart of a mirage. There were strange sounds coming from above.

As kids in the village, at night time, we used to be told the prophecy: 'One day, the sound of dogs barking will come from the sky.' But we'd laugh at this and reply, 'So? An eagle will snatch a puppy off the ground and carry its yelps into the sky! Big deal!' But this sound now was neither the sound of puppies nor eagles.

Suddenly, a crackle of thunder and lightning filled the sky, like electric wires colliding. I span round this way and that, out of sheer panic. My heart was racing. The sky fizzled and rumbled incessantly, as if mirroring what was going on inside my head. I was burning, it felt like there was a fire inside me and there was no one to put it out.

I looked up once more at the Iron Locusts. Locusts, hah! Now I understood why that woman had said 'Judgement Day is coming.' How could I not believe her now? Now the locusts were hovering directly above my head.

An army of Iron Locusts filled the horizon, and still more of them were coming in groups, moving in tight formation, each filling the gap left by the one in front. Sometimes people choose to be cynical about what humans are capable of creating. 'If it's man-made, it has a flaw,' my father would say. But nobody seeing this would deny that it was anything short of perfect.

Those in the east had built a perfect, mechanoid army, and my eyes now reflected the image of thousands, maybe even millions of Iron Locusts filling the skies. In the mouths of some, there was an occasional flash of light, in others a long, continuous flame. Their long legs dangled sharply into the air below them, like double-edged swords.

What was I supposed to do? The woman was still nowhere to be seen, but suddenly, with a rush, I remembered what she'd said: 'What can a man even do?' I needed to go to the Women's Village, quickly. Maybe that's where she went also.

With panic coursing through my body, I rushed down

from the summit. The Iron Locusts were still lining up on the horizon. There was so little time.

Rivers and springs nourished the earth as they flowed like sweet nectar beside the paths I ran down. Only yellow wheat and rice plants grew here. The more I thought about it, the faster I went. The Women's Village was a precious gem, nestled between four mountains. Black bread, yellow milk, curd from the hands of housewives and mothers. Each product brings another one with it. I was still walking through the fog, my heart thudding. The road was unfamiliar, never-ending. I felt as if I was going round in circles.

I need to speed up, I realised. *Everywhere is getting dark, with every moment the darkness intensifies. I can't see more than a few feet.* In the darkness, I didn't know where I was walking, but still I was going.

How quickly I was stumbling into the blackness, only beneath my feet, instead of rocks, smoke was spreading. White smoke. I had no more power or weight or balance anymore. I became like the smoke itself. Suddenly I tripped up and fell on my face. A cold sweat prickled my forehead. I slowly stood up and looked around. It looked like the earth was a blank white page with me standing in the middle. There was no path or anything to guide me. Where should I go, in which direction should I head? I have to do something. If there is no road, what is there?

I stayed still for a few moments. I took two or three deep breaths and I rubbed my eyes. There was no road where there should be, under my feet. I took a step forward into the nothingness, and as I did, my radio blared.

'Oh Captain, the population stays...' the voice was interrupted by static. 'Zzzzz... It will not be broken, not with all the bombs of the world...' More static. 'Zzzzz... dying... women survive... Zzzzz.'

That voice! It became like a road guiding me along. I

needed to go towards that voice, and the sound of the radio! Yes, I need to go back to the oak tree! Maybe the mysterious woman would also be there. That woman! What was her name again? Septa. Yes, Septa!

Slowly, I turned to where the radio's voice was coming from. It didn't sound very far away. I started to crawl, like an animal on four legs, or perhaps four hands. I sped up as the muffled noise of my radio continued, going back up the way I had come. It was all on instinct, of course, I had no idea if it was the right thing to do or not...

Halfway up, something suddenly passed across my vision. Was I imagining things? No, I was sure of it. Out of the corner of my eye, I'd seen a flash of light. I turned around slowly, and again light flashed across my face from above. I looked up, and my blood ran cold. Two red flashing lights hovered above me.

In that moment, I remembered a story my mother used to tell me, about the Gurê Mancho.[2] Even as an adult, I would occasionally remind my mum of it: 'Remember how you were always scaring me with stories of the Gurê Mancho, telling me he's going to come and attack me?' My mum would laugh at me under her scarf, and say 'Musa, my son, I was only joking. There is no such thing as the Manco Wolf, it's just a story.' But now I knew the Manco Wolf was real; it was standing right in front of me. Its eyes were red, its mouth rusty with dried blood, its legs made of iron, its chest a ball of metal cables. The red eyes stared at me. We face each other off, yet there is something very strange about its stance. Like it was waiting for something. Then in a moment, its eyes changed colour and it let out a strange sound...

'Xuuuurrrrrxurrrrr'

So many thoughts raced through my mind in that moment.

I couldn't help think of my mother and little sister and what they might be doing right now. Had these iron monsters reached them as well? And what was to stop them spreading further, beyond the Kurdistan? Oh, Mother, how could we have known the destiny that was written for us would eventually become that of the whole world!

Before I left my house that morning, my mother had made me a packed lunch of flatbread and cheese, wrapped in fabric. Who could have known what would happen to me that day? What would happen to any us? Maybe my grandma could have. In one of those strange prophecies, she once declared: 'A day will come when they will build houses on top of each other, and they will put dogs in these houses that are made from concrete. The sound of their barking will come from the sky. Children will keep pictures of their mother and father in their houses, but throw their parents out onto the streets. They will put plastic flowers on their balcony and instead of warm, home cooked food, they will eat only tablets. Nobody will cook food at home anymore. These people will forget the warmth of families.' Then she added, 'They will destroy seeds, and nobody will eat food that has been grown in the soil. They will push against nature so much that it will never forgive them, and one day it will take its revenge. Nature only forgives those who cherish it.' *Oh, Grandma! You used to say that we are in Noah's Ark, in these modern times. But where is the shore? In the east, all I can see are Iron Locusts.* I closed my eyes, wanting to block it all out forever.

And suddenly, I could hear the voice of the woman again. On hearing it also, the Iron Locusts' antennae lit up with bright yellow lights, and the same strange noise began to emanate from them:

'Dirrrdirrrdirrr. Ziirrrzireeeerrrrrddddd'

The woman who called herself Septa was ululating: her voice rising, expanding like a snowball rolling and rolling, gathering snow. It was as if the voice of the mountain itself were rising up through her.

Another voice came out of nowhere, abruptly cutting into Septa's:

'Taq... taq... taq...'

It was like the sound of hammers hitting iron, and together with the sound of the mysterious woman ululating, grew louder and stronger.

From Below

'Dear Listeners, good day from Radio Mahabad. Today is the 10th of February 1946. You're listening to *The Oak Tree*, my name's Ava Calali. Before we get started with today's edition of 'The Shining Star', here are the headlines: Ahead of today's election, Soviet leader Joseph Stalin has claimed, on Russian national radio, that [quote] 'another war is inevitable given the capitalist development of the world economy,' and committed that if re-elected he would commit more investment in national defence in advance of that war with the West...'

'For a hundred years, outsiders have come to our land only to strip it of its resources, to rob us of what is rightfully ours. Some come in the name of their god, others in the name of dictators, others in the name of foreigners' freedom. They take our girls, our women, together with our homes and land. They take everything that's ours and use it for themselves, all while the world looks on and applauds.

'But, Listeners, the Kurds are dignified people. Each tree must grow in its own patch of soil. Today our tree grew some branches, her leaves are blooming, this is a historic day. In today's programme, I want to open up a bit about a hundred years of heartache. For more than a century, snakes, mice and scorpions have been sucking the lifeblood of our homeland, and its people. Today is an historical day, one that will be written down in history. This afternoon there will be a meeting of the government. The President...' Zzzzz... Again, static briefly interrupted the announcement. '... on the top it's red, in the middle it's white, on the bottom it's green, on these colours there are two wheat plants, a mountain, a pine tree and a sunrise.'

Explosions sounded above and below. At the same time, the sound of a woman's voice was coming from my radio. I didn't understand a word she was saying. I felt like I was losing my mind. All around me, women were rushing towards Mount Zengê, pouring the unseen path from the Women's Village. I couldn't keep up with them, many had reached the mountain already. Groups of women, with their long, red hair braided into plaits, were thronging along paths around Mount Zengê, like a necklace adorning the neck of God. They were making fires on every small peak and outcrop. There was so much distance between us. Even if I had wings, I wouldn't be able to catch up with them. Sure, the place where I was standing was supposed to be a summit, but compared to Mount Zengê it was barely a pile of rocks. I could have seen more if only I was standing a few…

'Ssshhhh Musa, come this way!'

The woman's hand was on my shoulder. Slowly I turned towards her.

'Where did you go before? Who are you? Seriously?'

She smiled a little, and said: 'Like I told you before, my name is Septa.'

And like before, she took my hand and pulled me along after her.

'We should go back to your oak tree. We need your radio.'

'My radio?'

I suddenly felt very tired. My footsteps made no sound. I had no idea what was about to happen to us. We were walking quickly but my radio never sounded far away. Wherever we went, the voice seemed just as close.

'Dear Listeners, Today is 20th March 2046. You're listening to Radio Mahabad, my name's Ava. Before I start my programme, I want to talk about tomorrow's celebration. To mark the transition from the stars to the moon, and the beginning of Nowruz...'

'Hey, there's my tree!!'

Suddenly I saw her, the tree. Yes, I was still calling her a tree, though she had become little more than a burnt-up skeleton of one. We had walked for so long, but what was the point? As if we had only been circling around it. My one-eyed radio was still making a noise. Above it, one side of the sky was black, the other yellow. On the horizon, a myriad of iron machines, Iron Locusts, were still amassing, hanging there, like bloodthirsty bats, waiting to begin their swoop. I glanced again at the woman; she was looking at my tree. She stepped a little closer to it. Suddenly she grabbed the radio, snapped it from its branch, and yanked on the dial.

Zzziiiiiidddd

Strange sounds emanated from the box as she turned the button. But that dial was not supposed to be turned that far, I realised. What was this woman doing?

'Look here, that isn't some lump of iron, it's a radio!'

She didn't answer me, instead just looked into my eyes. She wasn't the same woman who'd taken my hand, before, and dragged me along. Her features were the same, but the way she held them had changed. A bitter feeling rose inside me. The hiss from my radio travelled out into the evening, into the cracks of the mountain. From that little box, a voice boomed, and with each turn of the dial, the Iron Locusts in the sky appeared to turn and pivot.

Suddenly, the top of Mount Zengê became shrouded in smoke. The Iron Locusts had moved before we even knew it. Their movement was so synchronised they seemed locked together in the pattern they made in the sky. The lights on their antennae first changed from yellow to red, but as they moved they turned them upwards, to flash dully into the empty sky.

Anyone who didn't know what was about to happen would have simply marvelled at how beautiful these new stars were. The Iron Locusts left in an ordered formation, perfectly synchronised with the movement of the radio's dial in the woman's hands. They flew towards Mount Zengê and began to circle it. That circle wasn't like the circle of a headscarf on the head of the mountain, it was like the circle of the snake, ready to strangle its prey. The summit was not visible behind them; swarm after swarm they were surrounding the mountain. The smoke from the fires lit by the women with red plaits had disappeared by this point. The strange woman stopped suddenly, and looked around, before returning again to the dial. This time she turned it in the opposite direction. She turned and a sound came from the clouds. A hard rain started falling. At that moment, the mountain echoed with the sound of thunder. Dust from the valleys began to rise up on the breeze to form a circle around the mountain. Suddenly a different metallic sound started to emanate from the locusts. Drops of rain were falling on them like bullets, causing steam to lift off them. Then followed lightning bolts taking them out one by one, leaving them lifeless, and plummeting to the earth.

'Lele![3] Did you see? Did you see?!'

The woman didn't reply. The radio's dial was still gripped between her fingers. The rain grew heavier, and the steam rising from the fallen Locusts filled the air. The mountain had become a graveyard filled with carcasses of the Locusts. Battalion by battalion they fell. They fell so fast that a blueness cleared above us, like the sky opening its eyes. Dazzling sunbeams, previously held captive by the Locusts, suddenly burst through. Maybe because of the heat they brought, or maybe out of pure coincidence, whenever the light landed on a crashed Locust it instantly exploded. Out of total devastation a few minutes before, a perfect scene was now emerging. The mountain seem to sparkle in the new light, as if it were covered in the dust of rubies and diamonds. The village women used to say, 'Zengê is enchanted. Its soil is gold, its rocks are steel. There are a thousand and one secrets here, and when there is danger, it changes its colours'.

The change happened in a moment… Once again, I turned towards the oak tree and the strange woman. Slowly she removed her hand from the radio dial. Again, it emitted the sound of a voice:

'May your celebration be blessed by the sunlight, dear Listeners. Today is the 21st March 2046. My name's Ava, I bring you greetings from the Women's Village in the Land of the Sun. Now, after a song of Mihemed Şêxo,[4] our programme, *The Oak Tree,* will discuss the unification of Greater Kurdistan.

'Oh, home sweet home. How sweet it is! The home is the crown of the world, beauty of the east. Oh home, home sweet home.'

'Hush, Musa! Open your eyes!'

Notes

1. Muhammad Mamle (1925-1999) was a Kurdish musician and singer, renowned for revitalising hundreds of Kurdish folk songs, as well as putting classic Kurdish poems, especially Hemn Mukryani's, to music.
2. The Gurê Mancho, or 'Manco Wolf', is a staple of Kurdish folklore, a fictional creature used to scare children from going out alone at night or wandering into the desert, variously described as a stealer of children, or an eater of them.

3. Lele: an expression of astonishment.

4 Mihemed Şêxo (1948-89) was a renowned Kurdish singer, specialising in folk songs, and political protest songs, among them 'Ay Le Gule' and 'Nesrîn'. Cautioned for his works by the Syrian Baath regime in Western Kurdistan (in Syria), he was variously exiled to Lebanon, Southern Kurdistan (in Iraq) and Eastern Kurdistan (in Iran).

Afterword

PUTTING TOGETHER AN ANTHOLOGY like this, with so many moving parts, inevitably takes time, and in the process we often saw things changing on the ground, for Kurdish people, that no one could have quite predicted. During this book's gestation period, a contagious excitement started to spread across all four quarters of Kurdistan, as well as among the Kurdish diaspora. Months before the general elections in Turkey (which eventually took place in May 2023), there was, for the first time in the twenty-year rule of Recep Tayyip Erdogan and the AKP, a feeling – whispered at first, then voiced loudly – that things might actually be about to change. Progress might finally be made, and the much sought-after goals of freedom, peace and democracy (in all their declinations) might really have a chance of materialising for the Kurds, way ahead of the schedule proposed in this book – the centenary of the Mahabad Republic, 2046. Hope, for a moment, stopped being confined to the imagination of authors, exploring fictional futures. It was widespread. And people started to express it. In a country where the censorship of the Kurds has been so extreme that speaking the language was illegal until the 1990s, and even three letters of the alphabet (Q, W and X) were banned for being 'too Kurdish' until very recently... in this context the new sense of optimism felt unprecedented.

Tragically it didn't last. With the eventual re-election of Erdogan, the Kurds' optimism was dashed and dark times loomed like never before. Suddenly, a future in which Kurds would be free to dissent, as well as speak, sing, and write in their mother tongue without censorship, seemed little more than fiction. Much more real, on the contrary, was their on-going persecution and repression. Meral Şimşek, one of this book's contributors is now living in exile in Germany, having been forced to leave her life, work and family behind after it became impossible for her to live in her hometown, Amed (Diyarbakır). In Turkey, she was put on trial, accused of 'making terrorist propaganda', found guilty (with a fifteen-year jail sentence) and facing fifteen years on other charges. The fictional story 'Arzela', published in this book, was cited in the trial as 'evidence' of such 'terrorism propaganda'. Meral was thus forced into exile, alongside thousands of other Kurds, but continues to write and speak out against the repression of Kurdish intellectuals and dissenters in all parts of Kurdistan.

Selahattin Demirtaş, a former co-president of the People's Democratic Party (the HDP, currently facing criminalisation) won't be able to get a copy of the book in which his story features because he is still in prison, and of course, nothing with the word Kurdistan printed on it would be allowed in jail.

Meanwhile censorship continues to show its ugly face elsewhere in Turkey. Just a few days before this book went to print, author Sema Kaygusuz was one of the jury members of the 2023 Antalya International Film Festival who, along with other filmmakers, quit the festival, after the government forced the removal of a documentary, in a stand against those who sought to 'identify criminal elements in films and normalize censorship measures.' The jury members refused to fulfil their duty if the film was not reinstated. The film, *The Decree*, by Nejla Demirci, which depicts the plight of the victims of the major government purge that followed the failed 2016 coup, was reinstated in the festival programme, only to be withdrawn again following threatening statements by the Minister of Culture. The festival, on its sixtieth edition, was eventually cancelled by the Antalya Municipality, the main organising body, thus bowing to pressure and threats.

Culture is being hit hard in Turkey, but after the elections president Erdogan also set in motion his war machine on a much larger scale, simultaneously attacking Rojava-Northeastern Syria and the Kurdistan Region in Iraq.

After the Turkish invasion of Serê Kaniyê (Ras al-Ayn) in Syria in 2019, Nariman Evdike had to flee her home town, and become an internally 'displaced person', moving with the rest of her family to the city of Qamishlo.

The situation in Iran and its Kurdish region, Rojhilat, is not much better. In September 2022, following the brutal killing of a young Kurdish woman, Jina (Mahsa) Amini, in the custody of the so-called 'morality police', who had arrested her in Tehran for not wearing the hijab 'properly', an incredible uprising erupted. Thousands of women, chanting *Jin, Jiyan, Azadi* (Woman, Life, Freedom) took to the streets for months, not just in Rojhilat but eventually across all of Iran. One year on, people are still protesting despite the Iranian government's violent acts of suppression.

And when, on 6 February 2023, a massive earthquake struck Turkey and Syria, both the Erdogan and Assad regimes were quick to weaponise the crisis against the Kurds, blocking convoys of emergency aid, medicines, food, heating fuel, blankets, etc., from entering Kurdish areas, and in the case of Turkey, allowing its occupying jihadist proxy forces to steal Kurdish-funded aid.

When the authors of this book first put pen to paper, most of these tumultuous events could not have been foreseen: neither the new glimmers of hope, nor the new disappointments. But as the stories in this book, not to mention the peoples' reactions to these events, both show, the sun may not have yet risen on the Kurdish dream... but it *is* there, just below the horizon, waiting to ascend.

Orsola Casagrande, Oct 2023

About the Authors

Qadir Agid was born in Amûde, and graduated with a degree in Kurdish literature in 2018. He is the editor-in-chief of *Nu Dem*, the first Kurdish-language newspaper in Syria. He has published four works of fiction and non-fiction, including one collection of short stories, *The Head of the Pain* (2018), as well as *Women in Kurdish Folklore* (2013), *The Amûde Cinema* Fire (2018), and *Translating Kurdish: Origins, Problems and Solutions* (2018). He is a regular translator of books from Arabic into Kurdish.

Yildiz Çakar was born in Amed (Diyarbakir) in 1978, and is a poet, novelist and playwright. She has published two collections of poetry, *Goristana Stêrkan* ('The Graveyyard of Stars', 2004) and *Derî* ('The Door', 2012), a book of short stories (*Duhok*, 2008), a guide to Diyarbakir city (2012), and a book of essays based on the Zoroastrian sacred text, *Avesta* titled *Leylanok* ('The Mirage', 2014). More recently she has published two novels, *Gerîneka Guernicayê* ('The Guernica Whirlpool', 2016) and *Ev rê naçe bihuştê* ('This Way Doesn't Lead to Heaven', 2019). She is a founder member of the Kurdish Writers' Association and a member of Kurdish PEN.

Orsola Casagrande (co-editor) is a Venetian journalist, film-maker and curator. She worked for twenty-five years for the

Italian daily newspaper *il manifesto*, and is co-editor of the web magazine *Global Rights*. Currently based in the Basque country, Orsola writes regularly on Kurdish, Turkish and Basque politics and culture for the Basque daily paper *Berria*, among others. She has translated numerous books, as well as written her own.

Selahattin Demirtaş is an author and former co-leader of the Peoples' Democratic Party (HDP), a progressive pro-Kurdish party with an emphasis on democratic values, feminism, and LGBTQ rights, and has been imprisoned in a maximum-security jail since November 2016. Since 2016, he has written and published two short story collections *Seher* (published as *Dawn* by SJP at Hogarth) and *Devran*, and one novel *Leylan* (2020). Born in 1973, he has been a member of Turkish parliament since 2007 and ran for presidency in 2018 while in prison, where he faces a sentence of 183 years essentially for giving talks as part of political campaigns and election rallies.

Ömer Dilsoz (real name Ömer Demir) was born in 1978 in the village of Gûzereşa in Colemêrg (Hakkari) Province, Southeast Turkey. At the age of 23, he published his first novel, *Wounded Hopes*, and has since published a further eight: *The Breath of the Earth, The Mirror of the Heart, The Yellow Bear, The Evray Mountains, The Judgment of Let My Word and You Be, Kundê Dager, Gêjevang,* and *Four Pages*. In addition to writing fiction, he works as a journalist. His work has also appeared in magazines such as *Gula Tamara, Nûbihar, Tigris, Vesta, Kulîlka Ciwan, Kovara W, Çirûsk, Peyv, Nûbûn,* as well as the newspaper *Azadiya Welat û Tûrik* and numerous websites including www.yuksekovahaber.com and www.nûkurd.com.

Muharrem Erbey is an author, human rights lawyer, and former chairman of the Human Rights Association, Diyarbakır Branch. In 2009 he was detained as part of the Turkish government's nationwide crackdown on Kurdish politicians, elected mayors, NGO representatives, journalists, and lawyers. After four years in prison, and a hunger strike, he was released on bail and currently practices as a lawyer in Diyarbakır (Amed) specialising in the plight of sick prisoners. He is the author of four books, including the short story collections *Lost Genealogy* and *My Father Aharon Usta*, and has had numerous stories published in magazines. His awards include the Ludovic Trarieux International Law and Human Rights Award, 2010, the Norwegian Pen Thought and Freedom of Expression Award, 2014 and the Tucholsky Award, 2014.

Nariman Evdike was born in Sari Kani (Resulayn) in Northeastern Syria, and studied Arabic literature at Al Furat University in Deir ez-Zor, and Kurdish literature at the Cegerxwîn Academy from which she graduated in 2015. Since then, she has written or contributed to three books: *Into The Sun* (2018), a collection of short stories based on the real-life accounts of wounded Rojava fighters; *Summer Dreams* (2018), an anthology featuring three of her short stories, and *Painful Memories* (2019), a novel she co-wrote with Botan Hoshe.

Mustafa Gündoğdu (co-editor) as born in the city of Dersim, and is currently based in London. He has worked as a coordinator for various human rights and conflict resolution NGOs over 20 years, where his roles included in-house translator (working on over 100 books and articles). He has since worked as a freelance editor and second reader on a number of Kurdish translations, including *Sara: My Whole life was a Struggle* by Sakine Cansız translated by Janet Biehl (Pluto) and *Uprising, Suppression, Retribution* by Ahmet Kahraman translated by Andrew Penny (Taderon). He is one of the founding members and former Coordinator of London Kurdish Film Festival, and has organised Kurdish film festivals and screenings in London, New York,

Dublin, Glasgow, Istanbul, and Busan. He is the author of numerous articles on Kurdish cinema published in Kurdish, Turkish, English, and Korean.

Ava Homa is an award-winning novelist, activist, and a lecturer at the California State University, Monterey Bay. Her debut novel *Daughters of Smoke and Fire* was listed as one of 2020's best books of the year in the *Wall Street Journal, The Independent,* and *The Globe and Mail,* won the 2020 Nautilus Silver Book Award for Fiction and was a finalist for the 2022 William Saroyan International Writing Prize. Her collection of short stories *Echoes from the Other Land* was longlisted for the 2011 Frank O'Connor International Short Story Award. Her essays have been published by the BBC, *Globe and Mail, Literary Hub, Literary Review of Canada,* and in several anthologies across the U.S., U.K., and Canada. She is a 2023 California Arts Council Fellow.

Hüseyin Karabey is an Istanbul-based Kurdish film director, producer and screenwriter. Graduating from Marmara University, his feature films include *Go: My Marlon and Brandom* (2008), *Don't Forget Me Istanbul* (2011), and *Come to My Voice* which premiered at the 2014 Berlinale, and won Best Film at Mar Del Plata Film Festival, Argentina and the Sofia Film Festival. He is the author of *Sessiz Ölüm* ('Silent Death') a compendium of testimonies on the use of solitary confinement on political prisoners, which led to his documentary of the same name.

Karzan Kardozi was born in Kurdistan and left with his family in 1999 due to war. Settling in Nashville, US, he studied Film Directing and Cinematography at Watkins College of Art, Design & Film. In 2015, Karzan went back to Kurdistan to make a low-budget documentary *I Want to Live* about the lives of Kurdish refugees from Syria. In 2023, he wrote, produced, and directed *Where is Gilgamesh?*, a film noir based on the Epic of Gilgamesh, shot on location in the Kurdistan Region of Iraq. Also a prolific writer, Kardozi wrote a series of short books in Kurdish titled *100 Years of Cinema, 100 Directors*, consisting of 50 volumes that chronicle the history of cinema.

Sema Kaygusuz (born 1972) is one of Turkey's leading female writers. She has published five collections of short stories, three novels, a collection of non-fiction essays, and a play, which have won a number of awards in Turkey and Europe and have been translated into English, French, German, Norwegian, and Swedish. Her short story collection *The Well of Trapped Words* was published in an English translation by Maureen Freely (Comma, 2015), and her novel *Every Fire You Tend*, was published in an English translation by Nicholas Glastonbury (Tilted Axis, 2019). She is of Kurdish heritage.

Meral Şimşek is a Kurdish author of novels and poetry, based in Turkey. Her poetry collections include *Refugee Dreams* (2013), *Clouding the Fire* (2015) and *Black Fig* (2017). Her first novel *Pomegranate Stain* was published in 2017. Her poems have won first prize and twice been runners up in the Martyr Deniz Fırat Turkish Poetry Prize. In 2018 she was named Best Poet in Diyarbakır's Golden Earth Awards. As well as working as a journalist, she also works as an editor and a songwriter.

Jîl Şwanî is a young author with roots in south Kurdistan. He moved to Denmark at age fifteen and since then he's been immersed in theatre, film, and writing. He was the host of a podcast called *What Happened Last Week in Kurdistan* and is currently writing a novel.

Jahangir Mahmoudveysi was born in Paveh City, Iran in 1961

235

and received part of his education in Qasr-e Shirin and Baneh City before returning to Paveh to finish his studies in 1988. Although trained and offered a position as a teacher, Waisi was denied a career in teaching due to political discrimination. He subsequently retrained and worked in the electrical industry. Waisi writes fiction, poetry and journalism, and has been published in literary journals such as *Sirwa, Mahabad,* and *Nimah,* and in newspapers such as *Azadi* and the websites *Nuryau Voice* and *Salam Paveh*. He won the short story of the year prize at the Hawrami Literary Festival and is a member of International PEN.

About the Translators

Dîbar Çelik is a translator and researcher based in Rouen. He received his MA and PhD in translation studies at Okan University and Boğaziçi University, respectively. He has previously translated *Treasure Island* into Kurdish as *Girava Gencîneyê* (2010).

Kate Ferguson is an Istanbul-based translator, and an interpreter trainer at Boğaziçi University. Together with Amy Spangler she co-translated *Dawn*, a collection of short stories by former HDP leader Selahattin Demirtaş, which received a PEN Translates Award in 2018. In 2013 and 2014 she was invited to attend the Cunda International Workshop for Translators of Turkish Literature where she collaborated on a translation of *Hah!* by Birgül Oğuz, winner of the 2014 European Prize for Literature.

Nicholas Glastonbury is a translator of Turkish and Kurdish literature. He is a doctoral candidate in cultural anthropology at the Graduate Center of the City University of New York, and a co-editor of the e-zine *Jadaliyya*. His translation of Sema Kaygusuz's novel *Every Fire You Tend* received a PEN Translates award and was long-listed for the 2020 EBRD Literature Prize.

Khazan Jangiz was born in Sulaimaniyah in 1997. She graduated in English Language and Literature and is currently working as a journalist and translator in the Kurdistan Region of Iraq.

Darya Najim was born in Sulaymaniyah, Iraq in 1992. She received a bachelor's degree in International Studies and a master's degree in Middle Eastern Studies from Lund University. She is a published poet, writer and translator. Her translations include a collection of poetry by Kajal Ahmed titled *A Handful of Salt* and a collection of Kurdish women's autobiographies titled *Kurdish Women's Stories*. She is currently located in Stockholm, Sweden.

Harriet Paintin has worked with languages since her BA in Hindi at School in Oriental and African Studies in 2014. Since then she has worked on various translation projects including campaign materials (for international NGO Survival International), websites, and journalistic pieces (published in *The New Internationalist*). She has been working with the Kurdish language since 2018, and works in a 'tandem translation' with her Kurdish husband Aras Almaree. Between them they speak seven languages, and often work on translation projects together. She is currently working on a Kurdish textbook for new learners of the language.

Andrew Penny is a regular translator from the Turkish. His translations include *Uprising, Suppression, Retribution: The Kurdish Struggle in Turkey in the Twentieth Century,* by Ahmet Kahraman. He has been interested in the Kurdish question for over 40 years and is a regular visitor to the Kurdish region. In 1991 he was translator and production assistant on the BBC Panorama documentary: *The Dream of Kurdistan* (17 June 1991).

Rojin Shekh-Hamo, (born, 1995 in Serekaniye), graduated in

English Literature at Tishreen University in 2018. She has worked as a freelance translator as well as a volunteer for the Tel Tamer based NGO, Hevy. As a translator she has worked on a research project into "Says", a Kurdish singing genre similar to Dengbêj, which preserves and celebrates Kurdish history and culture through folk song. Her translations of these lyrics (from Sinjar Yazidis and Rojava) have featured in two TV documentaries *Life is Beautiful* and *On the Rooftop,* and others have been produced for the archives of the Kurdish Heritage Institute. She has also worked as a translator (into Kurdish) of film scripts for the Rojava Art Academy, and of short stories from around the world for the Rojava Literature Committee.

Amy Spangler is a literary agent and translator based in Istanbul. Co-Founder of AnatoliaLit Agency, her published translations include *Noontime in Yenişehir* by Sevgi Soysal (Milet, 2014), *Dawn* by Selahattin Demirtaş (co-translated with Kate Ferguson, Hogarth, 2019), and *A Strange Woman* by Leyla Erbil (co-translated with Nermin Menemncioğlu, Deep Vellum, forthcoming).

Special Thanks

The author Selahattin Demirtaş would like to thank Mehmet Sait Aydın and Xelîl Semed for their contributions.

Mustafa Gündoğdu would like to thank Zınar Karavil for coordinating very smooth communications with Selahattin Demirtaş, whose story was written in prison. He would also like to thank Houzan Mahmoud and Tara Jaff for their recommendations, Hishyar Abid and Zeynep Yaş for their help with the Kurdish translations in the early stages, Darya Najim for her work in the Sorani, and his old friend and former colleague Andrew Penny for always being available when needed. Orsola Casagrande would like to thank Sevinaz, Azad Evdike, Meryem Kobane and Heval Nesrin.

The publisher would like to thank Will Forrester and translator Khazan Jangiz for their invaluable support.